We Need to Talk About Ross

PAUL HOWARD

Illustrated by Alan Clarke

PENGUIN
IRELAND

PENGUIN IRELAND

Published by the Penguin Group
Penguin Ireland, 25 St Stephen's Green, Dublin 2, Ireland
(a division of Penguin Books Ltd)
Penguin Books Ltd, 80 Strand, London WC2R ORL, England
Penguin Group (USA) Inc., 375 Hudson Street, New York, New York 10014, USA
Penguin Group (Australia), 250 Camberwell Road,
Camberwell, Victoria 3124, Australia (a division of Pearson Australia Group Pty Ltd)
Penguin Group (Canada), 90 Eglinton Avenue East, Suite 700, Toronto, Ontario, Canada M4P 2Y3
(a division of Pearson Penguin Canada Inc.)
Penguin Books India Pvt Ltd, 11 Community Centre,
Panchsheel Park, New Delhi – 110 017, India
Penguin Group (NZ), 67 Apollo Drive, Rosedale, North Shore 0632, New Zealand
(a division of Pearson New Zealand Ltd)
Penguin Books (South Africa) (Pty) Ltd, 24 Sturdee Avenue,
Rosebank, Johannesburg 2196, South Africa

Penguin Books Ltd, Registered Offices: 80 Strand, London WC2R ORL, England

www.penguin.com

First published 2009
I

Copyright © Paul Howard, 2009
Illustrations copyright © Alan Clarke, 2009

Penguin Ireland thanks O'Brien Press for its agreement to Penguin Ireland
using the same design approach and typography, and the same artist,
as O'Brien Press used in the first four Ross O'Carroll-Kelly titles

The moral right of the author and illustrator has been asserted

Set in 12/14.75pt Bembo
Typeset by Palimpsest Book Production Limited,
Grangemouth, Stirlingshire
Printed in Great Britain by Clays Ltd, St Ives plc

A CIP catalogue record for this book is available from the British Library

ISBN 978-1-844-88178-9

www.greenpenguin.co.uk

Penguin Books is committed to a sustainable future
for our business, our readers and our planet.
The book in your hands is made from paper
certified by the Forest Stewardship Council.

This book is dedicated to the memory of Redmond Walsh.
'I am somewhat of a bullshitter myself, but occasionally I like to
listen to a professional. Please carry on . . .'

'A dream may often become dearer than a child'

Brinsley MacNamara, *The Valley of the Squinting Windows*

Interviewer's Foreword

One Sunday morning, it wasn't too long ago, I paid twelve euro for a loaf of bread. It had caraway seeds in it. I sawed off two slices, ate one, picked at the other and three days later dumped what was left into the bin. I only mention it because telling your guilty tales of excess is suddenly in fashion. Everyone is at it. You've got to have a story that demonstrates how you, too, slightly lost the run of yourself during the good times.

One woman, who doesn't wish to be named, paid four hundred euro for a Barbara Cosgrove Blanche lamp in mustard, which, it turned out, jarred angrily with the colour scheme in her front living room. So she put the lamp, not in a discreet corner where it wouldn't be seen, not even in the hidden dark of the attic — she put it in a skip, then went back to Brown Thomas and bought another one, this time in ochre and brilliant vermilion.

My favourite story, though, is the man who pulled on a pair of jeans he hadn't worn for more than a year and discovered six hundred euro, neatly folded, in the front pocket. Imagine not missing six hundred euro.

On and on, they keep coming, conga-lines of listeners, phoning in to bare their souls. 'An orangerie, Joe . . . it's the same as a conservatory, except twenty grand dearer . . .'

Ireland is headed for what could be a long and hard period of recession. Construction is grinding to a halt, house prices are plummeting fast and the emigrant airbuses are filling up again. For ten years we lived the high life, though I'm not sure we were ever entirely happy at that altitude. Some inner guilt inside us. The consensus this morning is that a period of austerity would be good for our souls.

I switch off the radio, kill the engine.

Perhaps the worst money anyone spent during what will be remembered as the Celtic Tiger was the six-figure sum that Penguin Ireland paid Ross O'Carroll-Kelly to write a book called *1,001 Birds You Must Knob Before You Die*. After three years and twice as many deadline extensions, the project was scaled back to a less ambitious 501 birds. By the beginning of September 2008 he had completed only short, albeit graphically illustrated, profiles of Kristin Kreuk, Jessica Biel, Olga Kurylenko, Vanessa Hudgens and Lisa Scott-Lee. None was considered publishable due to reasons of decency.

Ross made a rather better fist of spending his advance, however, making a downpayment on the apartment I'm about to visit, the penthouse of a very fetching block overlooking the dual carriageway in Stillorgan.

I rap three times on the door and wait.

The Grange was billed as South Dublin's most prestigious new address. While it was under construction, the large wooden hoardings that hid it, like Christmas wrapping, from the view of passing commuters proclaimed, in bold, six-feet-high capitals, THE SPIRIT OF GRACIOUS LIVING – a piece of gibberish worthy of Edward Lear and yet a phrase that beautifully captured the essence of the times.

Who cares what it means? Just borrow the money and buy it.

The door is answered by a short, whey-faced girl, eighteen, maybe nineteen, pretty in a perfunctory sort of way, wearing nothing but a man's shirt and regulation Uggs. She regards me with a look of huffy boredom until I mention that I'm Ross's friend and the man who writes his books for him, and suddenly she can't do enough for me. 'I'm thinking of making French toast for breakfast,' she says sunnily, taking my coat, 'with *actual* vanilla pods. I'm Etain, by the way . . .'

She air-kisses me on both cheeks and I tell her I'm fine for French toast, thank you.

Ross is in the living room, playing some shoot-'em-up on a giant plasma-screen television, well into his third Heineken of the morning if the evidence on the coffee table is anything to go by.

When he sees me, he holds up an open palm and says, 'I've got a high-five here with *someone's* name on it!'

I gratefully accept it. He tells me that I'm the man and perhaps I mention, once or twice, that, no, he's the man.

'So, what have you been up to?' he says. 'Spending all that money you made off my back?'

'The usual,' I tell him. 'Burnishing your legend around town.'

I sit down. He studies me, taking in every detail. 'You certainly haven't been spending it on clothes,' he says. 'How did you get past the concierge dressed like that?'

I laugh – it's all you *can* do when Ross has you in his crosshairs.

'Seriously, Dude, there's a bag of my old clothes in the airing cupboard. I was going to send them down to Barnardo's. Take one or two things out and wear them if you're going to insist on coming here.'

'That's you, Ross – generous to a fault.'

'Well, your need is greater than Barnardo's, believe me.'

I ask him what he's been doing.

'Fock all,' he says proudly, which is what I suspected. Ross hasn't worked since his brief spell coaching the national rugby team of Andorra, and that was almost two years ago. He did spend the guts of a year in California, to be close to Sorcha, his estranged wife, and their daughter, Honor. But most of his days since then, I imagine, have passed rather like this one.

'I've had, like, a *few* offers,' he says, standing up to check himself out in a huge mirror over the artificial fireplace. 'There's a lot of teams out there who want me.'

His hand traces the torsion of his abdominal and pectoral muscles through his shirt. 'Hey,' he says, turning to me quickly, 'you might know this – is there an actual country called Luxembourg?'

'I'm about seventy-two per cent certain there is,' I tell him.

'Good,' he says, 'I thought it might have been the guys ripping the piss . . .'

I laugh. It's a knee-jerk.

'And you can quit that,' he says. 'You never saw *me* on *Blackboard* focking *Jungle*. It's like Fehily used to say – you'll never have a body like Atlas if you sit around reading one.'

He gives me the guns, along with a big stiletto smile, and he remains like that until I offer him a nod of acknowledgement. Then he drops to the floor, his hands behind his head, and starts performing sit-ups, each crunch punctuated by a steady rap: 'Fock Luke Fitzgerald! Fock Andrew Trimble! Fock Rob Kearney! Fock Shane Horgan!'

Etain appears, standing in the frame of the door. She doesn't comment on the scene, just asks Ross if he wants two slices of French toast or three. He pulls himself into a sitting position and says, 'None for me, Babes. I'm *actually* going to lay off the fatty shit for a while?'

'I *could* walk up to Stillorgan,' she says, 'get you some granola?'

'No, I'm actually cool.'

'What about fruit? There's caster sugar there and fresh ginger. I could do, like, a fruit salad. Or even coffee? Would either of you like even coffee? With just *actual* toast?'

We both tell her we're fine and she goes back to the kitchen.

'Mrs focking Doyle on E,' Ross says.

I laugh. 'I don't know, I think she's kind of sweet.'

'If she gets fake tan on that shirt,' he says, 'the next person you'll be singing her praises to will be a focking coroner.'

I tell him I heard about Ronan, his now eleven-year-old son, who is – what parents on this side of the city are all too quick to call – gifted. Last year, after taking two Las Vegas casinos for a total of $240,000, he was sent for testing and discovered to have an IQ of 130. In educational terms, he's already reached postgraduate level. Fifteen more points and he's officially a genius. The only problem is that they haven't managed to find a school for him that's suited to his intellectual needs.

'Chip off the old block,' Ross says, with rare self-deprecation.

'Maybe you should have had a paternity test done after all,' I say.

He laughs mid-sit-up, then reaches up for another high-five. 'Maybe I should,' he says.

I get down to business. 'You know Penguin aren't happy with you?' I say.

'Penguin?' he says, suddenly snapping to his feet and throwing a couple of punches at some imagined foe. 'Er, *why* exactly?'

'Well,' I say, taking in the four walls, 'it may have *something* to do with the fact that they paid for this place. And you haven't done any work yet.'

He shrugs. 'They were the times in which we were living, Dude. Anyway, I did *some* work . . .'

'Yeah – and it was all very, you know, anatomically correct. Except, obviously, Olga Kurytenko's four breasts . . .'

'Yeah, that was from, like, a dream I had? I probably shouldn't eat so much before bed. What can you do to get this Penguin crowd off my case, then?'

'Well, as it happens, they've asked me to put a proposal to you . . .'

'Go on.'

'For a *different* book.'

'As long as it's the old team back together again. I tell you shit and you write it down – that's the best way I work.'

'Well, what they want is basically a biography.'

'A biography,' he says, several times, trying the word out for size. 'A biography. Okay, continue . . .'

'You don't know what a biography is, do you?'

'Well, no, but I kind of presumed that was *your* department?'

'A biography is the story of your life . . .'

'Cool. But haven't I already *told* you the story of my life?'

'This would be written from the perspective of others.'

'Others? As in?'

'Well, anyone who's played a part in it. I mean, that last book we did, it threw up a lot of questions. Those sessions with that shrink . . .'

'Conchita.'

'Yeah, I thought she pulled a few psychological threads loose. But not enough for us to see, you know, exactly what's underneath. There's depths to you as yet unexplored.'

'Depths? Do you think so?'

'Yeah.'

He shrugs. 'My old dear never wanted me,' he says. 'My old man wanted me but never had time for me. That's my life in less than thirty words.'

'They also kept the fact of your son *and* your sister a secret from you.'

His eyes take on a yonderly look. 'I could give you even more shit on them than that,' he says. 'How *she* basically conned an old woman out of her business. How *he's* basically an even bigger penis than I've ever let on . . .'

'I think people *would* love to know more about them,' I say. 'The back-story. How did they meet? What was the attraction? And, yes, how *did* they make their money?'

'Fock knows *what* the attraction was,' he says. 'Did you see *her* on *Oprah*, the stupid scrod? She said writing has given her more pleasure than anything in life –*except*, obviously, the birth of her son. That's a lie – she *hated* having me.'

'Well,' I say, 'all of that – *if* it's true. But also you . . .'

'Me?'

'The man *behind* the myth.'

'Well, make sure and put one or two of the myths in as well, because they're all true.'

'People out there are gagging for you.'

'Yeah,' he says, visibly thrilling to the idea. 'I suppose if people are prepared to buy a book about Drico . . .'

'And the story of your life,' I say, 'so far, we only have *your* word for it? I've got to tell you, over the years I've been ghosting you, a lot of people have said to me, "I was there and it didn't happen like that at all . . ."'

He seems slightly needled by the suggestion. 'Like who?'

I pass it off. 'Well, I want to talk to as many people as possible. The guys obviously – JP, Oisinn, Fionn . . .'

'Good luck with that,' he says. 'They're not exactly a happy bunch of campers these days – that whole current economic tiger thing.'

I heard that Oisinn, who made millions from his perfume, *Eau d'Affluence – Essence of Tiger*, not to mention his brand of scented holy waters, had lost a fortune in the US stock-market crash. JP, who went back to work in his father's estate agency, is on a three-day week and is rumoured to be signing on for the other two days.

'That whole element is interesting as well,' I tell him. 'You and your friends were, I suppose, the first generation of Celtic Tiger cubs. It'd be interesting to see how you're all coping with the new economic realities.'

'Yeah, whatever,' he says. 'Just remember, what people *actually* want is a book about me. My life, my loves, some of the birds I've bedded down through the years. There's some stories out there about me. Here, take these names down – Rebecca Lane, Joanna Keyes, Sneachta Mullane . . .' He hangs his thumb out, scrabbling around for a memory.

'Etain,' I remind him.

'Exactly – she'd have one or two nice things to say about me from last night. Maybe have a word with her now before I throw her out. Of course, then some of the coaches who ignored my claims over the years and ended up having to eat their basic words. Eddie O'Sullivan's one, but there's others . . .'

I tell him not to worry, I've already drawn up the bones of a list.

'It's a pretty cool idea,' he says, admiring his reflection again. 'As in, getting the whole story, except from, like, *other* people's points of view? I suppose it's a bit like *The Hills*. Like, you hear Lauren describe some shit that happened and you think, yeah, I'm on *her* side on this one. Then you hear, like, Heidi or Audrina describe exactly the same shit, but in, like, a different way? And then you think, fock, now I'm on her side – er, *what* is going on with my brain?'

Etain reappears in the doorway, with – and I'm sure that the shock registers on my face – a second girl, equally pretty, but with a surly set to her face. Did he spend the night with both, I wonder?

'Ross,' the second girl says, 'we were thinking of going to, like, Yo Sushi – *if* you fancied . . .'

'I'm going to be honest with you,' he says, reaching into the pocket of his chinos and pulling out a small parcel of money, 'I hate long goodbyes. As we say in the game, last night was last night – this morning is this morning.'

'Here,' he says then, stripping a fifty from the top of the pile and handing it to Etain. 'Get yourselves a bit of breakfast somewhere. Should be enough in that for a taxi as well.'

She stares at the note in her hand, a look of outrage spreading across her face.

'You total wanker!' the other girl says, spitting out the words.

'Hey, there's a lot of bad words out there,' Ross says evenly, holding my shoulder for balance while stretching his leg behind him. 'I've been called most of them in my time. This dude here will tell you – he's known me, like, ten years. Look, last night was great. We all learned a lot about ourselves. But I'm telling you for your own sake – there ain't no pot of gold at the end of this rainbow.'

'Oh my God,' Etain says, 'I thought you were *such* a nice guy. You're actually a dickhead.'

The two girls make a furious exit, leaving a trail of invective in their wake. Etain, I notice, hangs on to the fifty.

'That *has* to go into the book,' Ross says, pointing at the slamming door. 'Wouldn't be a bad way to start it either.'

I gurn non-committally, then stand up.

'Hey, before you go,' he says, 'is this any good to you?'

He plucks a tattered, leather-bound journal from a bookshelf notice-ably light on books.

I hold it in my hands and let it fall open. 'What is it?' I say, my eyes straining to make sense of the crazy hieroglyphics.

'Father Fehily's journal,' he says.

'His journal?'

He nods. 'Yeah, no, he left it to me when he died – in, like, his will?'

I look at the inside cover. It says, *My Struggle, 1992–1999*.

'Now I'm kicking your orse out as well,' Ross says. 'You've got a seri-ous amount of work to do. Go and talk to some women – find the *real* Ross O'Carroll-Kelly.'

September 2008

Interview Tape 01
Tuesday 16 September 2008
Fionnuala and Charles O'Carroll-Kelly

The tune on the piano is Beethoven's 'Für Elise'. She's sitting in the Terrace Lounge of the Westbury Hotel – lips puckered, eyes lightly closed – rolling her head from side to side in an attitude of appreciation. A copy of Eckhart Tolle's *A New Earth – Awakening to Your Life's Purpose* sits closed on her lap. The entire scene feels like a contrivance, an assemblage of things put together to create a certain impression.

I clear my throat, a theatrical effort to get her attention. She opens her eyes and says, 'Oh! Oh, *hello!*' like our meeting is a chance affair, rather than something that was prearranged through her agent. She stands up, then extends her hand. 'Fionnuala O'Carroll-Kelly,' she says, like there's anyone in Ireland who wouldn't recognize her instantly. I can't work out if it's terribly conceited or terribly the opposite.

She looks well – far younger than her reputed sixty-one years – whip-thin and tanned, with a tightness in her features that suggests what is referred to in her new home of Los Angeles as 'work'. She is warmer than I imagined, but with a feyness about her – her words, her manner, her whole aspect at times seem to belong to a different age. She asks me if I'm going to 'take tea', a phrase I didn't think still existed outside the pages of Jane Austen.

Her voice has that congested, adenoidal timbre so often associated with South Dublin women of a certain social class. 'You must – simply *must* – try their smoked salmon sandwiches,' she says. 'The smoked salmon here is famous – or deserves to be.' No words pass between her and the waiter. With apparent effort, she scrunches her face into a smile and cocks her head slightly, then ten minutes later the waiter returns, carrying a three-tiered plate, with a selection of sandwiches, scones and cakes arrayed on each level like spokes on a wheel.

In between we make small talk. I ask her about her new life in

America, where she's become a household name since her appearance on *Oprah* in July. Her newest book, *Presidential Erection*, has caught the prevailing wind of the cultural zeitgeist in the lead-up to the most eagerly anticipated American election in a generation, topping the *New York Times* bestseller list for five weeks. The book, written in her 'famously breathless style', tells the story of Teri Chasey, an ambitious Washington-born campaign worker leading a double life as adviser to Democratic candidate Samuel Aldous, an African-American, and Republican candidate Rabaul Williams, a septuagenarian Vietnam War hero. Chasey also happens to be, in the words of the dustjacket, banging both men.

I compliment her on how well she looks. She thanks me and tells me it's possible to live on scrambled tofu and watercress juice in LA, 'which it simply *isn't* here'. After more conversational footsie, I bring up the subject of Ross. I watched her interview with Oprah, I tell her, and was moved by the warmth with which she spoke about her son. 'Those tears,' I say, 'were obviously genuine.'

Fionnuala: Well, of course they were genuine. I was discussing what, for me, *is* a very emotional subject. Ross and I share this – I would say – bond. An amazing bond, which I don't think any mother should be ashamed to discuss openly ...

We are, all of us, unreliable narrators of our own life stories, but I'm at a loss to reconcile these two accounts. Ross says Fionnuala never wanted him. Fionnuala says that she and Ross share a bond.

'You're really that close?' I ask, trying not to sound too incredulous.

Fionnuala: Oh, yes. Don't get me wrong, we have our disagreements like everyone else. But we have this wonderful emotional connection. *And*, I would say, there's a reason for it, though it's something I find very difficult to talk about. I wouldn't even let Oprah go there – I *told* her – for fear that I'd just ... break down. But I never knew my own mother. She was mad, you see. For the birds. In an institution from the time I was, oh, three, four years of age.

'I had no idea.'

Fionnuala: Well . . . So I have no real memories *of* her, except as this, you know, catatonic woman in a raggedy old nightdress, who my father and I would go to visit on Sunday afternoons, in this old hospital – loony bin, for want of a better phrase.

I used to write letters to her as well, like you'd write up your news in school, all the things that happened in the week. This was when I was seven or eight years old. My father would sit me down, every Wednesday night, and he'd say, 'Let's tell your mother what's been happening, shall we?'

I'm not sure if he ever posted them . . . I mean, I doubt he did. She wasn't capable of reading or understanding them. But *he* was quite anxious that I didn't forget her. That I didn't forget I *had* a mother . . .

She's still alive, you know.

I shake my head.

Fionnuala: Ninety years old.

So I was determined to have this connection with my son – to be the mother that *I* never had. I mean, yes, I'm a feminist – and I want you to put that in – but a belief in equality between the sexes isn't incompatible with a belief that we should also celebrate our essential differences – that which makes us different. And what makes *us* different – *as* women – is this wonderful gift called mother-hood, which *I* define as being responsible for the care, for the nur-turing, for the growth and development of this person, both before *and* after they're born.

And motherhood, as I told Oprah, is one of the few things in life I did get right. That and my writing. And business obviously – the florist shops. My cooking. And my role as an advocate for those with no voice . . .

If you were to ask me what it was that made me so cut out to *be* a good mother, I would say it was a combination of, firstly, desiring this bond that I never got to experience with my own mother and, secondly, simply the fact that I like to give *of* myself. I'm a very giving person. You only have to look at my charity work to see that.

Nineteen ninety-four, I think it was – the year of the famous Rwandan thing. Terrible, terrible genocide. Either the Hutus were killing the Tutsis or the Tutsis were killing the Hutus, I can never remember which it was. But . . . there . . . was . . . bloodshed! I'm sitting in the Gables. Brunch with the girls. Angela, Delma, maybe one or two others. And I can feel it – you know, the expectation coming from them. This awful thing that's happened on the television – what's Fionnuala going to do about it? Because let's be honest, she's the only one.

At that stage, I wasn't even thinking about how I might go about healing the divisions in the country. It was very much a case of, Fionnuala, think practical, think short term. *Do* these people need something to eat? Could *I* or any of the girls take in an orphan or two? Just until the worst passed, obviously.

Ten days later, I'd arranged a charity golf classic, which was an enormous success.

Giving, giving, giving . . .

I tell her I hope she doesn't mind me saying it, but Ross often talks about her in a way that's ill at odds with her image of herself as a mother, writer and, well, campaigner.

'Have you read *any* of *his* books?' I ask.

She stares off into the middle distance, then after a long pause speaks as if weighing up the likely consequences of every word.

Fionnuala: He made some things sound far, far worse than they were. But everyone has his or her own version of the truth, don't they? Who am I to say mine is any more valid than his?

No, I wasn't *always* the perfect mother. But Ross had a very, very happy childhood. It's disappointing for me that he's never included any of the nice things in his books – all the fun we had, the tender moments we shared, the three of us, as a family.

I suppose that's the nature of memoir.

Of *mémoire* . . .

Her phone trills on the table in front of us. The ringtone is 'Me and Mrs Jones'. Ross mentioned she had a thing for Michael Bublé. She answers with an enthusiastic, 'Hello, Darling', and I find myself wondering is there a new man in her life. 'Yes, I'm in the Westbury, with this writer friend of Ross, taking afternoon tea . . .'

With her free hand she indicates the miniature Battenberg slices, then mimes eating one — a suggestion to me. I pick one up, take a bite.

'Why don't you pop in — say hello? Oh, wonderful. We'll see you then.'

When she hangs up, she says, 'Charles is coming in. Can you believe that — he was on Grafton Street, picking up cigars!' The surprise must show on my face because she feels it necessary to add, 'Yes, it *is* odd, isn't it? Charles and I are better friends now than when we were married . . .'

It's not so much funny as bizarre. Her first book, *Criminal Assets* — a thinly veiled autobiographical account of her marriage to the disgraced businessman and politician — contained enough hard evidence for the Criminal Assets Bureau and the Revenue Commissioners to build a case against him. From my conversations with Ross, the book was Fionnuala's revenge on Charles for fathering a child outside their marriage. I make a botched attempt to bring it up. 'Charles and Helen . . .' I say, '. . . I hear they're, em, back together again — as a couple?'

'Helen Joseph was always the love of his life,' she says, fast-tracking my line of questioning. 'Oh, I knew all *about* Erika, before you ask. I knew about her before she was born . . .'

This comes as a huge surprise to me. 'I just presumed you found out, maybe three or four years ago,' I say, 'and wrote *Criminal Assets* as, I don't know, a kind of revenge . . .'

She tosses back her perfectly coiffed hair. 'Revenge *was* my motivation,' she says. 'But I knew about his affair — if you want to call it that — for years and years. *And* his daughter. The thing is, I didn't think it affected me. It *didn't* affect me. Not until I went through the change. You know . . . the menopause.'

'And he ended up doing, what, two, three years in jail?'

'Like I said, it was the hormones.'

'But he doesn't hate you for it?'

'You've met Charles . . .'

'A few times,' I tell her. 'It's usually been with Ross, after rugby matches.'

'Then you'll know. He doesn't have the capacity to hate.'

I hear a sudden greeting roared from the far side of the lounge and turn to see Charles – big and bluff – juking his way, between tables, over to where we're sitting. Heads turn in annoyance as he calls out, 'Emily Brontë, eat your bloody heart out,' and other *bons mots*.

They embrace each other. Fionnuala holds him at arm's length and tells him he looks wonderful and Charles tells her that the new book is a triumph – her best yet. I rise partway in my chair and Charles turns to me, clearly not remembering my name, and says, 'Oh, yes – Ross's pal,' then shakes my hand while squeezing the top of my arm with a giant, ursine paw.

I'm not sure if he got the long and rambling voice message I left. Ross told me he's busy – 'as focking usual' – with various business ventures, which include a cheesemongers that he and Helen are opening in the Merrion Shopping Centre and a proposal, along with Hennessy Coghlan-O'Hara, his solicitor and friend, to convert Mountjoy Jail into Dublin's first six-star hotel. The sense of gloom about the world economy hasn't caused him to so much as break step.

'Those books that Ross writes,' he says, reversing his bulk into the chair opposite, 'terribly good fun, of course. But it's like I always say to Fionnuala – reading them, you'd think we didn't love each other. Sometimes, whatever way *you've* twisted his words, it's almost as if we don't like each other – which isn't the case at all. Memory, of course, can be a notoriously unreliable adjutant. So to answer your question [he waves his mobile phone at me], I'd be more than happy to talk to you, if only because there *are* specific things that I'd like to see corrected – the record set straight and so forth.

'We – and I think I speak for both of us here, Fionnuala – would like people to see that Ross doesn't come from one of these, you know, *dysfunctional* families that you see on the television . . .'

'Well,' I say, 'the tape is still running.'

Charles: Well, what we've often said to Ross about his books is – where's all the fun we had? Where's the joy?

The day Ross took his first steps – that, for instance, is a story that's not been heard before. We were living in the famous Glenageary at the time, and I'd often take the little chap out into the garden, just the two of us and the Gilbert ball that I bought the very day that Fionnuala had it confirmed she was pregnant.

It was important – I think we would have *both* been firm believers – to familiarize him with the shape and feel of the ball.

Now, to cut a long story short, I *always* made sure to bring the ball back into the house after we'd finished playing. Didn't want to leave it lying there in the garden. As we all no doubt know by now, this would have been one of the less affluent parts of Glenageary in the 1980s – they wouldn't have known anything about rugby in that part of the world. Had they *seen* this ball, some of the neighbours we had at the time – I see Fionnuala nodding there – would have considered it something akin to voodoo.

I suppose there was a genuine fear that they might kill Ross.

Fionnuala: Oh, I feared for *all* of our lives.

Charles: Very occasionally, though, I would forget to bring it in and that's precisely what happened on this one particular day that I'm telling you about. I spotted it through the kitchen window and I remember saying to Fionnuala, 'I'd better get that in. No point in rubbing the neighbours' noses in it, *etcetera*.'

So I had Ross with me and I was walking him like so – holding his hands while he put one foot in front of the other. The next thing – we're a couple of feet away from the ball – he breaks loose, quite literally shakes his hands free of mine, runs unaided to the ball and kicks it. It must have travelled twenty feet. Of course, I *would* say that – I'm the proud *old dad*, as he calls me.

I remember walking into the kitchen and saying to Fionnuala – do you remember this, Darling? – I said, 'I hope you're ready to see this little chap of ours become huge in the world of international rugby.'

I'm far more interested in hearing about Fionnuala's relationship with Ross than Charles's meandering reminiscences. 'So you were pregnant, what, three, four years into the marriage?'

Charles: That's right. And – much as it'll embarrass Fionnuala here – I can tell you the night it happened, too, because I've done the arithmetic a thousand times. It was the day we beat Herman and Susan Downing in the mixed-doubles final in Sandycove Tennis Club – 6–2, 4–6, 6–5.

We celebrated that night with a bottle of Château Margaux 1970, if you don't mind – a second anniversary present, if you remember, Darling, from your father. Tom Doorley reviewed the self-same wine only a week ago. Pleasantly silky, with imposing aromas of leather and cedarwood – *his* words, not mine.

Well, we both ended up rather drunk and I don't think I *need* to explain the hows, the wherefores and the whatnots of what ensued. Just to say that what happened, happened, and we were delighted with the outcome.

Fionnuala: I was sure it was going to be a boy. I somehow formed that impression from the beginning. I don't know why.

Charles: And naturally my heart quite literally leapt.

Day and night, I prayed for a son. Secretly, I think every man prays for a son.

So, armed with this information, I took the unilateral liberty of phoning old Denis Fehily in Castlerock. *My* old *alma mater*.

I said, 'Put his name down. Future star of the school team and so forth.'

Which, of course, he proceeded to do.

Oh, put this in, too – big part of the story. Hennessy and I were in the Berkeley. Just watched Ireland lose to England on television. Twenty-four to nine. Check it if you want, but I think you'll find I'm right. The 1980 Five Nations was terribly disappointing – you would never have believed a Triple Crown was only two years away. By then we were famous in the Berkeley, especially on big match days. Anyway, Hennessy turns to me and he says, 'Charles, I get the feeling that if it's a boy, he's going to play for Ireland one day.'

Which was a lovely thing to say. He didn't *have* to say it.

I said, 'Damn it, Hennessy, I have the self-same feeling.'

Fast-forward a few months. I was on the golf course when I got the call. Elm Park. The sixth. A tough hole. Requires two perfect shots to reach the green – a 150-yard-long drive over water and a deceptively tricky long iron shot onto the green, which – as if it weren't difficult enough – contains an eight-foot depression separating front and back, making it a very difficult two-putt to the pin.

None of your so-called mobile phones then, of course. Tom from the bar took the call. Came tearing down the fairway, shouting and waving his arms. I said to Hennessy, 'Hello – what's all this how-do-you-do?'

Oh, yes, that's right, Hennessy skewed his tee shot to the right. Wanted a Mulligan. Not on your life, I said. That was us – the best of friends, but always super, super competitive. And there *was* money riding on it.

Tom said, 'Charles, quick. Fionnuala's been taken in.'

Now, Hennessy – if you could put this in – was calmness personified. Said, 'Forget the clubs, Charlie. *I'll* bring them back for you. You just go.'

And there *I'd* been, trying to screw him over a shot.

So anyway, jumped into the car, still in all my golfing gear, if you can believe that – shoes, glove, visor, crazy when I think back – and hit Merrion Road like the proverbial man possessed.

Fionnuala: Ross was born in Holles Street, which wouldn't have been my choice.

But there just wasn't time, was there, Charles?

Charles: Unfortunately not. I parked in Merrion Square. Tore into the hospital, looking for news and so forth, only to be told that Fionnuala was *in* labour, quote-unquote.

Remember, in those days, men didn't attend the birth – or very seldom. They tended to head for the pub. Which – and you can quote me on this, if you like – is what *I* proceeded to do.

I left word with the nurses that I was repairing to the Horseshoe Bar for the duration and was contactable there.

Now a lot of the rest of that day is a blur. I know that at some point Hennessy arrived in with a couple of chaps from the Law Library, a bottle of his beloved XO was produced and, well, you can imagine the rest. Don't think I need to paint you a picture.

There was rugby talk. There was golf talk . . .

It was just before eleven – four minutes to eleven to be precise, because I told Hennessy to mark the time – when the call came. Fionnuala had given birth to a baby boy. Nine pounds.

Now, I walked into that ward, saw him lying there in his little crib and I can honestly say that it was love at first sight. We literally could not take our eyes off each other.

Such a beautiful little baby – eyes, nose, fingers and so forth. Put all that in.

Fionnuala: I was dead to the world. The birth took a lot out of me.

Charles: So I'm left sitting there, in this armchair in the corner of the ward, this little bundle in my arms, and I said – and I remember this like it was yesterday – I said, 'Well, Charlie, you've really gone and done it this time . . .'

But you can understand why it was such an emotional thing for me, sitting there, looking at my own son. This was a new start. I said to myself, this little chap's going to live up to my expectations just as I failed to live up to *my* father's . . .

My jaw almost comes unhinged when I hear that. *This little chap's going to live up to my expectations just as I failed to live up to my father's* . . . I wonder is he even aware of what he just said.

Fionnuala: At the time, we were living in that awful place . . .

Charles: Glenageary. One of these famous *housing* estates. Private, I hasten to add, though near enough to Sallynoggin, in geographical terms, for certain sections of the media to make mischief later on, when they were writing about our rise from – inverted commas – penury to affluence.

But looking back – yes – *I* remember that whole period as an exciting episode in our lives. It was even an adventure to be living *in amongst* other people. Made us appreciate what we had later on.

Fionnuala: Oh, come on, Charles, we were living in squalor. Net curtains, coal fires, free newspapers . . .

We were living like animals. Quite literally.

One of these awful *ice-cream vans* would come around every day, encouraging all sorts of people out onto the street.

I mean, this was the kind of thing you were seeing, day in, day out . . .

Charles: Fionnuala has a slight tendency towards exaggeration when she talks about those days. Glenageary was her Vietnam, I rather think.

Fionnuala: There was one Saturday afternoon, I was coming home from somewhere and I saw the man who lived *next door* – never knew his name, no interest – quite literally lying down underneath his car. It happened exactly like that – two little legs sticking out.

You remember, Darling, I said to you, 'Dear God, Charles – what's *happening* out there?' and you said, 'He's, em – I believe the phrase is – *tinkering*.'

Oh, I just burst into tears. I cried, I think, for three hours straight.

Charles: Looking back now, benefit of hindsight and so forth – I hope you don't mind me saying this, Darling – but I think Fionnuala believed she possibly married beneath herself when she married me . . .

Fionnuala: I would agree with that, yes.

Charles: Fionnuala was engaged before, you see.

Engaged before? Has this family no end of secrets?

Fionnuala: Yes. To Conor.

Charles: Chap called Conor Hession – a good guy, as it happens, and a bloody good rugby player, if you don't mind me saying, Fionnuala. Played centre for Conleth's. In fact, it was always said that if he'd moved to a decent rugby school – Rock, for instance – he'd probably have played for Ireland at schools level.
   Lot of money there, of course.

Fionnuala: Oh, yes, they were *fabulously* wealthy.

Charles: The Hessions were one of those families, no one was ever really sure *what* they did. It was all inherited, you see. His great-grandfather on his mother's side was a Lord of some description.

Fionnuala: Lord Rath-something-or-other. If you check *Burke's Peerage* . . .
   But Conor and I were childhood sweethearts.

Charles: Fionnuala's dad, Ted, he was in the bank racket. Did well enough, I think it's fair to say. House on Dalkey Avenue. Branch manager and so forth. He was English, of all things. Served during the war, although he didn't see any real action. Spent most of it guarding a munitions factory near Aldershot. That's where he met Fionnuala's mother, wasn't it? She was a char–

Fionnuala: A tea lady . . .

Charles: Oh, that's right – in the local golf and country club, where Ted played off six.

Fionnuala's mother was originally from Rathdrum, in Wicklow. Anyway, after the war, for reasons best known to themselves, they came to Ireland, where Fionnuala here was born. Ted returned to the old banking game. But he had to raise Fionnuala on his own – did you tell him about your mother, Darling?

Fionnuala: Yes.

Twice a week, we ate in restaurants, my father and I. This was at a time when no one in Ireland went out to dinner. This was the fifties and early sixties – there wasn't any money around. So we really *were* a cut above. The Royal Hibernian. The Russell Hotel. The Shelbourne, naturally. This is where the wealthy ate. Oh, and the Beaufield Mews. Their wonderful lamb shanks. And fabulous rose garden.

So this was my childhood.

My father had this thing about education – its importance. I went to Miss Meredith's on Pembroke Road, which later became Pembroke School. Of course, Maeve Binchy – who's since become a dear, dear friend – famously taught me Latin for the Leaving Certificate.

She'll be embarrassed by that because I'm revealing her age now!

But wonderful, wonderful memories of school. This three-storey Georgian building. They used to cook the dinners in the basement. Even now the smell of cabbage takes me back there. And tiny classes – eleven, twelve children. All *good* people as well. They didn't take trade. It was sons and daughters of lords, diplomats – that type of thing.

No rubbish.

Angela Hutton – my dearest, dearest friend – was in Meredith's, too. We represented the school in tennis – doubles. She'll tell you all about that if you talk to her. We used to use the courts at St Conleth's, which wasn't too far away. And that's how Conor and I met, yes. We tended to mix with them a lot. There was a sort of cross-pollination between the two schools.

Oh, I must take a note of that phrase – I want to use it in one of my books.

Charles offers to fetch a pen and some paper from the hotel reception. 'Inspiration,' he proclaims loudly. 'Who knows when it will strike!'

The conversation is skittering around like a drunken sailor. But, unsure what it is I'm looking for, I decide to go with it. What attracted her to Conor, I ask, though I suspect I already know the answer. Was he handsome?

Fionnuala: Oh God, no! He really *was* something of an eyesore. I would say that, in the beginning, whatever attraction there was, it was all from the other side. Oh, he loved me in my tennis skirt – certainly from the way he used to stare at me, though I know that makes me sound terribly full of myself.

I *did* have good legs. Always very tanned.

She runs her hand down the side of her leg, from the top of her thigh to the middle of her calf. Her hand lisps off the nylon. I wonder for a brief moment is she flirting with me.

Fionnuala: The way these things worked was, Conor and I would have been aware of each other – and then we got together . . .

Let me think. Yes, it would have been after a rugby game. One of my friends might have had a brother or a boyfriend who was on the team with him – you know, we all tended to have coffee together, a big group of us, after the games. That's how we socialized – we met in each other's kitchens and sitting rooms.

Yes, it was in Conor's house, now that I think about it, a beautiful place in Enniskerry.

All very innocent . . .

Charles returns and hands Fionnuala a pen and several sheets of hotel letterhead. She scribbles the word *cross-pollination* while Charles picks up the thread of the conversation.

Charles: We – and what I mean by *we* is the chaps at Castlerock – we tended to concentrate our energies on the girls from Wesley College. Prods, you see – considered to be of lower moral virtue.

Sex wasn't a *mortal* sin to them – it was a misdemeanour or some-such. This was all talk, of course. None of us had a notion about that whole *demimonde*, if you'll pardon the French. You know, we were terribly green when I think back.

Helen was the first girl I ever kissed – *really* kissed, as opposed to all the silly childhood business. Yes, I met her at one of these famous record hops, in Blackrock Bowling and Tennis Club, there on Green Road. Twelfth of June, nineteen hundred and sixty-two. That made us, what, sixteen, seventeen?

Of course, the backdrop to all of this – as it were – was the music of the fifties, to say nothing of the world-famous sixties. Buddy Holly? Little Richard? Chuck Berry, for heaven's sake!

Fionnuala: To us – our *set* – rock and roll was something that was considered very much vulgar.

Charles: You got the rockin' pneumonia? I expect, you'll need a shot of rhythm and blues. Me, I got the old rollin' arthritis, and that's with a capital A. Roll over, indeed. And tell that Tchaikovsky to do likewise.

Fionnuala: We called it idiot music.

We were more interested in what I would call *high* art. Opera – that kind of thing. Luigi Alva. Alfredo Kraus. Tito Schipa. These were the records that Conor and I listened to. Yes, especially the *leggiero* tenors. Fritz Wunderlich. Ferruccio Tagliavini.

Poetry as well. Oh, we used to read to each other in front of a huge fire in the drawing room. That was the kind of thing we did. All the time.

Do you see the picture I'm painting here? Yes. *Very* romantic.

Oh, Yeats – we were both huge fans of Yeats.

'Which of his poems in particular?' I ask.

Fionnuala: Well, no *one* poem in particular – just all of his *œuvre*.

In fact – yes – people are always coming up to me and saying that they can hear the language and spirit of, you know, Yeats *suffused* through my own work. Which is always lovely to hear.

Charles: Oh, there's no doubt you're stirring up the sediment of old memories now, with your questions and what have you.

With Helen, I'll confess, one of the big attractions – aside from her being such a striking-looking girl – was the fact that her parents owned their own jukebox. In the house, yes – the most extravagant thing I'd ever seen. This was bloody Booterstown Avenue, nineteen sixty-two, sixty-three. Can you imagine how exciting that was for a chap of seventeen? All these records. Well, you might well need some loving and kissing and hugging, but you'll just have wait until Bobby returns!

You will indeed, young lady!

Helen's uncle, you see – it would have been her mother's brother – he was some big noise in the music racket. In Chicago, of all places. Emigrated and did terribly well for himself. And he sent her this *thing* as a gift.

Well, to me, it might as well have been sent down from space. This magical machine, beaming out all these wonderful sounds. Bobby Vee. Buddy Holly. Bobby Darin. Paul Revere and the Raiders. To say nothing of the Big O.

Then Elvis, of course . . .

Fionnuala stands up and announces that she has to go to the 'powder room'. Our eyes follow her to the ladies', then Charles frowns importantly. 'An interesting postscript to the story of the day Ross was born – Hennessy did, in point of fact, bring my clubs back to the clubhouse, but my driver was never the same again,' he says. 'Every tee shot I played seemed to be a couple of degrees off. Then I noticed a slight kink in the shaft. I asked Hennessy about it. Did he *drop* the bag or something – benefit of the doubt and so forth – but he always said no. But my game suffered for a long, long time afterwards . . .'

I tell him I'm surprised to find him and Fionnuala on such good terms.

He shrugs. 'We like each other very much,' he says, as if it were self-evident. 'We always did.'

'You just married the wrong people?' I suggest.

'How could I possibly say yes to that?' he asks. 'Look at our wonderful son.'

'All that time in jail,' I say. 'You're not bitter?'

'You know, Father Fehily – Ross's old coach *and* mine – used to say that feeling bitterness was like drinking poison and expecting someone else to die.' He nods sagely. 'I went to jail because, in the political climate that pertained at that time, certain figures – I won't give them the pleasure of naming them – considered it expedient for *someone* to *do time*, inverted commas. There wasn't anything in Fionnuala's book they didn't already have. I was going down, with or without it.'

I tell him I'd like to speak to Helen. 'Do you think she'd be prepared to?'

'Helen Joseph?' he says, his eyes narrowing. 'This is all very thorough this, isn't it?'

'Well,' I say, 'it's supposed to be a biography of Ross and I figured, you know, *she's* a major part of the story now, isn't she? The mother of his half-sister?'

He hesitates. I ask him if he's come up with a name for the shop yet. 'Oh, yes,' he says. 'Cheeses Merrion Joseph!'

I tell him it's inspired. He brightens at that. 'Come by the shop then.'

Fionnuala arrives back from the ladies' and mentions another engagement. I think she says Bikram yoga.

Charles has to go, too. He's expecting a delivery – six loaves of *Montenebro*. He asks me if I've ever tasted it, but doesn't wait for an answer, just tells me it's a smooth, semi-soft, chalky-white cheese – Spanish – that yields a complex goaty flavour, not unlike a *Montsec* or a Harbourne Blue.

We gather up our things. Perhaps I linger for a beat, because Fionnuala says, 'You have enough there, do you?'

'Well, no,' I say. 'We've barely scratched the surface. I *would* like to meet you again, if you're not too . . .'

'I'm here for a few weeks,' she says. 'But I'm *very* busy. Everyone wants their piece of me, as you can imagine.'

I'll call, I tell her. She says we might be able to arrange something. As I make my way down the Westbury's staircase, I hear her rebuke Charles good-naturedly about his cheese intake. 'I'm going to have to talk to Helen,' she says. 'You know I worry about your heart.'

I step out onto a cold, rain-slicked Grafton Street, trying to imagine the two women in Charles O'Carroll-Kelly's life sitting down to discuss his cholesterol levels. As it happens, it's an image all too easy to conjure up. Fionnuala and Charles might not have had the perfect marriage. But they might well have the perfect divorce.

Interview Tape 02
Tuesday 16 September 2008
Ross O'Carroll-Kelly

I walk back to Stephen's Green Shopping Centre, where I parked earlier. A car has pulled in behind me, waiting for another driver to vacate a space, so I sit and listen to Matt Cooper. Lehman Brothers, one of the world's oldest investment banks, has collapsed – the biggest bankruptcy in US history – and, given the grave tone of the coverage, it seems it's somehow bad news for everyone.

There's a sense of gloom about the place, of old certainties slipping away.

I switch off the radio and retread my conversation with Charles and Fionnuala. To understand Ross and what it is that makes him tick, I need to get a perspective on his childhood. But right now, I know far less than I did this morning. Was his upbringing the idyll that Charles suggested? Is the 'amazing bond' that Fionnuala claims she shared with Ross a product of her imagination? And why is Ross so angry?

A sharp rap on the window snaps me from my reverie. 'Are you still driving this piece of shit?' he says, opening the door and slipping into the front passenger seat. 'If you want, I could park it outside Ronan's gaff for a night. You'd probably get two or three hundred yoyos back on the insurance.'

'Not all our daddies are rich,' I tell him. It's intended as a piece of repartee, but he just says, 'A-focking-men to that.'

Then he asks me how it went.

'It was a bit, I don't know, *unfocused*?' I tell him. 'I suppose it was more background stuff than anything . . .'

A look of outrage crosses his face. '*I* don't give a fock about your interview,' he says. 'I'm, asking, what did *she* say about me?'

'Oh, this and that,' I say. 'She's had kind of a sad life, hasn't she?'

'I don't believe it,' he says, with a kind of sneering delight, 'you *fancied* her . . .'

'I didn't fancy her,' I tell him.

'You focking filthbag. What was she doing – banging on about her legs?'

'Well, yeah, she might have mentioned them.'

'Yeah, she used to do that when the goys came to the gaff ... You filthy horndog.'

'You never told me you had a granny still alive.'

'Yeah, but she's Baghdad.'

'So I believe.'

'Like mother, like daughter.'

'*And* you never told me that your mother was engaged before.'

'What's that got to do with anything?'

'Well, nothing I suppose. Except that if she'd gone ahead and married that other guy, you wouldn't have been born at all.'

He looks at me like he believes me to be quite mad. 'How do you work that out?' he says. 'I *would* have been born – it's just someone *else* would have been my old man.'

I don't have time to explain the rudiments of genetics to him. 'Speaking of your old man,' I say, 'he showed up.'

'What, while you were with her? I'd say your ears are focking ringing, are they?'

'You never told me about them either.'

'Told you? As in?'

'As in, they're best friends ...'

He shakes his head, trying to banish the thought. 'Sick, isn't it? But go on anyway, give me a flavour of the kind of shit they were saying about me – probably all lies.'

'As it happens,' I say, '*they* were talking mostly about themselves ...'

'What? No focking surprise there.'

'Your dad – he didn't get on with his *own* father, did he?'

'I don't know – I wouldn't think so.'

'Any idea why?'

'Because he's a focking tosser. Why do you think? I don't *actually* believe you? We're talking about a man and a woman who never told me I had, like, a son? Who never told me I had, like, a sister? And you're looking for reasons to feel basically sorry for them?'

'I'm not looking to feel sorry for them,' I say. 'I'm trying to understand where everyone's coming from – by going back to the beginning. I mean, you – do you have, like, a first memory?'

He picks up my iPod, desultorily turns the clickwheel. I know from bitter experience to stay quiet, let him make the first move. After a moment or so of sulky contemplation, he says he's ready to share.

Ross: I don't have, like, a *first* memory as such? *He's* always crapping on about rugby matches he *says* he took me to, but I don't remember any.

The one thing I do remember about *him* was that he used to always, like, jiggle the loose change in his Davy Crocket. He'd be standing there and all you'd hear would be *chink, chink, chink, chink.* I must have thought, 'Yeah, this focker's all right for a few squids.'

The old dear I would have fewer *fond* memories of? You know, when I think about her now, I think about that bird in *Little Britain* – a writer as well – big focking porker, lying on the sofa all day, ploughing chocolates into her face. She was focking huge when she had me – did you know that? I'll see can I get one or two pictures. Definitely bang them in the book. She's supposed to have put on, like, seven stone – it's, like, yeah, *and* the rest.

The weight she gained during her pregnancy – is that the reason he thinks she didn't want him?

Ross: No, she *didn't* want me – that's an actual fact. I know she's probably spun you some focking story, happy families, blahdy blahdy blah.

But don't buy it. As in, *seriously* don't buy it.

Believe me, underneath all the niceness, I was, like, a major inconvenience to her. I mean, why do you think it was four years before she had me?

'I did wonder about that,' I tell him. 'I thought maybe they were trying for a while.'

Ross: No, they weren't. I was a total accident. *She* didn't want kids. Seriously, if I hadn't come along, they wouldn't have even stayed together. They'd have got, like, separated years before they actually did.

'Why do you say that?'

Ross: Because *she* was off her cake and *he* was doing Helen on the side. Not that I've anything against her – she's actually a really cool person. Way too good for *him*.

I'm thinking about all the Plimsoll lines of childhood, wondering would any of them stir even one happy memory in him. 'Do you remember, for instance, your first day at school?' I ask.

Ross: Nope. I remember *going* to school? But it would have been later. I remember *him*, sitting having breakfast, looking at me. Little Einstein – this is what he used to call me. I'd come downstairs already dressed for school and he'd look at me over the top of his *Irish* focking *Times* and go, 'Look at him there! Little wheels in his head whirring away already! He has a mind like motorway traffic, Fionnuala – thoughts and ideas bustling to get into lane.'

Of course, the big joke was, I couldn't even read until I was, like, fourteen.

'Why did you never tell anyone?'

Ross: Obvious – didn't want people knowing I was stupid.

I mean, it wasn't *even* that I was stupid? It was just, like, when I looked at letters, all *I* could see was shapes. Honestly, when I heard other kids reading in class, I'd look over their shoulders and think, what the fock are *you* seeing?

The other, I suppose, reason is, who was I going to tell? The old pair were never around.

'Where were they?'

Ross: *Any* focking where. *She* was off campaigning. *He* was off, I don't know, doing whatever dodgy shit they sent him down for. The point is, whatever bullshit they try to fill your head with, I'm telling you as a basic fact, they did not want to know me.

Not until I made the S. Oh, yeah, then they were all of a sudden *trying* to get in with me? *He* was like, 'Why isn't Warren Gatland here to witness this performance?' and all that. You know what he's like.

And I was just there, '*Whatever.*'

And then *her*, tarted up to the nines. It was like, heels? In focking Belfield?

From my conversation with Charles, it seems he wanted his son to play rugby more than anything else in the world. I ask Ross, rather indelicately as it happens, if he played the game as a means of winning his father's approval.

Ross: His *approval*? What the fock would I want his approval for?

They were a disgrace, the two of them. Especially *her*. She'd be actually flirting her orse off with my friends, if you can believe that. Oh, yeah – she thought she was a big-time MILF.

All the guys would be like, 'Hey, Mrs O'CK,' giving it loads. And Oisinn'd be there, '*Chanel No. 5* – classic, like the lady,' and she'd be there, totally loving it. I'd be like, 'Cop yourself on, you ugly smelt.'

I want to ask him about that. I've never observed him in the company of his mother, but I've seen him around his father many times and never have I heard him say anything remotely hostile to him. All those stinging insults and clever put-downs – are they just lines he wishes he'd said at the time, if only he'd had the courage to give expression to his anger?

Ross: You think I make that shit up?

'I don't know,' I tell him.

Ross: Okay, you need to see me around them, and soon. Whoa, the shit I'm going to throw at them.

'You don't have to – it was just a question.'

Ross: No, it was the old dear painting lovely rosy pictures for you of what we're supposedly like – and you bought it. You bought it, Dude, in a big-time way.

'She just said you never talk about the many happy times you had as a family. You never talk about the tender moments between you . . .'

Ross: *She* said that?

'Yes.'

Ross: Fine. I'll tell you what, put *this* story in. There was one time – can't remember what game it was, all I know is that we won – *her* and the rest of the Senior Cup Mums had, like, dinner somewhere. Maybe the Unicorn? Anyway, doesn't matter, she gets up the next morning, hungover to fock.

I'm in bed with this bird, Jessica Tohill – a friend of Sorcha's from, like, UCD?

'Your bed at home?'

Ross: Exactly. Night of passion, blah, blah, blah . . . Anyway, I didn't even try to sneak her out of the gaff. I was going to, but then I thought, I don't give a fock if the old pair know. I was like, 'Let's go downstairs, get a bit of brekky.'

Down we go. Jessica's wearing – I shit you not – a pair of knickers and the rugby jersey I was wearing for whatever match it was the day before. And I'm wearing literally just my boxer shorts – washboard stomach, the whole bit.

So the old dear happens to be in the kitchen, obviously hungover. Doesn't know what to say when *we* walk in – because it's obvious what's been going on.

Eventually, she just looks Jessica up and down and goes, 'Excuse *me* – in my day we had a thing called respect.'

I just turned around to Jessica and went, 'Ignore her – our hammering probably kept her awake all night!'

He asks me what I think of the story and I say Oedipal. He asks me what Oedipal means and I tell him it means hilarious. He says, 'Make sure and put it in then – give people a flavour of what I'm like. There's loads of stories like that about me – most of them true, I can tell you.'

I mention that I'm going to see Sorcha tonight. He's immediately defensive. He asks me why. 'You *are* still married to her,' I say. 'She's the mother of your daughter. I think that makes her relevant.'

'Obviously this book's going to be a stitch-up,' he says, shaking his head like he's disappointed in me. 'By the way, you have three Mel C songs on your iPod.'

'So?'

'Not even Spice Girls songs – *actual* Mel C singles,' he says, his face lit up like a pinball machine. 'Dude, you know what would have happened to you if you'd gone to Castlerock?'

'I'd have been taken for a homosexual and beaten to a bloody pulp?'

'Spot on,' he says. 'Mel focking C. Now – speaking of guilty focking secrets – did the old man mention where they got the name from? As in, why I'm called Ross?'

'No,' I tell him.

'Good,' he says, pushing open the door. 'And if Sorcha mentions the hickeys I had on my neck the night of her debs, it was from paintballing. And I focking mean that.'

Interview Tapes 03 and 04
Tuesday 16 September 2008
Sorcha O'Carroll-Kelly (*née* Lalor)

Sorcha is prettier than I remembered.

That's the thing about Sorcha – she's always prettier than you remembered.

She's wearing a pleated floral dress by Erdem, which I know because I complimented her on it, with a Juicy cardigan in baby pink and her hair cut in a style known as a pob. She air-kisses me on both cheeks, then conducts me into her showhouse-tidy home, saying it must be a year since she last saw me. I say it's longer.

'It *is*,' she says, 'because I was in the States for, like, two years pretty much. Oh my God, did Ross tell you I spent six months working with Stella McCartney?'

He didn't, but I say he did.

'We're, like, best best friends now.'

'Wow,' I think I say.

'You're going to think this is, like, majorly stalkerish of me, but I'm having my shop converted to, like, wind-powered electricity? *And* I've started stocking vintage. Oh my God, she has been *such* an inspiration to me.'

She slots a dark blue capsule into the Nespresso Lattissima, then asks me if I want a coffee. In her voice, there's the faintest suggestion of a Californian accent. But then, wasn't there always?

'Black,' I say. 'No sugar.'

'I really should get rid of this thing,' she says. 'Foil capsules – Stella would have a fit if she knew! But the special edition flavours this Christmas are going to be caramel, mandarin and crystallized ginger, which is like, *oh my God*! I shouldn't know that, by the way. It's just I'm friends with a girl from my J1 who works in the store on Lexington Avenue . . .'

The machine ejaculates coffee into a mug that says SLEEP IS A SYMPTOM OF CAFFEINE DEPRIVATION. She hands it to me.

I ask her about Erika. 'She's working for me in the shop,' she tells me. 'Well, she's actually in *charge* of the vintage? It's in, like, a second unit I've taken next door, although there's a door linking the two shops. They're called Sorcha and Circa.'

'The news must have come as a shock,' I say.

Sorcha: Well, especially the way Ross dropped it on me. You know he came over to the States for, like, nearly a year after Andorra?

Well, we were actually having lunch in Ketchup – as in Ketchup from *The Hills*? As in, the place where Lauren and Heidi ran into each other for the first time after the big fight, and Spencer sent over a drink for, like, Lauren and Jason, being – oh my God! – *such* a wanker.

Anyway, that's where Ross decided to finally tell me. Just, like, dropped it into the conversation? As in – oh, by the way, your best *best* friend is actually my sister. I was like, *Oh!* My God!

I wonder how the various inter-relationships have resolved themselves.

Sorcha: I actually rang Erika, told her to basically come over. See, she had, like, a major falling out with her mum? You would, wouldn't you? Imagine keeping something like that from her. So she needed, like, head space and I was like, 'Well, Ross and I are over here. California is everything that people say it is – that's it, I'm booking you a ticket,' which is exactly what I did.

'So it's not weird?' I ask.

Sorcha: I *thought* it was going to be? But, like, it actually *isn't*? Erika and I are, like, best friends forever. But now we're, like, related as well. Or we are until the divorce comes through. How *is* Ross? I haven't spoken to him this week.

I tell her about *1,001 Birds You Must Knob Before You Die* and we laugh like a couple of parents hearing their child's very first f-word – we both know it's wrong, but we also know it's not as wrong as it is funny. Sorcha shakes her head and says he'll never change. I tell her I hope he doesn't. After a wistful silence she says, 'Me too.'

When I arrived, I noticed a copy of *Dreams from My Father* poking out of her Treesje Asher Grande bag in the hall. 'I see you're reading Barack Obama's autobiography,' I say.

'I'm, like, *re-reading* it?' she says, I think rather defensively. 'I've been, like, a huge fan of his, since even *before* he won the nomination?'

I ask her what in particular drew her to Obama and she shrugs and pulls a face, as if it were a ludicrous question, then says, 'Hope,' and then a moment later, 'Pretty much hope. Pure and simple.'

The book turns out to be a handy conversational segue. I tell her I'm writing a biography of Ross – authorized, of course – and I wondered would she be prepared to talk to me.

'It pretty much depends?' she says. 'As in, what do you want to know?'

'Well,' I say, 'what do you want to know when you sit down to read *Dreams from My Father*? Or any account of someone's life? You want to know the whys. Why he is who he is today.'

She laughs, possibly at the scale of the job I've taken on, though more likely at my equating Ross O'Carroll-Kelly with Barack Obama.

'Well, first,' she says, 'I have a little girl who needs to be in bed.'

I hadn't thought about Honor, sitting so quietly in the next room that you'd never have known there was a child in the house. Sorcha goes out and returns, holding her hand. The last time I saw her, she was a tiny, organic satin-swaddled bundle in Sorcha's arms. Now, she's a walking, talking little person with a bright little face – and beautifully dressed, like her mother.

I do a quick mental count – she must be four now.

'What do we say to the man?' Sorcha asks her.

'*Ni hao*,' Honor says.

'No, you're saying goodnight. What do you say?'

I tell her it's fine. Really.

'What do you say, Honor?'

'*Wanv an*,' Honor says.

'Very good,' Sorcha says, bending down to gather her up. As she carries her out of the room, she stops to tell me that one of the things she loved most about the States was that diversity was *such* a major thing. Poet, one of Honor's playdates, was, like, part Asian-American?

While she's upstairs, I look over my crib notes – written on the back of an eflow toll charge I received in error – and realize that everything I want to ask Sorcha can be distilled down into one question: what did she see in Ross?

I figure she's asked herself that a dozen times a day since she was in her teens. When she returns to the kitchen, she answers the question without it ever being asked.

Sorcha: I suppose he *was* really, really good-looking? I mean, *everyone* thought so, certainly everyone in Mount Anville. Apart from the nose obviously.

And he was a rugby player, which was *so* my type at the time.

I knew him for ages, as in I knew *who* he was? I think every girl in South Dublin knew who he was – he was *the* guy to try to, like, *be* with.

I would have known a little bit about him through – well, you know him – Fionn de Barra? Well, I knew Fionn from the Model UN.

But the first time I plucked up the courage to go and – oh my God – *actually* talk to Ross was in Eddie Rocket's in Donnybrook . . .

I tell her I've heard contradictory accounts from Ross of the first time they met. Sometimes he says they've known each other since they were fifteen, other times he says seventeen.

She sits on the high stool beside mine.

Sorcha: That's him trying to be cool. It was 12 February 1998 and he knows it, because he sends me a card every year on the anniversary?

'Really?'

Sorcha: Even *since* our separation, which is very sweet.

It was after a game. I can't remember who they played, just that they lost and that Ross was, like, devastated.

I went over with him – he was sitting with Christian and I was actually with Erika – isn't that *so* weird? – and, without thinking, I just went, 'Hey, congrats!'

Oh! My God! I still can't believe I said that. It was just nerves. He was like, 'Er, we *lost*?'

I was like, 'Oh, I know – but congrats anyway. I thought you had an amazing game,' because I was always good at, like, thinking on my feet. I captained the Mount Anville Irish debating team two years in a row.

Okay, again, this is going to sound, like, majorly stalkerish? But I knew that his mum did a lot of, like, charity work, especially for Africa. My mum actually played in the Rwandan Emergency Charity Golf Day that Fionnuala organized in Foxrock.

'It's funny,' I say, helping myself to one of the Fair Trade stem ginger cookies she's laid out, 'Fionnuala was actually talking about that thing today.'

Sorcha: Oh, you saw Fionnuala? *Oh! My God!* Doesn't she look *so* amazing since her blepharoplasty?

She doesn't wait for an answer. I don't have one anyway.

Sorcha: Anyway, so my mum had played in her golf tournament. And, as it happens, I was, like, heavily involved in Amnesty International at the time. Aung San Suu Kyi . . . *all* the big prisoners of conscience – these were, like, major heroes to me. I thought, okay, it might help my chances if I slipped that – you know, the whole charity, caring-about-others thing? – into the conversation.

But it was actually him who brought it up. I happened to have a lot of my Amnesty stuff with me and he went, 'What's that?' and I was like, 'It's a report on the refugee crisis in Central and part of Eastern Africa. Thousands of refugees are being murdered or are dying from starvation or disease after being expelled from camps in Burundi, Rwanda and Zaire.'

He was like, 'Cool,' though not cool as in cool that all those people were dying. He meant cool as in it was cool that I cared about world events. He meant it, even though he *was* actually flirting with me?

He bought me and Erika a malt each. Oh my God, I still have the straw – as in the straw I used to drink it.

Christian, who's – oh my God – *such* a nice guy, had to go. Erika headed off as well. But Ross and I ended up sitting there for, like, hours, until the staff started giving us *major* filthies.

We weren't, like, with each other that night – as in *with* with? We were just, like, talking. But of course every girl who walked into the place – especially Muckross, who hated our actual guts because they were total wannabes – they were there just going, 'Oh my God, she's *so* going to end up being with him.'

Literally, I didn't notice the time go. It was, like, nine o'clock and I was like, 'Oh my God, I have to go,' because I had to be at the orthodontist at, like, eight the following morning . . .

I don't know – is this the kind of thing you're looking for?

I don't know what I'm looking for, but I tell her to keep talking.

Sorcha: I was getting, like, a new gumshield fitted for hockey?

Anyway, I went into the house and I was, like, oh my God, walking on air. Mum was already in bed, watching television, and I went in to her, as I always did – my mum's my *actual* best friend? And straight away she knew by me. She was like, 'What's the smile for?'

I was like, 'What are you talking about?'

She was like, 'Sorcha, you're glowing!'

I was like, 'Mum, today . . . I met the boy I'm going to marry.'

Mum was like, 'Oh my God, Sorcha, I'm so, so happy for you.'

It hits me, like a pail of ice water, the likeness between the mother Ross claims to hate and the woman Ross chose to marry.

'When did you first realize,' I tentatively ask, 'that Ross was . . . how can I put this . . .'

Sorcha: Sexually incontinent?

'Well, okay – yeah.'

Sorcha: Oh, pretty early on. Which makes me sound like *such* a sap for always taking him back. I mean, there were always, like, rumours when I was going out with him – he kissed *this* girl, or he was getting grinds from *that* girl.

And girls would come up and say it to your actual face. It'd be like, 'Oh, I scored your boyfriend,' but I'd be just like, 'Er, *loser?*' you know – *wanting* to give him the benefit of the doubt?

But we were out in his car one day, going somewhere – you remember the black Golf GTI he had? Anyway, I remember, whatever way the sun caught the windscreen . . . there, on the inside of the glass, were two footprints.

I laugh, as a reflex. 'Footprints?'
Sorcha laughs too.
'Whose feet were they?'

Sorcha: Oh, I'm pretty sure a girl called Labhaoise Dent? She was the only girl I knew with size ten feet – she played, like, basketball. Ross was seeing her behind my back.

I ask her a question then that has fascinated me for as long as I've known Ross. 'Have you ever considered the possibility that he hates women?'

Sorcha: *Hates* women? Er, I would say the opposite was the case, wouldn't you?

Lamely, I agree with her. I don't know how to tell her that sex can be as much about hatred as about love.

I ask her about the photograph on the mantelpiece. I'm surprised to see an image of them on their wedding day on display in the house. After all, it ended, just like their marriage, in tears and public ignominy.

Sorcha: Well, it wasn't, like, a total disaster? We got a beautiful, beautiful daughter out of it. And that day – it was the day that, I suppose, Ronan came into our lives. And I don't think any of us can even imagine life without Ronan now.

'I hear Cillian's no longer on the scene?' I say, a speculative edge in my voice. She quickly seizes on it.

Sorcha: Ah, you're asking me if I want Ross back. And the answer is – oh! my God! – *no*? We're actually *really* good friends now. Neither of us wants . . . the other thing any more.

I nod dully. 'Why do you think he hates his mother and father so much?' The question catches her offguard.

Sorcha: Whoa – where did that come from?

'Well, he's always talking in his books about how much he despises them. And the names he calls them . . .'

Sorcha: That's just talk.

'You've never heard him call his mother Pollock Face?'

Sorcha: No.

'Or his father Penis Features?'   *L 7932*

Sorcha: *Absolutely* no way.

'And you, of all people, would have, wouldn't you? If it was true.'

Sorcha: It's like, how *could* he hate them? I mean, Fionnuala is – oh my God – *such* an amazing mother. Look at all the things she's achieved. And she's had a lot to put up with, especially from Charles, who – don't get me wrong – I actually love to bits as well.

She suddenly remembers something.

Sorcha: Can I say one thing, like, *for* Ross? Okay, it's easy to be, like, hard on him? But this I will say. He's an amazing father. He is *so* good with Honor.

'*And* Ronan, I presume.'

Sorcha: Oh my God, yeah – he's really making up for lost time there. You heard Ronan's, like, a genius, did you? Well, nearly.

'I heard.'

Sorcha: But Ross is making sure he still has, like, a normal child-hood. You know that nuclear fallout shelter at the bottom of his mum and dad's garden?

Ross *has* mentioned it. Many times, as it happens. When he was a little boy, Charles, apparently, promised to turn it into a den, but according to Ross never found the time.

Sorcha: Ross turned it into a boys' room for him and Ronan. Just like he said he would.

Keeping the promise that his own father failed to honour. Sometimes those who are most determined to break from the past seem most enslaved by it.

But enough archaeology for one day.

As I stand up to leave, I ask Sorcha if she's worried about the gathering financial crisis. 'Oh my God, *yes*,' she says. 'It's like, *who* would have seen Habitat pulling out of Ireland?'

'Not me,' I say. 'I thought there'd always be a market for disco balls and framed prints of Borneo pygmy elephants.'

My sarcasm is lost on her and I feel suddenly bad. She says, 'It *is* a case of, oh my God, who's next?'

Then she puts her hands up to her mouth, suddenly remembering something important. She says she must RSVP her friend Claire – as in, Claire from Bray – who's getting married the day before Christmas Eve. The invitation asked guests to specify their special dietary requirements.

'Did you also hear,' she says, sounding unusually pleased with herself, 'that I'm, like, a coeliac?'

Interview Tape 05
Thursday 18 September 2008
Oisinn Wallace, JP Conroy, Fionn de Barra

'A *lot* of water,' JP says.

He means under the bridge, since we last saw each other, and he's right. These three, they used to crackle like exposed wires – but not now. They're barely recognizable from the cocksure alpha males I once knew. Oisinn doesn't look the better for all the weight he's lost – he looks ill, his complexion bleached out, his face crosshatched with three-day-old stubble. JP's hairline is retreating like a beaten army, exposing a heavily corrugated brow. Fionn is still Fionn, but minus the happy optimism that made him such good company – it might be in deference to the other two.

The tremors from the Lehman Brothers collapse are already being felt, here in Kiely's of Donnybrook. The ISEQ has been plummeting, with billions wiped off stocks – it seems some of it belonged to Oisinn.

'There's worse to come,' JP says, with a kind of grim relish. 'And we're talking way, way worse. You can see today, Lehman has just, like, devastated confidence in capital markets. I'm telling you, within a week, the Irish banks'll be on their knees looking for money.'

I think about JP in his carefree youth, his spindly body twisted up through the sunroof of his father's BMW E39, shuttling through the sink estates of West Dublin, shouting 'Affluence!' at the people.

'Especially,' Fionn says, 'because property developers and construction firms are their biggest clients – and *they're* all going bust.'

I mention one big-name developer who's supposed to have spent his last million on minders, to keep his angry creditors at one remove. They look at me blandly. Anyone who's been at a dinner party in the past six months has heard the story.

'*Everyone* said buy property,' Oisinn says. 'Put it in bricks and mortar – you can't lose.'

Fionn gives a rueful laugh. 'You know I'm teaching Leaving Cert. History this year?' he says, pushing his glasses onto the bridge of his nose. 'Well, I was talking to them today about Michael Davitt and I was think-ing, you know, for centuries, landlords were the most despised people in Ireland. They were the bane of our lives. We fought the Land War so ten-ant farmers could own the land they worked and control their own des-tinies. Then, what, a century later, we all have a few bob and what do we want to be? Focking landlords. No offence, Oisinn.'

Oisinn shrugs it off. 'I bought a lot of property,' he explains. 'A couple of houses, but mostly apartments – thirty altogether. And at this moment in time, only seven of them are occupied. Which means every month I'm paying the mortgage on twenty-three apartments, which by the end of the year are going to be worth about three-quarters of what I paid for them.

'I mean, I've got a letting agent trying to get people into them, but it's basically a tenant's market. People go and look at three, four apartments, then they ring up the next day and say, well, this other crowd are prepared to let me have a two-bed for two hundred less a month than you're asking – how low are you prepared to go? A year ago, it was the opposite.'

'Wasn't it inevitable,' I ask, 'that supply would eventually outstrip demand?'

No one answers. And no one objects when I offer to buy a round.

'Let's talk about Ross,' I suggest. Downturned mouths curl up into fond smiles. 'He's oblivious to all this,' JP says and they all laugh. 'Hasn't worked a day in nearly two years and he's like, "Global financial crisis? What global financial crisis?"'

'His reputation as a ladies' man,' I say, 'does he exaggerate it?'

JP purses his lips and blows hard, like it's so big a question, he doesn't know how to begin tackling it. It's Oisinn who answers.

Oisinn: I'll put it to you this way – if you want to know how Wesley went from being, you know, a pretty innocent teenage disco to, I don't know, the last days of the Roman Empire, then basically, talk to Ross. Goes back to when we were, like, fifteen, sixteen.

'I don't understand.'

Oisinn: Well, before *he* arrived on the scene, birds were into that whole preppy look – pink airtexes, penny loafers, maybe a cable-knit sweater thrown over the shoulders.

Ross comes along and suddenly the birds were wearing, you know, half-nothing – *all* to try and snag him. Skirts and dresses cut to here. Heels, for fock's sake . . .

JP: It's true – he influenced the way an entire generation of teen-age girls dressed. He'd score someone one week who was wearing, I don't know, a certain thing. Then the following Friday . . .

'Everyone was wearing something similar?'

JP: No – something *more* revealing. I'm telling you, every time the bar was raised, the skirts went up an inch as well. All that bare, goose-pimpled flesh. This was, like, October, November.

Oisinn: The focking St John's Ambulance were treating, what, nine, ten cases of hypothermia every night?

JP: A few of us used to, you know, sneak in the old Crouching Tiger, Hidden Naggin.

Believe it or not, Ross was the only one of our gang who didn't actually drink.

Oisinn: He didn't have time.

JP: No, there'd always be, like, a queue of girls waiting to talk to him. The rest of us were just, like, dining off his scraps.

You're going to have a difficult job, if you don't mind me saying, separating the man from the myth. Because most of the myths about Ross are actually true.

Oisinn: He scored thirty girls in there one night, though that was later on, in Anabel's. Still a house record as far as I know.

Fionn: Personally, I don't know how he coped with it. Especially then, when we were on the Senior Cup team. I mean, his love life was like a plate-spinning act. He had things going all over the place.

Oisinn: Yeah, at any one time, there would have been, say, six birds who believed they were his girlfriend. Not just believed – I mean, he would have told them. And they'd all be at every match. He'd have one in the Mounties crowd, which was usually Sorcha. There'd be one where the Alex girls stood. One in the Loreto Foxrock huddle. One in Muckross. One in Holy Child. One in Andrew's. And he had to stop them all finding out about each other. He'd fob one off while he talked to another. He's got another one waiting for him in Eddie Rocket's and another he's promised to call in an hour. And maybe another who's already gone home happy because he's dedicated a try to her.

Fionn: I mean, the tension involved in that . . .

Oisinn: You know how hard it is to keep *one* girl happy.

JP: He was actually like one of those old women you see doing the bingo – playing, like, ten cards at once.

Oisinn: Although every so often it would all, like, blow up in his face. Who was that bird – remember before the Skerries match?

JP: Was it Beulah Brogan?

Oisinn: I think it was Beulah Brogan. It *was* Beulah Brogan. And she was beautiful – you *had* to see this girl. She was, like, Rathdown. Anyway, the usual Ross – strings her along. He's getting his bit and whatever. But then she finds out about maybe one or two of the other girls he's stringing along as well. Has a total knicker-fit.

JP: Goes home crying to her old dear.

Oisinn: Exactly. The next thing, the old dear comes to see him – I shit you not – immediately before the actual match.

JP: Which, in fairness, *was* bang out of order.

Oisinn: She's all, 'So *you're* the famous Ross O'Carroll-Kelly?' and she's looking him up and down, basically trying to make little of him in front of his team-mates.

I'm pretty sure Beulah was there as well, obviously morto, trying to melt into the crowd.

So Ross looks the mother straight in the eyes and goes, 'If you want to know why I dropkicked your daughter, it's because she has tits like a seven-year-old boy – and I can see now where she got them from.'

No one laughs, not even Oisinn. It's like he's suddenly realized that it might have been funny once, but only in the context of the times.

'I've heard that Ross was shy to the point of being socially retarded as a child. Did his sudden adamantine confidence come from his success with girls?'

Oisinn: I would say it came from rugby – I don't know what you guys think.

JP: I would agree with that. See, it's, like, you've no idea how good this guy was. I mean, you couldn't see him *not* making it one day?

There are many legends regarding the famous Castlerock College Dream Team of 1998 and 1999. One has it that Father Fehily fashioned them in the manner of a master race. In the early hours of this morning, struggling to make sense of Fehily's tiny, crabbed handwriting, I read something very illuminating.

I ask if I can read them something from their old headmaster's journal.

'It was a fateful hour,' it says, 'on the first of September, nineteen hundred and ninety-two. I was returning from my lunchtime constitutional, on a crisp afternoon in early autumn, my mind strafed with questions of an ecclesiastical nature, my soul, in truth, as lonely as Field Marshal von Leeb in the forlorn hours after the loss of Tikhvin.

'My eyes were drawn to the area of the lower field, where a group of boys were involved in an *extempore* game of rugby.

'The smallest of them was little more than four feet tall, yet, already, he kicked a dead ball like no player I've seen, child or adult, before or since.

'The tallest of the group – he with the eyeglasses – moved with the nimble dispatch of the impalas I once watched in wonderment in the Botswanan *bushveld*.

'There was yet another – impossibly old-looking for his twelve years – who was as wide as he was tall and went through others with the irresistible will of a Panzer . . .'

They're all smiling.

JP: That actually happened. It was us three, then Ross and Christian. There's loads of others who've, like, *claimed* they were there that day? But take it from me, it was just us – as in the guys.

Oisinn: The thing is, we weren't all friends at the time. I mean, me and Fionn were – from the time we were in the junior school. Then Ross and Christian were mates . . .

This has always confused me. Again, Ross has told me contradictory accounts of how long he and Christian have been friends. Sometimes it's since they were eight, sometimes ten, other times not until they joined the senior school.

Oisinn: I don't think Ross likes remembering being in primary.

'Why?' I ask. They exchange looks.

Fionn: What you've got to bear in mind is that Ross, then, isn't the Ross you know today.

'So what was he like?'

Oisinn: Focking weirdo.

Fionn: Well, I think he'd admit himself that he was a bit, I suppose, withdrawn. Didn't say a lot. Kept himself to himself. I would say Christian was the only friend he had . . .

Oisinn: Well, they were friends insofar as Christian was just as weird as he was – used to just, like, follow him around the place.

See, Ross had, like, a different upbringing from the three of us? He wasn't one of the Lucky Sperm Club, as we used to call ourselves, as in his old pair didn't come from money. I know his old dear had the flower shop, but they were living in the Noggin, which was the major skeleton in his closet.

Of course, that eventually got out.

'Ross told Conchita, the shrink he was seeing in Andorra, that he was bullied in school . . .'

I leave it there, suspended. No one says anything, but there's an unmistakable air of collusion about their silence. Oisinn's effort to change the subject is artless.

Oisinn: Going back to that day you were talking about, I'm trying to remember how it ended up the five of us being there.

JP: Well, I know how *I* ended up being there. See, I'd come from, like, Willow Park, so I didn't know anyone in the secondary school. My old man, as you know, is in the property game and he would have been pretty good mates with Ross's old man.

So, big school, total stranger – my old man would have said, 'Find Charlie Kelly's boy. He'll make sure you're okay.'

Of course, Ross was four foot nothing. Afraid of his own shadow.

Fionn: I would imagine — and it's an educated guess — that Ross was drawn to Oisinn because of his size. He could protect him. That's what I *think*.

JP: So that's how we all found ourselves there. That fateful day.

The way it happened was Oisinn and Fionn were, like, throwing the ball to each other. And Oisinn, typical, totally cockeyed, sends it flying over there. I'm there, tagging behind Ross and Christian. I mean, it sounds like something from a movie, but this is exactly how it happened. Ross picks up the ball, spots it, takes three steps or whatever it was backwards, four steps to the side, then kicks it maybe forty yards, straight between the posts in the lower field. The angle had to be seen to be believed.

Oisinn: It was unbelievable. I mean, I think I even said to him, 'Do you mind me asking, where did you learn to kick a ball like that?'

He was like, 'Doesn't matter. He's a penis.'

I read them the next paragraph from Fehily's journal.

'More than the talents of any one individual player, there was something in their collective character that told me that history might well be at hand. Sweet Divine Lord, tell me — is this day really the harbinger of the glories for which I have prayed? In my mind, already forming, are the beginnings of a strategy . . .'

JP: Yeah, that was it. Denis would have seen the whole thing. So he comes over and it's, like, Ross he talks to. 'You have the facial aspect of someone I know, my child — what is your name?'

Ross tells him and then it's, like, big smile from Fehily. 'Your father is Charlie Kelly. Did *he* teach you to kick the ball like that?'

Ross has his head down.

'And pass it like you do?'

Ross just nods.

Oisinn: '*Look* at me,' Fehily goes. 'A boy who plays rugby like you do shouldn't be afraid to look anybody in the eye.'

JP: Yeah, so Ross looks up and Fehily goes, 'You're going to see, my child, that you're so much better than you think you are.'

I read on.

'These boys have stirred something in me, to the point where I believe I've been called to this post by history. They are young, but they are malleable. I will shape them to my will. For it is my destiny, I believe, to create *mein* own *Herrenvolk*.

'It is many the hour that Noel Lambkin and I have spent debating the politics of genetics. *Mein freund* from the science faculty considers my beliefs to be based on a nineteenth-century racial ideology that was discredited by science and perished with the victory of the Allies. Yet still I cleave to the notion of a supreme warrior class, in the manner of the original Aryans who invaded northern India in the second millennium, before The Coming.

'A supreme class of people who will destroy the *Untermenschen* of Blackrock College, Terenure and Clongowes Wood. Obliterate. Eradicate. Liquidate . . .'

Oisinn: Yeah, what that was, was he told us to follow him, the five of us and of course we thought we were in, like, major shit for something. So he brings us up to see Fanny Vickers, who cooked the dinners for, like, the teachers and the boarders.

'This is the future,' he says to her. 'These boys are going to bring glory to the school.'

Fanny's just like, 'Imagine that!'

He's there, 'I want you to cook these fellas steak – every lunchtime, every day.'

Fionn: We all remember the steaks.

Oisinn: Taking a shit was like having a baby – you'd be screaming for an epidural.

I laugh.

Ross was the team's undoubted leading man. In one report in

the *Star*, Derek Foley memorably described the other fourteen players on the Castlerock team as 'scrub nurses deferring to the master surgeon'.

I ask if they consider the quote fair.

Fionn: I would say it was, yeah. Look, don't get me wrong, we were all good players. But if you were a few points down with a couple of minutes to go, you just knew — give the ball to Ross . . .

JP: He'll do the necessary.

Fionn: Absolutely.

I wonder aloud then, if Ross was so much the physical reference point of the team, why didn't Father Fehily appoint him team captain?

JP: He did. Ross captained us the year we won the S.

'But not the previous year,' I say, 'when you lost in the final. Oisinn, you were captain, weren't you?'

Oisinn: I think he felt Ross's game might suffer if he had to carry, like, the extra burden of captaincy. He wanted him to be just free to play his own game.

'In many ways,' I tell them, 'I'm more interested in *that* year than the year you actually won it. I think it's just more interesting. Ross missing that kick. I mean, I've watched it a hundred times on YouTube. It was right in front of the posts — how many yards out? Did he have, like, a meltdown or something?'

Oisinn: He'd a lot of shit on his mind.

JP: Sorcha told him she was pregnant.

I hear the opening music for *Six One*. Raised voices implore the barman to switch it off. Too much bad news. There's a group of girls in the corner feeling guilty about their bellinis.

Ross's friends sink into a collective funk again, as if suddenly remembering their situation. In an effort to cheer them up, I tell them about the listeners I heard confessing their sins of profligacy to Joe Duffy. Oisinn says he used to make all of his calls on his mobile phone, even when he was at home, because he couldn't be arsed getting up to get the house phone.

They all stare into space, their minds abstracted somewhere else.

Interview Tape 06/A
Saturday 20 September 2008
Ross O'Carroll-Kelly

'Just bumped into Drico coming out of the gym,' he says. That's his opening line.

He sounds irritated.

I've just turned left onto the Leopardstown Road and I don't have my hands-free in the car. I try to cut him short with a promise to call him back later.

'He said you haven't even talked to him yet.'

'Ross, who are you talking about?' I ask.

'I'm talking about Brian O'Focking Driscoll. This is one of the greatest rugby players of, like, all-time and he'd have loved to have had me playing alongside him in the centre for Ireland – he'll tell you that himself, *if* you bothered to even ask him. Have you talked to Rog yet?'

'No.'

'What about Dorce?'

'Look, to be honest, Ross, I'm not really sure how any of those guys fit into the story . . .'

'Because they're huge fans of mine. That's what people want to read about Ross O'Carroll-Kelly – how all the greats rate him. What kind of a focking book are you writing?'

I tell him okay, I'll think about ringing Brian O'Driscoll.

'*And* Rog,' he says.

'And Rog.'

'Hey,' he says, 'did you hear the other major news? Renards is reopening as a sports and karaoke bar.'

'Jesus!'

I *hadn't* heard. I noticed a new trend in the newspapers this weekend – they're all looking for signs of Ireland adjusting to its reduced economic circumstances. Ross's old hangout pitching itself to the stag crowd might be the best indicator there is of a country cutting its coat according to its cloth.

'Anyway, I can't really talk,' I tell him, 'I'm in the car . . .'

'Where are you?' he asks.

'Just coming up to Leopardstown.'

'Why Leopardstown?'

When I don't answer immediately, he says, 'You're seeing a man about a dog.'

It would be too easy a punchline to say yes.

Interview Tape 06/B
Saturday 20 September 2008
Conor Hession

A racing reporter friend points out Conor Hession, standing in the queue for the Tote. He has the cut of a man for whom time has stood still, dressed in woollen trousers and an old, careworn, thorn-proof jacket. There's a slightly vulpine aspect to him, his features bunched in the middle of a florid little face, carpeted with absurdly generous sideburns. From the look of him, I imagine he has quite a disputatious streak.

I walk over and introduce myself and he reacts like a man expecting a writ, taking an instinctive step backwards, but without taking his eyes off me. I tell him my business, then I mention Fionnuala O'Carroll. He lifts a staying hand and says, in a voice that's surprisingly sissified, 'No, I will *not* speak to you, either on *or* off the record. I will not pay that woman the courtesy of . . .'

Whatever feelings he has about her suddenly overcome him and it's as if he can't form another word. He turns on his heel and walks away, the tails of his jacket flapping furiously behind him.

I consider staying to watch a race or two, but change my mind and make my way back to the car. I've just turned the key in the engine when I spot Conor on the far side of the car park, semaphoring wildly, like a runway controller, to try to get my attention. I kill the engine, get out and walk back to him.

'I expect *she* spoke to you,' he says. 'Filled your head with all sorts.'

I tell him she spoke to me, yes.

'Come on then,' he says. 'Somewhere quieter.'

I walk with him back to the main stand, then up two flights of stairs, while passers-by nod in acknowledgement and call him Mr Hession.

There are twenty people, maybe more, in what turns out to be his private box, standing around languidly, drinking, alternately studying the form and the passing canapés. He leads me briskly through the room and out onto a terrace overlooking the racecourse. It's bitterly cold, especially for September. There are chairs scattered around but he remains standing, so I do too.

Conor: Fionnuala O'Carroll is the most conniving, calculating person it's ever been my misfortune to meet. Svengali could have taken her correspondence course.

And that's all I'm prepared to say . . .

Clearly he's prepared to say a lot more. He wants to be indulged. I suggest he must have felt something for her, to stay with her for as long as he did. Was it seven or eight years? They were together through the last two years of school and all through college . . .

Conor: I wouldn't have said it was love, if that's what you're asking. I would say, for beginners, Fionnuala is incapable of that emotion – either giving or receiving love. What she is capable of – and eminently so – is manipulating people into *believing* that she's in love with them and that they're in love with her. Does that make sense?

'I think so.'

Conor: You see, her original interest, from recollection, was Des Reston, one of our second rows. She *pursued* him, you could say. But that all changed when she saw where I lived.

'This was the house in Enniskerry?'

Conor: Yes. Look, I wouldn't make any claims for myself – I was quite an unsightly looking thing, even in those days. Terribly shy, too – never so much as kissed a girl – so any attention from the fillies was, well, you know . . .

All these questions about the house. How many bedrooms? How many reception rooms? How many acres? How long had it been in the family?

This was the first time I'd ever spoken to the girl.

Then she asked for the, om, grand tour — *she* called it that. Lots of whooping and hollering from the other chaps as we slipped out of the kitchen. *I* didn't know what was happening — still wet behind the ears.

She pumped me expertly about the Morbier longcase in the vestibule, the chandaliers, the Constable in my father's study. Same thing. How old? What kind of price do they fetch?

Then — this is the truth, as true as we're standing here — we walked into one of the bedrooms and Fionnuala closed the door behind her. I didn't notice. I was too busy blathering away. The next thing, she's, om, taken off her jumper and she's unbuttoning her blouse.

I nearly had a heart attack. I was quite a nervous person then. I said, 'What ... what are you doing?'

Or maybe I didn't say it — maybe she just saw my reaction.

'Drop the little-boy-lost act,' she said, 'and take off your trousers.'

I said — funny to think of it now — I said, 'But this is Mummy and Daddy's room.'

'Did anything happen?' I ask.

Conor: No, nothing happened. Of course nothing happened. I was terrified of her.

But then she was suddenly my *girlfriend*. I don't even remember how it happened precisely. It's an odd thing to say, I know, given that we were together for, om, all those years, but there was no discussion about it. I think, from that day in the house, it was just assumed — and I was too polite to say otherwise.

But now you're getting me talking, you see. And I've already said more than I want to say, thank you very much ...

'You sound like you were frightened of her.'

Conor: Yes and I know it makes me sound somewhat less of a man for saying it, but it's true. I think it was clear to me that she was

quite mad. You know her mother was loopy? Well, I think Fionnuala was inclined that way, too.

'Why do you say that?'

Conor: It was just . . . she always seemed to be acting. It was like
she was playing out a part in some nineteenth-century romance
novel. I remember one night she handed me a book of poems and
got me to read to her – this is the truth – while she lay back on
the Rococo chaise, pressing the back of her hand against her
forehead.

Then Mummy had this huge collection of records. She used to
buy them when she and my father went to France. Hundreds of
them, mostly opera. Tito Schipa. Riccardo Stracciari. Domencio
Viglione-Borghesi. And Ernest Lough – yes, the boy soprano.

What Fionnuala would do was, she would call to the house when
she knew I wasn't there. Her father would drive her, drop her off
and she'd sit in the library with Mummy listening to these records.
Ingratiating herself is what she was doing.

I'd come home and they'd have Alfredo Kraus or maybe Mario
Sammarco on – we had this old gramophone, one of the original
models – and Fionnuala would be sat there with her eyes closed,
bloody . . . *conducting*.

I think about her sitting in the lounge of the Westbury and I can't sup-
press a smile.

Conor: My father hated her. He absolutely despised her. Oh, he
didn't care that she knew it either. He'd say to her, straight out, 'Are
you not expected home, Girl?'

Because she was forever in the house, you see. Even when I
wasn't there, she'd call to see Mummy. She could manipulate her.
But my father saw her for what she was – a prospector is what he
called her.

And then . . .

This is the story I *wasn't* going to tell you . . .

'I'd like to hear it.'

Conor: Well, she started to, om, *say* things about him. My father, I mean. The most awful things. She said to me one night, 'I don't like the way he looks at me.'

I said, 'What are you talking about?'

She said, 'Open your eyes, Conor. I think it's pretty clear to every-one that your father desires me.'

Desires me! I mean, it came out of nowhere.

Then – it might have been a short time later – she came back from the pantry one evening with this story about my him sup-posedly staring at her while she fixed us something to eat. 'Undress-ing me with his eyes,' is what she said. 'He had me down to my bra and panties, Conor, and I know, just know, that he was doing the most unspeakable things to my body. I mean, bestial things.'

Then she said, 'I want you to say something to him?'

This was *me* – I'd never said a cross word to my father in my life. Wouldn't dare. As it was, I could barely look him in the eye.

'It makes me uncomfortable,' she said. 'And if something is mak-ing me uncomfortable, it's your responsibility to do something about it. That's what love *is*. Not that you'd know anything about it, being raised by nannies.'

She could really wound you when the mood took her.

So I *did* say it to him. I mean, Fionnuala kept at it, chipping away. She said, 'What if he cornered me one night and just *took* me? Took me for himself. That would be rape, Conor, and for the rest of your life you'd have to live with the guilt of knowing that you let it happen.'

She'd get inside your head and . . .

Well, I was persuaded to say something. I was very frightened, of course. I was, om, trembling when I knocked on the door of his study. And even that was something one *never* did – it was a rule of the house that he was never to be disturbed while he was working.

I said the things that Fionnuala had told me. I told him I was sure it was all a huge misunderstanding, but she did feel uncomfortable around him and if that was the case, then . . .

He stood up, walked around the desk, then slapped me hard across the face. 'Stupid boy!' he said.

And they were the last words he spoke to me for four years.

He waves at somebody through the glass doors. I follow his line of vision. 'That's Abigail,' he says. 'My wife . . .'

After a moment's silence, I realize he's awaiting my judgement. 'Very nice,' I say, though what I mean, I suppose, is that she's done a good job of preserving whatever it was that first attracted him to her.

'Where did you go to college?' I ask.

Conor: Trinity, of course. I studied Law and German. Fionnuala did cookery or somesuch.

'Catering and Hotel Management,' I remind him.

Conor: Yes, you're quite right! Because she would tell people she was *reading* Catering and Hotel Management. Reading it! In Cathal Brugha Street! Although she *was* an extraordinary cook. You see, I think she took over the role of the homemaker when they packed her mother off to the funny farm.

If I was being suspicious – and you always had to be where Fionnuala's motives were concerned – I would say that she chose cookery in college to let my mother see what a wonderful wife she'd make.

You could say it was her apprenticeship.

'Is it true you were engaged?'

Conor: I did buy her a ring. Gave it to her one night in the Red Bank, a wonderful fish restaurant on Dame Street that we both liked – you wouldn't remember it. Best baked sea bream in Ireland.

It wasn't an engagement ring as such. There *were* diamonds in it. But I certainly didn't propose marriage.

You see, that just shows how terribly conflicted I must have been. Together for all those years, I must have felt I had to offer her *some-*

thing. But at the same time, I knew that my father, who still wasn't speaking to me, was never going to give us his blessing.

I *was* terribly conflicted now that I think back. I think, yes, that's why I produced this ring, which *looked* like an engagement ring but was really just a symbol of my, om, confusion . . .

I was about to do the final year of my degree. Fionnuala, if memory serves, was finished with whatever it was she was doing and there was a sense of, you know, what's next?

Of course, she had no intention of ever becoming a chef or working in a hotel. There was an expectation there that she was going to marry me.

I told her I was planning to, om, do my Master's when I finished my degree. I had no real interest in doing it, if the truth be told, but it was my way of stalling.

Perhaps what I really wanted was Fionnuala to tire of it – the waiting – and end it *for* me, do what I hadn't the backbone to do.

But Fionnuala was, om, nothing if not resilient. Oh, she hung on in there. Decided to go to teacher training college then – again, buying herself time.

At the same time . . .

'What?'

Conor: I suppose, in a perverse sort of way, I didn't want to lose her. I'd become, om, oddly reliant on her. One would have to have been – *that* many years with someone *that* controlling. She told me how I should dress, who I should be friends with – oh, everything.

Then he does something that truly surprises me. He asks after her. 'I've read one or two of her books,' he says, stealing a surreptitious look over his shoulder. 'Abigail has no idea, of course – she wouldn't have them in the house. Very entertaining, though.'

I tell him I'll pass that on if he wishes. He says no.

Conor: You know, I went about it in a very cowardly way, looking back. Breaking up, I mean. Didn't handle it very maturely. But then,

I didn't have much character about me. You have to remember, the two people who'd had the greatest bearing on my life were Fionnuala and my father, two very controlling – very similar, actually – people.

My father and I ended up having this, om, summit. I was doing my Master's at the time, so it must have been *more* than four years we didn't speak. More like five.

Anyway, he sat me down, said it was time I decided once and for all what my intentions were regarding *this person*, as he called her. I was just so relieved that he was speaking to me again, I think I would have agreed to anything he asked me.

He as good as said that if I married her, I wouldn't inherit.

But even then, I was a coward about it, you see. Kept trying to find the moral steel from somewhere to tell her. I think she knew, though. For the next few months – even though I never told her what way I was thinking – she sensed that I was disengaging. She just got tired of waiting around. Gave me an ultimatum – marry me or I'm gone, that sort of thing. I don't know what she saw in my eyes – some flicker of something. And then she *was* gone.

And now you can go too . . .

Interview Tapes 07 and 08
Thursday 25 September 2008
Erika Joseph and Sorcha Lalor

'I was interested in buying this dress, but it's got, like, one or two sequins missing from it?'

'Yes, it's vintage? This is the vintage *section* of the shop?'

'Vintage? Vintage, as in . . .'

'Well, vintage is a classic designer piece that's been previously owned . . .'

'Oh . . . So what'll you give me off it then?'

'Give you off it?'

'It's been worn . . .'

'No, that's its charm, you see. Someone has worn this dress and loved it so much, she felt it was a joy that should be shared. The girl we bought it from? She spent an hour saying goodbye to it . . .'

'Really?'

'Cried her eyes out. We had to get security to drag her out of here. *By the ankles* . . .'

'Oh my God. Well, I *do* love it. *And* it's from the hem that the sequins are missing. I mean, who's going to see . . .'

'Exactly. And do you mind my saying, it makes you look really thin – accentuates your clavicles.'

'Okay, I'll take it.'

I'd heard about the change that had come over Erika, but I had to see it with my own eyes to believe it. Gone is the old hauteur, the tense lines of her beauty, the torqued-up snigger with which she used to celebrate the misfortunes of others. There's a lightness about her, from her laugh to the manner of her dress, eschewing the old black for white linen trousers and pink cardigans and only the subtlest hint of make-up, to enhance, not to distract. The *über*-bitch who could flay you with just one whip-sharp put-down has transformed herself into a kind of Julie Andrews of retail.

'The divorce parties,' I say. 'That was going great for you, wasn't it? What happened?'

'I just decided it was wrong,' she says, carefully refolding a black satin boat-neck top. 'It *was* wrong, making money out of other people's unhappiness?'

I nod, then compliment her handling of the last customer. I ask her if she thinks vintage will catch on here. Will Irish people buy second-hand clothes for twice their original price, especially in the current economic climate?'

'You mean the recession?' she says. 'Well, Charles says a recession's nothing to be frightened of.'

'And he should know,' I say. 'He made his millions during the last one. So did all of his heroes, come to think of it – JP McManus, Dermot Desmond . . .'

'Don't get me wrong,' she says, 'it would be, oh my God, *so* terrible if people ended up losing their homes? But Charles says that what's happening is part of a natural cycle. As in, we're poor, we work hard and we all become wealthy. But wealth dulls our wits. It makes us complacent. So then we have to learn it all over again, the things that made us rich in the first place – how to streamline, how to undercut, how to give people what they want . . .'

I suspect that might not be ten-year-old clothes and today's prices.

'It's *Charles* then?' I ask. 'Not *Dad*?'

She laughs. 'You know what, we tried it for a little while? Like maybe a week? But it was just, like, *too* weird. So we decided on Charles . . .'

'It's been, what, two years now? Is everything, I don't know, normal now? I mean, how do you feel about them keeping that from you for all those years?'

Erika: The way I look at it is, what happened back then happened. Mum and Charles were both married to other people and everyone involved tried to make the best of a bad situation. And they made choices, which might not have been the best choices, or maybe they were. Who are any of us to say?

Look, it took me a while – and a lot of counselling, believe me – to get to a place where I can say that. You know I didn't speak to my mum for, like, a whole year?

'Yeah, I heard.'

Erika: Which was just, you know, crazy. Because there I was, over in the States, trying to form a relationship with Charles by phone from the other side of the Atlantic. And, I suppose, redefine what-ever relationship I had with Ross. And at the same time, my mum and Charles were, you know, restarting where they left off all those years ago. It's an amazing love story really – they'll tell you all about it, I'm sure. Anyway, Mum was the only one I wasn't actually *talking* to? Which was stupid.

'So, what, you woke up one day and saw sense?'

Erika: Actually, it was Fionnuala who talked sense into me. Well, you know she's living over there now? Well, we used to see her all the time, Sorcha and I. We used to go for, like, lunch and treatments together. Anyway, there was one night she took just me out, to Geoffrey's, which is this really, like, upmarket restaurant in Malibu. They have, like, valet parking? And she told me that she blamed herself because she basically told Charles that he couldn't have any-thing to do with me.

'And she felt, what, guilty about that?'

Erika: About a lot of things. But especially that. She told me all sorts – she didn't have a relationship with her own mother, see.

'I know – she was in an institution.'

Erika: Well, she said, 'You have your mother *and* your father now. They're not perfect, but none of us is. Don't act out of anger – I learned that the hard way. Don't waste your life away focusing on your pain. And if you can avoid it at all, don't grow old with regrets.'

    I just, like, burst into tears, took out my phone, rang Mum.

'She's certainly an *interesting* woman,' I say.

Erika: Yeah, she's amazing.

'What about Charles? Had you ever met him before you found out he was your father?'

Erika: Once – and it's quite a funny story actually. It was in their house.

'In Foxrock?'

Erika: Yeah, I would have been about sixteen, seventeen? Sorcha had decided to break it off with Ross – yet again! – and she asked me to come along for, like, moral support. Charles came in. 'Ah, young Sorcha!' he shouts at the top of his voice. 'How wonderful!' House shaking to its foundations.

I laugh.

Erika: Then he said, 'And who, pray tell me, is *this*?'
   He told me recently that he thought his heart had stopped when he saw me. He said the only way he could think to describe it was that he found himself suddenly staring into his own eyes.

'He knew immediately?'

Erika: Well, no, Mum used to send him photographs of me every year, usually on my birthday. He actually rang Mum that night and said, 'I've just met her. God, Helen, isn't she beautiful!'

She tosses back a curtain of hair.

Erika: So, what, you're writing a book about Ross? Is his head not big enough as it is?

'I think Ross may have the wrong end of the stick as to what kind of book it's going to be,' I say. 'He might not be happy with the finished product.'

Erika: He's telling everyone it's going to be, like, a tribute to him? I heard him on the phone the other day to Laura Woods, coaching her what to say in case you rang . . .

I laugh. Then she says something that rocks me back on my heels.

Erika: You will be fair to him, won't you?

'As fair as I can, I suppose.'

Erika: Because he *is* actually a nice guy. I know that's going to sound, like, weird coming from me.

'I mean, you really hated him.'

Erika: I know.

'Like *really* hated him.'

Erika: I know. We didn't get off on the right foot, put it that way. Look, I knew Ross, or I knew all about him, for about six months before Sorcha was ever with him? He was actually seeing Brooke, this girl I knew from, like, horse-riding. Have you heard this story before?

'It sounds like one of the few I haven't.'

Erika: Well, one Friday night, he turns up at Brooke's house in Sandymount with a bunch of flowers. So she's all delighted with herself and her mum's going, 'What a lovely young man,' and she offers to put them in a vase. As she's arranging them, she finds this playing card, stuck down among the stems. The queen of hearts.

And on it's written, 'We'll always love you, Diana,' and then all these kisses.

'*Princess* Diana?'

Erika: He took them from the memorial outside the British Embassy.

'Jesus!'

Erika: Stole them. So that was the first thing I ever knew about him. I told Sorcha. I was like, 'Do yourself a favour, Girl. The guy's a loser.'

'But, what, now you're suddenly a fan?'

Erika: He can be an idiot – you know him. But he has got a heart of gold.

'Yeah, I'd go along with that.'

Erika: He's unbelievably loyal.

'As long as you're not sleeping with him.'

Erika: Exactly – I'm talking about to his friends? And you've seen him around Honor and Ronan. He's an amazing father. And there's a lot of so-called good people you couldn't say that about . . .

'Ronan would be, what, your nephew now?' I say, still trying to get my head around all the new configurations. 'I haven't seen him for nearly two years.'

Erika: Oh, you'll barely recognize him. He's like a little mad professor.

She giggles – a noise I've never heard her make.

It's at that point that Sorcha walks in from the non-vintage part of the shop. She tells me she was going to phone me.

Sorcha: Oh my God, after you left the other night. See, I kept thinking about what you said? About Ross hating his mum and dad?

Erika: *Hating* them?

Sorcha: That's what he said. And I thought of, like, loads of really nice things he did for them over the years. Like, Erika, do you remember the day his granddad died?

'His granddad?' I say. 'That'd be Fionnuala's father?'

Sorcha: Exactly. Oh my God, Ross was *so* amazing. Fionnuala *always* talks about it. He was the one there with her when she, like, got the news? And he took total charge. Made her tea – loads of milk and sugar, good for shock. He actually went upstairs and picked her out a lovely outfit – I remember Fionnuala saying it was exactly what she'd have chosen herself – and he drove her to the hospital to say her goodbyes.

All the ringing around her friends, Ross did it all. There were people calling around to offer their sympathies and of course Fionnuala was thinking, oh my God, I've got *nothing* to offer them. She goes out to the kitchen and there's Ross, spreading and slicing – enough sandwiches to feed an army.

I mean, I was there, in the actual house. There was even, like, mango and crayfish.

Fionnuala was like, 'Thank you, Ross,' and Ross was like, 'That's okay, Mum.'

Now, does that sound like someone who hates their mum?

An old lady, looking woefully lost, blunders into the company. 'Is it all second-hand?' she wants to know.

'Vintage,' Sorcha says, with a degree of tartness.

Erika smiles sweetly.

'I was with War on Want for years,' the woman says. 'Aren't you very good, all the same, giving up your time?'

Interview Tape 09
Friday 26 September 2008
Ross O'Carroll-Kelly

I'm sitting in Gourmet Burger in Dun Laoghaire, reading about panic spreading like a pathogen across the country. The *Evening Herald* says that people are turning up at their local banks and leaving with every cent they own stuffed into their Bags for Life. Could this all be a bad dream? It seems like only a year ago we were spending our SSIAs on hot tubs and Alaskan holidays. Now we're burying our life-savings in the garden.

I close the paper and stare out the window at the rain coming down in heavy stair-rods – the perfect correlative for the collective mood. The world has a sense about it tonight that someone should be collecting two of every animal.

'Did you see the George Hooks that focking waitress was giving me?' Ross has arrived.

'Holy shit, she's a ringer for Tinsley Mortimer . . .'

I ask him how he is and he tells me to shut the fock up and listen.

'I've been working my hole off for you,' he says. 'I've come up with, like, two or three people who can give you the goods on my old pair. Audrey Mannion is this friend of hers – *ex*-friend, who she fell out with years ago over the flower shop I was telling you about. Audrey was friends with Mrs Goad, who the old dear basically swindled. Audrey is, like, Sophie's old dear? Hates my old dear with a focking passion. Number's on that . . .'

He pushes a large manila envelope across the high table to me. 'What's *in* it?' I ask.

'Loads of, like, newspaper clippings,' he says, 'all about Conalswood . . .'

Conalswood is the infamous dormitory suburb on Dublin's western-most outskirts, built by Charles and Hennessy with the aid of bribes to politicians. 'You need to talk to the two journalists who wrote all that shit.

Dude called Toft from the *Times* and a dude from, I think, the *Sunday Indo*. But *definitely* talk to them. I'm sure they've got loads of shit they *couldn't* actually publish?'

I thank him for the trouble to which he's clearly gone. 'Well, the public needs to know what these people are actually like,' he says. 'So, who else have you been talking to?'

'I met the guys,' I tell him.

'So I hear. What was Fionn saying? He's a focking steamer, isn't he?'

I shake my head. 'Why is everybody gay to you?'

'Oh, so you're defending him?'

'I'm not defending . . . Look, I'm saying there's nothing to defend.'

I've always believed that Ross has an affection for Fionn that he can't express except through casual abuse.

'Aren't most rugby players gay anyway?' I ask, feigning innocence.

'Excuse me?'

'All those games you've told me about involving, I don't know, biscuits and mince pies and slapping each other's nipples. You're telling me there's no sexual subtext to that?'

'There wasn't. There isn't.'

'Flicking each other with wet towels? Wedgies?'

'Whoa, I know what you're doing,' he says, pointing a finger at me. 'You're yanking my wire.'

'It was just a question,' I say, struggling to hide a smile.

'Do you know how many birds I've been with in my life? Do you want me to go through the Mount Anville class of 1999 yearbook with a highlighter pen for you?'

'Forget I said anything.'

'Do you know what, if you'd said that to me in front of the rest of the guys, I can guarantee you this – your underpants would be hanging from one of those focking streetlights out there . . .'

'Which, of course, would prove *your* case beyond doubt . . .'

He smiles. 'You know, there was a Celine Dion song on your iPod as well – and it wasn't *even* the one from *Titanic* . . .'

'I met Erika and Sorcha today.'

'Whoa, what were *they* saying?'

'Nice stuff, actually . . . Can I ask you something? You and Erika – *before* you knew you were related – it is true that you two . . . I mean, does that ever come up?'

'No.'

'Never?'

'No – and that's another thing you're never allowed to mention again in my company. So, what was Sorcha saying?'

'Again, all good stuff. In fact, she said you're very nice to your parents.'

'She's out of order there,' he says. 'And we're *talking* bang.'

'Well, she also said you were great to your mother when your grandfather died. She says she saw, you know, genuine love between you two . . .'

He adjusts his features in a look of shock, then looks around for someone to share his outrage.

Ross: I can't believe I'm having to constantly justify myself to you. You're asking me was I *nice* to my old dear when her old man died? Who the fock wouldn't be? Her old man had just *died*.

Okay, I'll tell you an even better story. About her dog . . .

From the sudden warmth of his expression, I know he's going to tell me some awful atrocity story, just to crush the joy out of the moment.

Ross: She had this dog called Alexis. Little focker of a thing. It was just this, like, ball of fur – this golden-brown colour? – with this ugly little face sticking out, like a fox. *Yap, yap, yap, yap, yap.* One of them.

The point is, she was always focking barking at me. Or snapping at me.

'How old were you at the time?'

Ross: I was a baby.

I wonder what kind of mother goes out and buys a dog when she already has a new-born baby to look after. One whose husband has just fathered a daughter with another woman? Or perhaps I'm overreaching.

Ross: And *she* never stopped her, of course – as in, the old dear.

I had this toy – it was, like, a rubber King Kong? Anyway, I loved it. Whatever. So one day the dog takes it and she brings it to her little basket in the old dear's bedroom and she starts chewing it, as in chewing its actual head off?

So of course I'm thinking, hey, I'll just take it back. So I stick my hand in to get it and she goes for me. If I hadn't pulled my hand away, she'd have seriously savaged it.

And that was the end of King Kong.

But then, of course, I suppose every week I was getting bigger and bigger, just growing – as you do. So I noticed that suddenly the dog was becoming more and more, like, wary of me? *She* stayed the same size, you see. Took me a while to cop it, that there'd been this, like, change in the whole, I suppose, balance of power between us?

I mean, she'd still bark at me, but I'd just, like, growl back at her, then she'd focking run and hide behind the old dear.

Then one day she bit me. And the old dear had to get her put down . . .

He smiles thickly, almost carnally. He wants me to ask what happened next. I oblige.

Ross: Basically, I remember always looking at the dog, thinking, I'm going to focking fix you in a big-time way. I'll get you back for King Kong. And loads of other shit.

I would have had, I suppose, all sorts of tortures planned for her, but the trick was to do it without leaving a mark. To basically do something without it looking like I did anything?

God, that waitress can't *actually* keep her eyes off me.

Anyway, I'd pretty much given up on the idea when this particular day, I walk into the sitting room and there she is, asleep in front of the fire. See, she'd baskets all over the focking house.

Instantly, I knew what I was going to do. Looked over my shoulder. Old dear was in the kitchen. Old man was, I don't know, somewhere else. The usual. Shut the door, quietly. Tiptoed over to her. She was totally out of the game. Very gently, grabbed her sort of snout, then sort of, like, prised her jaws aport. She had, like, shitloads of teeth, we're talking millions of them, small but unbelievably sharp.

She started to wake up, so I knew I had to be quick.

I put these two fingers on this hand here – the left – between her jaws, between her two sets of teeth. Then, with the other hand, I hit her the most unbelievable thump on the nose – in the same way that you'd punch, like, a cow?

Crunch! Her teeth sank into my fingers. It was pure focking agony and I let out this scream, as did the dog. I had a quick look at the old fingers and I'd actually managed to draw blood.

Of course, the old man comes pegging it into the room, followed by the old dear. *She* ran straight for the dog – I remember that.

I'm crying, as in really crying – because it actually *was* pretty sore? – and the old man's, I suppose, comforting me.

Of course, the dog hasn't a clue what happened. She's still groggy because it *was* a hell of a dig she got. Her eyes are all over the gaff and she's got, like, froth coming out of the side of her mouth.

So the old man – this is pretty funny – *he's* thinking about my rugby career. 'No permanent harm done,' he says, 'though I think someone's going to be passing off his other hand for a little while.'

Then he turns around to the old dear and goes, 'That's it, Darling. We're going to have to get rid of it.'

I swear to God, she actually looked at *me*. The old man had to go, 'The dog, Fionnuala! The dog!'

The waitress Ross has been talking about stops by the table and asks him if he'd like something to eat. 'Yeah,' he says, looking her up and down, 'but you're wearing them, Babes.'

I watch her cheeks kindle. She fidgets with her menu. I offer her a polite smile by way of apology and tell her I'll stick with the coffee. She turns away.

'Someone wants me bad,' he says.

'Obviously. So were you there,' I ask, 'when the dog was put down?'

I'm wondering is there a link between this and any of the other animal cruelty stories that are a recurring theme in his life story. There was

Oreanna's cat. There was Oreanna's dog. I think I remember him, somewhere in his distant past, throwing a poodle into a garden with a Rottweiler.

Ross: Too focking right I was there. Big-time. I would have, like, insisted on it? Just to be in the room when they gave her the jab. Make sure *my* boat-race was the last she saw. Let her know it was a case of, you know, no one focks with Ross O'Carroll-Kelly!

He stands up, calls me a loser, rather gratuitously I think, and announces that he's going. He gives the manila envelope two sharp taps, then says, 'Get the goods, Dude – start doing some actual work.'

I watch him intercept the waitress on her way to the table with my coffee. A short conversation takes place. Ross says something to her and she offers him a smile bookended by the most perfect dimples. He pulls out his phone and she dictates her number to him. On his way out the door, he waves the phone at me and shouts, 'Oh, gay, am I? Put that in your focking book.'

Interview Tape 10
Saturday 27 September 2008
Helen Joseph and Charles O'Carroll-Kelly

The smell assaults me the moment I step onto the travelator – earwax, except a thousand times more pungent, stealthily making its way through the Merrion Shopping Centre. There's a commotion happening outside the shop and I have to struggle against an angry current of bodies to reach the door. Charles opens it no more than a few inches, a gap just wide enough for me to insinuate myself through.

'The Barbarians are at the gates!' he says, barking like a coxswain. 'It's the *Vieux-Boulogne*, I shouldn't wonder. Arrived last night. They wash the rind in beer, of all things.'

'Is that what the smell is?' I ask.

'Yes, something to do with the way the beer reacts with the enzymes.'

'So who are all those people – the other shop-owners?'

He doesn't answer, just bangs on the inside of the window and shouts, 'It's actually quite a mild cheese to taste!'

A voice behind us says, 'I don't think that's going to cut any ice with them, Charlie.'

Helen is strikingly attractive, pretty and petite, with strawberry-blonde hair – a real surprise – pinned up, to expose a long, graceful neck. I can see Erika in her jade-coloured eyes and slightly timorous nose. She shakes my hand and introduces herself, then turns to Charles and says, 'Why don't you go out and speak to them?'

'Because what if it's not the *Vieux-Boulogne* at all?' he says. 'What if it's the *Reblochon*? Or the *brie de Meaux*?'

'Charlie,' she says, smiling sweetly, 'whatever it is, you need to go out there. They have businesses to run, too.'

After a brief hesitation, Charles opens the door, squeezes out through it and surprisingly quickly the clamour dies down.

'He has a way with people,' Helen says, still watching him through th
window. 'He doesn't always realize it . . .'

I look around the shop. The walls have been stripped back to the origin
brown brickwork to give it a farmhouse kitchen aspect. There's no coun
ter yet, no display. The shopfitters are due this morning. We sit on upturne
wooden crates.

I've come, I suppose, to hear the love story that Erika mentioned. 'Yo
and Charles,' I say, 'it must be some story.'

'And you want to hear it,' she says.

Helen: Well, I should start by saying that he's the most adorab
man I've ever met. Honestly – before *or* since.

He was always so, well, charming obviously. So chivalrous, whic
I loved. Very old-fashioned in that way, even for the times – I'r
talking about the late fifties, early sixties. Even the way he dresse
He always seemed to be five years behind whatever was the fashio
And of course he had that lovely bumbling way about him. Yo
know what he's like.

His first words to me were: 'Charlie Kelly's the name – wonder
if you were, em, interested in a dance and so forth.' It was 'There
No Other Like My Baby' by The Crystals. Haven't forgotten it t
this day. And he's still Charlie to me – I presume you have notice
that. Our first date, he took me to see *Escape from Zahrain*, with Y
Brynner, in the Deluxe on Camden Street.

Oh, yes, I was smitten. You see, *everybody* loved Charlie. Everyor
who met him adored him. And the most charming thing about hir
was that he didn't know. He genuinely didn't know.

He had this wonderful warmth to him. Could be gauche as he
of course. When he said the wrong thing, which was often, it w
always at a couple of hundred decibels. But you never cared becau
you knew his heart was in the right place.

He was just this lovable lug of a thing.

And a hopeless dancer. Because he was big – as he is now. We
over six feet. I was barely five, by the way. And no sense of rhyth
whatsoever. When he was on the dancefloor, he was a danger t

other people. I'm sure people were maimed by him. But no one ever told him because you just didn't want to hurt his feelings.

Outside, there's a sudden dam-burst of laughter. Charles is working his magic.

I tell her I find it difficult to reconcile the Charles she talks about with the media image of the man – the land speculator who made a fortune off the back of corrupt property development and the local politician famous for his extremist views, often aired in the letters pages of the *Irish Times*, where he once described flooding in Ringsend as a modern-day Exodus, with God, in his anger, smiting the welfare classes.

Helen: I always put that down to his father.

'His father?'

Helen: It's the kind of thing *he* said all the time. And Charlie always tried to *be* like him. I don't know why. God forgive me, he was a horrible, bitter little man.

He'd ignore Charlie, for no reason at all. This was when he was a little boy. I mean, there wouldn't have been a row or anything. Charlie would say something to him, maybe ask him a question, and if his father didn't feel like answering him, he wouldn't. Sometimes he'd go weeks without speaking to him. There was only the two of them in the house, because his mother died when he was still a baby. But can you imagine how lonely that was for Charlie growing up?

The door suddenly opens. 'Going to give this lot some of that wonderful *Raschera* we were saving for the opening,' Charles says. He disappears into the room at the back of the shop, then returns a moment later carrying a large box. 'Détente has broken out, I'm happy to report, though the offending cheese is going to have to go, I'm afraid, but it's a small price to pay for, quote-unquote, peace in our time!'

He steps outside again.

Helen: I used to say to him, 'Why don't you sleep here?' you know, whenever his father took one of his moods. We lived quite close – we were on Booterstown Avenue, they were on Cross. See, there were very few cars about in those days, so distance was a huge issue, which it isn't today, of course. Back then, you did your courting locally. I think most marriages among people of our generation were determined by geography as much as by love.

My parents would have been happy for him to sleep under our roof. I think they'd have let us sleep in the same bed! Oh, they worshipped him. It was like, you know, he'd come through the door – the big voice again – and the house felt suddenly full. Something nice to say to everyone.

They thought he was great. Everybody did . . .

Outside, the crowd disperses. Charles returns, looking especially pleased with himself. He leans against the wall, next to where we're sitting.

Charles: I expect you're telling him about the famous good old days.

Helen was terribly exotic, you know. Not unlike Debra Paget.

Helen: Oh, Charlie!

Charles: Wasn't only me who said it. We were quite the little movers in our day, weren't we? And when we weren't reeling and rocking, let me just say, we were eating our famous knickerbocker glories. Of course, O'Connell Street at that time wasn't the no-go area it is now, oh no, it had all these wonderful ice-cream parlours. You had Caffolas. You had Forte . . .

Helen: The Rainbow Café.

Charles: Of course, the Rainbow. This is where Helen and I would spend our Saturday mornings, talking ourselves hoarse, naturally. Oh, we had wonderful times in there. Every Saturday morning, no matter what was going on in our lives. Sometimes just the two of us, sometimes with friends.

You know, it was one of the only times you met people from the other side of the city. It was where southside and northside met. So you were meeting people from all these far-off places – Clontarf, Portmarnock, Malahide. And sometimes even country people. And *mixing* with them, as if they were just the same as you.

Helen: And the music. The Rainbow had a jukebox. So it was Jim Reeves – 'Put Your Sweet Lips A Little Closer To The Phone'. And then later on, where we were in college, it was The Beatles. 'Please Please Me', all those.

Charles: My father, I should probably say, Helen, wasn't exactly enamoured with all the – quote-unquote – rocking and rolling I was doing, was he, Darling?

Helen: Well, he was a very serious man, wasn't he?

Charles: Yes, a bit dour, you could say. He was an engineer, of all things. *From* Dublin, though he worked for years in Belfast, in the shipyards. He would have been one of the few Catholics there. I think the experience accounted for what I always called the Calvinistic streak in him – thought there should be a high ratio of misery to pleasure, that kind of thing.

One of the things I remember was, he used to tie his shoelaces so tight that his feet would swell up. I remember staring at his feet, the mark of the boots on them – the little laceholes and everything. I don't know how he managed to walk.

But work hard, live modestly – that was his thing. No time for nonsense.

Losing my mother can't have been easy, of course. She was from up there – Larne, though they moved down here after they got married. Died of tuberculosis – bloody awful thing – when I was still a baby. The old boy, well, he never got over it.

It suddenly occurs to me that Charles and Fionnuala had almost identical childhoods – both were only children, both were raised by overweening fathers. But that's jumping ahead of the narrative.

Charles: It was very seldom I ever saw the old boy happy. Sport was about the only thing. I remember sitting with him, listening to Ronnie Delaney win in fifty-six. The famous Turkey Trotter, because of the way he ran. I remember him shouting, 'Here he comes – right from the back of the field. The bloody Turkey Trotter.'

Gold for Ireland and whatever you're having yourself.

He was a bloody good miler himself, you see. Ran until well into his forties. And rugby. He loved rugby. Rather famously won two Ireland A caps on a development tour of Uruguay.

Yes, we went to all the games together. Jackie Kyle – I often tell Ross, I'm one of the lucky ones who can say they saw him play numerous times, though I was too young to remember the famous Grand Slam.

No, there *were* happy times – don't do him an injustice. I remember when I was a boy, there's that wonderful photograph of all those chaps sitting on that girder, having their lunch, high over Manhattan. Well, he *had* that photograph in this little box of things he kept. Might have clipped it out of the *Irish Times*, which he bought religiously by the way. Used to tell me that the chap on the end – far right – was my grandfather. And, you know, for years and years I believed him. *Wasn't* him, of course. My grandfather was a labourer – worked on the famous Shannon Scheme. Cap S, cap S. In Ardnacrusha, naturally.

I think my father's problem was that he had all these hopes for me.

Helen: He wanted Charlie to be an engineer as well.

Charles: And I went and bloody well disappointed him.

Helen: Don't talk like that.

Charles: He was always in awe of people who built things – ships obviously, skyscrapers also, but his favourite was bridges. I think that's what he wanted me to do.

He was – you can use this word – obsessed with bridges. Had all these books. The Sydney Harbour Bridge – the span of the steel arch is five hundred and three metres and weighs thirty-nine thousand tonnes. Had all these facts and figures in his head. One point two million steel rivets to hold the Golden Gate together. This was the kind of thing that interested him.

Anyway, I was never going to be building bridges. Didn't have the grey matter, I'm afraid.

I remember having this, oh, terrible row with him when I told him I wanted to drop mechanical drawing to do business organization. He really was furious. Oh, he caused a right how-do-you-do, of course. Marched me up to Castlerock, shouting this, that and a fair portion of the other.

'What kind of a school . . .' and so forth.

Father Fehily – oh, God rest poor Denis – he took him into his office, told him I was probably making the right decision. And a very mature decision for a boy of fourteen. Said I had an excellent aptitude for figures and that business was probably my calling. As for drawing, well, I couldn't draw the bloody curtains – still can't, to this day! But as far as my father was concerned, I'd humiliated him . . .

His mobile phone rings, cutting him off mid-flow. It's Hennessy.

'Hello there, old chap,' Charles says. 'We're here talking about a subject I know is dear to your own heart – namely, the good old times. You'll have to have a word with this chap yourself, Hennessy – tell him all about *our* carry-on over the years . . .'

He mouths an apology to Helen, then takes the phone through to the back room.

Helen's voice drops to a minor key.

Helen: He would have done anything to win his father's respect.

'Including rugby?'

Helen: Charlie wasn't *interested* in rugby. His father brought him to all the games, but I never once heard Charlie talk about it. He told me himself he only played it because he thought it would make his father like him.

I remember when he made the school team. They lost in the first round to Pres. Bray. But Charlie wasn't upset because they were out of whatever cup it was. He was upset because his father hadn't come to see him.

I tried to pretend he had – you'd have done anything to protect Charlie's feelings. I said I saw him there, but he knew I was lying. He cried his heart out. He was a big stupid softie anyway, but he really cried that day.

'So, what, you and Charles were together just at school?'

Helen: No, *and* college. We were in college together – what would have been the College of Commerce in those days, in Rathmines. Charlie did Business and I did Secretarial.

Oh, he was the same old Charlie in college. You could hear his voice around every corner. Always putting a smile on people's faces. I tried to persuade him to run for student president. It would have been a landslide – you know, that's how popular he was. Of course, he had no idea. His father was constantly undermining whatever confidence he had in himself.

My parents would have encouraged him a lot. They would have been very business-minded. My father had just gone into haulage. This was when he was in his late forties. He actually quit his job as assistant transport manager with PJ Carroll and built up this truck business from nothing. Transporting cigarettes at the start, then later coal. My mother did all the books.

Charles returns again and rejoins the conversation.

Charles: Yes, Helen's father — James, if you don't mind — he very kindly offered me a job. This was way back, just after I started college. It was Helen's eighteenth birthday, if I remember correctly. He and Mrs Joseph took us to the Bianconi in the Royal Hibernian Hotel — my first time in a restaurant, if you can believe that.

Over dinner, he asked me if I'd one day consider joining the firm. Think he may have foreseen me eventually taking over the business. No son and heir, you see. There was just Helen and her older sister, Francesca.

Helen: Well, I think he would have seen you as a future son-in-law anyway.

'So why did you decide to move to America?' I ask her.

Charles: You were offered a job, weren't you? Through your uncle — in, what, Chess Records? Wonderfully exciting because they specialized in the same early rock and roll that we loved, then jazz, rhythm and blues, gospel . . .

Helen: You've got to remember, Ireland was a different country then. There was no money around. No confidence about the future.

Charles: Oh, none of our Celtic Tigers, if you don't mind.

Helen: You got whatever qualification you could, then you got your airline ticket — that's the way it was.

Charles: And the A&R division, where Helen was going to work, their job was to scout and recruit new acts. So it was hugely, hugely glamorous.

Helen: I got the offer in the summer of sixty-seven, the year I finished in Rathmines. If I took it, they were going to send me to college at night and train me up as an accountant, which was, you know ... those sorts of opportunities didn't come around every day, especially for a woman in the Ireland of the sixties.

I talked to Mum and Dad. And Mum, especially, was of the view that I should go. You know, much as she loved Charlie, her attitude would also have been, what's for you won't pass you by. What's meant to be will be.

They smile at each other.

Helen: 'In the end, she was right.'

'Did you consider maybe both of you going?' I ask.

Charles: Oh, naturally. But, well, I didn't want to leave my father. I suppose *I* felt I had something to prove to him. I stayed home because I wanted him to see, up close, if you will, the success I was going to make of my life.

Helen: We did think at that point that it might only be for two years, maybe three.

Charles: So we said we'd endeavour to keep it going, long distance.

Helen: I still have all his letters he wrote. And they still make me cry.

Charles: Yes, I kept Helen's for years. But later on, well, Fionnuala would have been quite insistent that I, em, dispose of them.

Helen laughs.

Helen: The letters, they made it harder, not easier, to keep the relationship going, because every time you read one, you felt your heart break all over again.

The job was great. I was mixing with all sorts. Met anyone who *was* anyone at the time. John Lennon, Mick Jagger, Janis Joplin, Donovan. I met The Zombies. I almost met Bob Dylan.

And in my heart of hearts, I knew it wasn't going to be just two or three years. I knew, deep down, that I wasn't coming home.

Charles: I said I'd wait. As long as it took.

Helen: But that wasn't fair to either of us. It was upsetting me, thinking about what I was putting him through. We both had to move on. I didn't want to stand in the way of him meeting some-one really, really special. So when I went home that first Christmas, I very reluctantly ended it.

Charles: In the Rainbow – do you remember?

Helen: Of course. Christmas Eve. And, Charlie, you were so good. You could see it was tearing me up inside, so you didn't make it difficult for me . . .

And we said our goodbyes, the two of us blubbing away like goodness knows what, our ice cream untouched.

Charles: Of course, then, for two or three years I went completely off the rails. Started playing more rugby, golf and tennis than was good for me. Egged on, in no small measure, by our friend, a certain Mr Hennessy Coghlan-O'Hara, with whom I'd managed to get myself entangled.

Oh, he's happy to speak to you, by the way. He's Ross's godfather, of course – a central character to the story. Give him a call. Or, better still, we're having a retirement party for him on Monday. Shanahan's on the Green. You should come along.

The shopfitters arrive, carrying long lengths of lacquered red timber, and I take it as my cue to leave. 'Sorry about the smell,' Charles tells them, as he conducts me to the door.

Charles and Helen's story – of love lost, then, half a lifetime later, found again – contains enough saccharin to be an instant made-for-TV movie. Yet it's a story full of hope and optimism and the blithe spirit of never-say-never – a happy story in these iconoclastic times.

I step outside, then turn and tell Charles that I've one last question. 'The name, Ross,' I say, rather cheekily. 'Where did it come from?'

He smiles fondly at some hidden remembrance.

Charles: I'm going to tell you, much to his chagrin, I suspect – hates his *old dad* embarrassing him and so forth. Fionnuala and I, well, we tired the bloody moon with our ruminations on the question of what to call this new son of ours.

I suggested Mike, William or Jack – and of course, *you* know where I'm coming from with that. Mike after Mike Gibson, with his wonderful hands and rapier-like boot. William after Mr William James McBride Esquire – aka Willie John – as you know the great Irish lock. And Jack after Jackie Kyle – Doctor Jackie Kyle, if you don't mind – for my money possibly the greatest fly-half to ever play the game.

I couldn't choose between them – just as I couldn't choose between them as players. Make sure and put that in.

So what happens is, we get the little chap home from the hospital and the next thing there's a knock on the door. Who's this? *etcetera*. Of course, it's none other than Hennessy – bottle of Champagne in his hand.

I mean, can you picture it?

The minute I open the door, the singing starts. 'Congratulations'. You know that one? Congratulations and jubilations and so forth. Well, I make no apologies for saying it, I was an enormous fan of Cliff Richard. Still am, if the truth be told. 'Please Don't Tease'. 'Bachelor Boy'. 'The Minute You're Gone'. Cliff Richard, Adam Faith, *all* those. I mean, I've gone on the record as saying I was a rock and roller, haven't I?

'Yes, you have.'

Charles: Well, cut a long story short, a lot of drink was taken and Hennessy suggested Cliff as a possible name.

So, like I said, buckets of drink consumed at this point, I thought, why *not* Cliff? Then I thought, maybe Fionnuala wouldn't buy it. She was by no means a fan.

So then Hennessy suggested using the Irish variation.

And *ross* happens to be the Irish word for a cliff. Or a steep promontory.

Interview Tapes 11 and 12
Monday 29 September 2008
Tom McGahy, Eoghan Clark, Eabhan Warren, Alan Sutton, John Crabtree

When Father Denis Fehily died in 2006, so too did the era of rugby-above-all-else at Castlerock College. Within three days of taking over as the first ever lay principal in the school's ninety-six-year history, Tom McGahy lifted the ban on the playing of other sports by the students of the college.

Since then, Castlerock has gone on to enjoy success in sports as varied as trampolining, field archery and ju-jitsu, while the playing of Gaelic football – once described by Fehily as 'a cross-eyed *citeog* bastard of a game' – is now tolerated, if not encouraged.

In April 2008 the school announced that, for the first time in its history, it would not be entering a team in the following year's Leinster Schools Senior Cup. Hundreds of former students resigned from the Castlerock Old Boys Association in protest, while a number of high-profile donors, including Charles O'Carroll-Kelly, withdrew their support for a new science wing, work on which has been suspended indefinitely.

McGahy rode out the crisis and insists he has no regrets. 'Overall,' he says, in an academic monotone that puts me in mind of Ferris Bueller's teacher, 'I would say that our involvement in rugby had a mostly deleterious effect on the values of this institute of learning.'

We're sitting in the staff canteen, an austere-looking room with formica tables and hard plastic chairs scattered around and walls painted institution magnolia.

As well as McGahy, four other teachers have agreed to speak to me – but only in general terms – about the school's experiences with rugby and rugby players.

John Crabtree, a shiny, rotund man with an impossibly black pompadour and a perspiration problem, was paid, among other things, to teach Ross History, but swears he met him only once. Eabhan Warren – pretty, blonde, a nimbus of patchouli and other pleasant smells – not surprisingly saw a lot more of him in her Chemistry class, even though he didn't take Chemistry. Eoghan Clark, a balding, vinegary sort of character, is head of the English faculty, and Alan Sutton, a foppish type with the look of a student more than a teacher, coached Ross and his friends for their first, ultimately unsuccessful, tilt at the Schools Cup in 1998.

It's Eoghan Clark who brings up the subject of the steaks.

Eoghan: Fillet steaks, I might add.

John: Well, the steaks weren't the thing – that is to say what we, the teachers, objected to wasn't the steaks *per se*.

Eoghan: No, it was children – only twelve, thirteen years old – being permitted to eat in here, in the staff canteen.

Tom: I think what Eoghan is trying to say is that anyone who has ever been involved in the teaching profession will tell you that to maintain discipline, you *have* to have parameters. These boys were accorded the same privileges as we were. The effect that had was to erode the respect with which we were viewed by the general student body and create disciplinary problems, the effects of which are still being felt to this day.

Eoghan: Tom was our shop steward and he tried to raise the matter with Denis. And he told you – didn't he? – in no uncertain terms . . .

Tom: Well, it's unhelpful to keep raking over . . .

Eoghan: 'You're an excellent Civics and Geography teacher. I'm sure you'll have no difficulty finding employment in another school.'

And he emphasized the Civics, didn't he? Made you feel like it wasn't a valued part of the curriculum.

Tom: Look, without getting into recriminations, I'd like to outline for you, if I may, some of my own personal thoughts on the subject of rugby in schools, because that, after all, is what we're here to discuss.

Firstly, in a very general sense, I would have an issue with the way that success in sport – and particularly rugby – is prized over academic achievement in so many of our elite secondary schools. That's the first thing. Secondly, I would have a difficulty with the manner in which, remember, *adolescent* athletes are presented as something approaching God figures to the rest of their peer group. And thirdly, I would worry about the pressures placed *on* their fragile psyches by the excessive exposure of their successes and failures in the national media . . .

Eabhan: Tom, we all read your Op Ed piece in the *Times*.

Alan: Yeah, and it *is* worth saying, Tom, that rugby *can* perform a valuable role in teaching boys important things like self-esteem, teamwork, how to minimize errors, how to make better tactical choices, how to deal with adversity, how to live with their mistakes. Life lessons . . . You know, one of the things I've always loved about rugby is that everyone, irrespective of their size, has a part to play . . .

Tom: That, I *would* humbly suggest, Alan, was not our experience. See, this was Denis's great claim, of course – that it took boys and processed them into men. Our experience was the opposite – an excuse for a permanent adolescence, a *lifetime* of adolescence in the case of some I could mention, but won't . . .

The entire subculture – and I said this in my *Times* piece, Eabhan, thank you very much – is very American. Just to give you a bit of context, that's where we appropriated the schools rugby model from – the States. High school footballers presented as – a phrase I'm sure Denis would have loved – *über*-heroes.

Let's be honest, the American school system hasn't exactly distin-
guished itself by turning out happy, well-adjusted young people, has
it? And, to quote myself again, football, more than anything else,
polarized the student population in the US, creating communities
of so-called jocks and non-jocks, an adversarial environment that
has been blamed on an increasing number of school shootings.

Eabhan: Oh, for God's sake, Tom!

Tom: Well, having spent three years teaching at a high school in
Wilmington, Delaware, Eabhan, I think my views on this subject
have at least some wherewithal.

John: Well, what it *did* do, in the case of this particular group we're
talking about, is it taught them that they could exist outside the
rules that applied to the rest of the student body. They could act as
they pleased. They were untouchable.

Tom: Let's not refer to any *particular* group, shall we? Let's keep it
general.

Eoghan: Tom, we all know who we're talking about here. These
boys were Denis's project. I mean, Mary Shelley couldn't have
written it.

John: Eoghan's right. You tell kids they're a master race and they'll
behave like one.

I ask if I can read them something – an extract from Father Fehily's journal, from 12 January 1998, two days before Castlerock played Gonzaga in
the first round of that year's Leinster Schools Senior Cup.

'Tonight, I am exalted, for tomorrow, at assembly, I shall impart to the
boys the joyous news that 1998 – this year of years – shall be known
henceforth as the Year of the Eagle.

'And oh, and oh, and oh – how fitting.

'The eagle is the most majestic of all His creatures, ruling the skies with graceful imperiousness. And in the same way, Castlerock boys are the very finest species of men – better than anyone else in the entire world.

'I shall leave them in no doubt as to this fact. They look down on the rest of the world from a position of exalted greatness. My message shall be – kill, have your fill and let others feast on the carrion.'

One or two shake their heads, though no one seems particularly surprised by the language.

John: I'm telling you, if anyone ever wondered how an ugly, five foot, nine inch, failed painter from Vienna convinced one of the most sophisticated, logical-thinking nations in the world to do the evil things they did, then all they'd have to do is listen to that eagle speech he made. And see the effect of it.

Eoghan: Nine hundred kids stamping their feet, chanting, 'You can't knock the Rock! You can't knock the Rock!'

I said it to you, John, didn't I? I said, 'They'd march into the Sudetenland now if he asked them.'

Of course, Denis would have considered that a compliment.

John: 'We go the way that Providence dictates with the assurance of a sleepwalker . . .' That's a direct quote.

'From Fehily or Hitler?' I ask.

John: Both.

I mean, it was a rugby match!

Alan, you were in the dressing-room – Lord knows what *you* heard.

Eabhan: Sorry to cut across you, Alan. Can I just point out – I know I seem to be playing devil's advocate here – but it wasn't exactly out of keeping with the ethos of the school . . .

Tom: That's not fair.

Eabhan: What I'm saying is, it wasn't the only area of their education ...

Tom: No, I can't let that pass. That's a gross ...

Eabhan: Tom, I didn't interrupt you.
   Thank you!
   What I'm saying is, it wasn't the only area of their education in which they were being taught that they were, you know, special. I mean, read the prospectus we send out every year, Tom. The barristers, surgeons, stockbrokers, opinion-formers of tomorrow – that's what we tell them. We were doing exactly the same thing. And continue to – albeit with fewer references to the Nazis.

Eoghan: I don't think it's the same thing at all. There was an ugly edge to the whole rugby thing. That poor girl from whatever school it was. Pelted with eggs. Turned out she was allergic to dairy. Her whole head swelled up. Lucky she didn't die. Three boys, all on the Senior Cup team, suspended for a month – but the suspension was deferred until the summer holidays.

John: Denis took a call once – a woman tried to get on the Dart in Dun Laoghaire, only to have her way barred by one of our students. And you know who I'm referring to. 'Sorry,' he told her, 'this is a Rock carriage.'
   You want to know what Denis said to her? And I heard this with my own ears. He said, 'Well, if he said it was a Rock carriage, then it is written.'

They all laugh, despite themselves.

Eabhan: These stories, what I would say also is, they shouldn't be divorced from the context of the times. We had a lot of obnoxious kids in the school around that time – they weren't *all* rugby players, I can tell you that.

John: Now, I *would* agree with that. I don't think the phrase Celtic Tiger had been coined at that point. But, economically, Ireland was entering a new era. And the kids were different, no question. They looked you straight in the eye when they spoke to you . . .

Tom: They considered that they knew as much as you did, that they were your equal.

Eoghan: They'd put their cars in our parking spaces.

I know that Ross, in particular, has fond memories of doing that.

The coming recession, according to a piece in this morning's *Independent*, is going to be a curiously middle-class affair, affecting solicitors, architects, stockbrokers and bankers. 'As teachers, do you think the generation of young people we're talking about – who've never known hard times – are in any way equipped to deal with what seems to be coming?'

I'm thinking about JP and Oisinn.

John: I would say no.

Look, just going back to what was being said there about the famous eagle speech. That match – I can't remember who it was against . . .

Alan: It was Gonzaga.

John: Well, what *I* remember about it was what I would call the ugly air of triumphalism that accompanied it. And it *wasn't* just the players, you're right in that, Eabhan. This extended right into the crowd.

This song they had. 'We're Rich And We Know We Are'. And they were waving huge wads of money! I mean, kids! Probably more money than most of us earned in a week.

That's not rugby. That's a question of values.

So I don't know, can people who grow up with that, really obnoxious wealth, adjust to having no money at all? It'll be hard for them, but it'll be no bad thing.

I have just one more question. Rumours about drug-taking have long cast a shadow over the achievements of the so-called Dream Team that reached successive Schools Cup finals in 1998 and 1999. At least one coach went on the record with his belief that certain Castlerock players were being powered by more than just creatine.

Alan: There's no truth in that, insofar as I'm aware.

It's far from a categoric denial.

Eoghan: A certain rugby correspondent, with a certain daily newspaper — this is true — he's supposed to have phoned his desk after the Gonzaga match and said he wanted to write an article about drugs in schools rugby. The sports editor said, 'The players?' and the guy said, 'The players, the fans, their parents . . .'

Tom: We wouldn't want the school's name associated with drugs, though.

John: Sure, I heard one father — won't name the individual involved — clap his son off the pitch shouting, 'Not only beat them — rubbed their blasted noses in it! Well done, Kicker.'
 Now, with parents like that . . .

Interview Tapes 13, 14 and 15
Monday 29 September 2008
Hennessy-Coghlan O'Hara and
Charles O'Carroll-Kelly

Everyone is agreed. Shanahan's won't be affected one bloody jot, what-ever happens to the economy, not while they're serving Angus Beef like that – certified Irish as well.

It's late. Rivers of wine have been consumed, but no one's in any hurry to leave. Thunderclaps of pompous laughter can still be heard from vari-ous corners of the restaurant. But there's a sense that this could very easily turn melancholic.

Various people stop by to talk to Hennessy. 'Excellent speech,' they tell him. 'The old law game's going to miss you,' and Charles says, 'Well, he had to go some time – see if he can't get that bloody golf handicap of his down!' and everyone reacts like it's the first time they've heard it tonight.

Hennessy is telling a barrister friend, who I'm sure I recognize, that he's been asked to front an ad on daytime TV for a personal injuries law-firm called Quidz In.

'Back to where it all started,' the friend says. 'One business guaranteed to thrive in bad economic times – personal injuries claims. You'd have to wonder what way it's all going to go, though, wouldn't you?'

They're calling today Black Monday. Irish bank shares suffered their greatest fall in more than a quarter of a century, as international investors and corporate deposit-holders lost faith in Ireland's financial institutions. Anglo-Irish is supposed to be on the verge of collapse tonight. Some are saying the whole lot could go.

There must be a lot of worried men in this room. A lot of men putting on a front. I watch Charles swirl his brandy around in his glass. If there's a purpose to it, I presume it's to release the flavour.

There are lots of questions I want to ask him. Is he worried? And if not, why not? Why is a man with his unquestioned business savvy opening up a cheesemongers while the rest of the world is bracing itself for a return to the days of the Great Depression? Who's going to pay fifteen euro for a block of *bleu de Bresse* when their bank branch could be boarded up in the morning?

But it's Hennessy's night, and it seems impolite to talk about anything else. So I ask Charles how they met.

Charles: What you're asking me is how it all started – the famous team? The Dynamic Duo, as we've been called. Well, it's one of these long stories, as they call them.

See, I never really had a best friend before. Helen would have been the closest thing to it, I suppose. Lots of friends, but never a chap I would have called my – inverted commas – right-hand man.

Hennessy's a few years older than I am – he won't thank me for reminding him. Look at him looking at me out of the corner of his eye there . . .

'I'm sure Ross told me that you two were in school together,' I say. 'That's not true, then?'

Charles: You must have picked that up wrong. Hennessy's Clongowes. To the core.

No, we didn't hook up until the late sixties – sixty-eight, sixty-nine, that type of thing. I'd have been twenty-four, something like that.

I suppose the only advice I'd give to anyone who's going along to meet Hennessy is make sure you're wearing some class of corset – because your sides are liable to bloody well split, as mine have many, many times over, what, forty years of friendship?

Hennessy is a lot drunker than I thought, judging by his slanting expression. I draw him into the conversation. His past has always intrigued me. I ask him if his name was really Frank Awder. 'Did Ross get that right?'

Hennessy: Ah – that's no secret. It's been in the papers. Hey, I was young. Naughty boy. Bit of embezzlement, bit of cheque fraud, that kind of shit.

Charles: He used his time inside wisely – not unlike my good self, if you don't mind my saying, old scout.

Hennessy: Yeah, obviously I wasn't cut out for business. Was, I'd never have been caught. Ah, I needed a change of direction. Studied the law.

Charles: Personal injuries was his thing when I met him. Spent a year or two in New York, didn't you? Saw how they did things over there. Came back with all sorts of ideas.

Hennessy: You know, I had the first ever freephone number in Ireland? I'm kind of proud of that – 1800 CLAIM.

Charles: *You may have had an accident. You may not even know you had an accident. We'll get you ten witnesses.*
   This was a little routine he used to do for my benefit, knowing full well I'd near rupture my bloody pancreas laughing.

Hennessy: That wasn't a routine – that was my first radio ad.

Charles: See what I mean? This *never* stops!

'So, how did you meet?'

Charles: Well, it all came about – like so much else in my life that I have to be thankful for – through rugby. Wonderful, wonderful rugby.
   One of my first clients when I went into the old insurance racket – which I'll talk about later – he was playing for the famous Wanderers FC. *FC*, mind – no R – which'll tell you how old it is. A bloody good club – still is, to this day.

But Arthur, this is the chap – still good friends – he remembered me from school. Seems we crossed swords in one or two friendlies. He was St Michael's.

So anyway, Arthur says, you know, where are you playing your rugby these days? I told him, truthfully, that I wasn't playing any. Hadn't since school. Now, he was *literally* shocked. Capital S. Talent like that, going to waste, *etcetera, etcetera.*

Harsh, yes – but exactly what I needed to hear.

So I toddled out one night to Wanderers.

Hennessy: I was on the thirds – played hooker – but for me it was just a social thing.

Ah – we were all big drinkers on that team. None of us could fucking run any more.

So one night, *he* shows up – this big, lumbering idiot here. Said he played a bit of rugby. We'd all heard that one before. Charlie Kelly. Played number eight at school. But what we needed was someone at loosehead. So we stuck him in there. You know, he wasn't bad. Bit soft. Bit windy.

Charles: See, this'd be typical of us now. He'll say something like that, then I'll say something back and, before you know it, you've got full-scale repartee on your hands.

But that very first training session, well, I was probably a bit intimidated by him, if the truth be told. He was *captaining* the team and, as I said, he was a bit older, so I was gung-ho to impress. I acquitted myself rather well, I think. Went back. Changed. And of course, Hennessy here didn't say a word to me in the dressing-room. Playing his cards close to his chest, as per usual.

But afterwards I went along to the bar and there he was, sat there, smoking one of his world-famous Cohibas. Thought he was awfully young to be a cigar smoker. Then he offered one to me, which, incidentally, he was never *known* to do to anyone – Arthur or any of the chaps will tell you – and that was an indication, I'm pretty sure, that he respected what I did out there on the field.

And, well, we've been firm friends ever since.

It was Hennessy, believe it or not, who got me my membership for Milltown. He proposed me. *And* – let me tell you – Riverview.

You're talking about two people who just hit it off. Famously. *From* the get-go.

Anytime anything's come up over the years, Hennessy and I have always been in agreement. Haughey or Colley? Haughey. Campbell or Ward? Campbell. BMW or Mercedes-Benz? Always BMW – except for that W126 sedan you bought that time, Hennessy, and, I'm pretty certain, regretted.

Hennessy: Charlie was a fucking basket-case when I met him.

He twirls his finger around his right temple, the universal sign for madness.

Charles: Well, I would still have been pining for Helen, I expect.

Hennessy: Nice piece of ass is what you needed.

It's the first time I've ever seen Charles's face colour with embarrass- ment.

Hennessy: Maeve – my *first* ex-wife – she had one or two friends, even a sister, who were sweet on him. And the sister – whoa! – I mean, she was great and you're talking to someone who knows. Joyce, she was called – up in the paints age-wise, but, whoa, what a broad!

I told Charlie here all about her. Says, I sampled the goods, I can vouch for her. Ah – he wasn't interested. In anyone. He was that way for years.

Charles: I suppose I wanted to concentrate, at that time, on growing the business. I started off in insurance, you see. That was what was important to me, as well as the rugby and the golf, naturally.

Hennessy: Ah – you were another Willie Loman. Dreamer. Too nice, too. Didn't know how to work the angles.

Charles: Oh, I remember *that* conversation. Happened at the Wanderers' annual dinner. Pork steak and home truths – am I right? You called it as you saw it, Hennessy. 'With *your* brains,' *etcetera, etcetera*.

You see, the problem was, my confidence was very much shot at that point. Because the word on the old transatlantic grapevine was that Helen had met a new chap – Tim – which was all very quick, if you ask me.

Hennessy: So I starts taking him out a bit. Showed him a thing or two. He's still a kid in my eyes – wanted him to see what's out there. Ah – he was too much about this Helen, see.

That time, you had the Metropole Ballroom . . .

Charles: Ah, the Metropole!

Hennessy: Up over the cinema on Abbey Street. Had dances every Sunday, half-two till six. I was a regular. Older broads, lot of them loose.

Charles: They certainly weren't the Wanderers crowd.

Hennessy: I was married. But, hey, so was half the men in there. You just got to be careful. Make like you're going to the flicks. Looking at the pictures they got in the foyer – Edward G. Robinson, all those. Jean Harlow – I liked Jean Harlow. So you're taking an interest in these pictures. Nice and casual. Quick look around you. No one looking, so you slip upstairs.

You got Victor Silvestre and all these dancebands. Looks nice and civilized. Whole lot of waltzing and foxtrotting going on. But there's an edge, see.

Most exciting thing ever happened at a Wanderers dance was, you know, word gets round that some broad's not wearing a bra, so you spend the whole time walking around, looking to see them little nipples. Jesus – what are we, teenagers?

The Metropole was different. You foxtrot with the right lady, next thing you know, you're back in some flat on Pearse Street. Or somewhere strange, like Drumcondra.

I took Charlie there once, maybe twice, but he wasn't happy, was you? Kind of scared the broads off. Says to me, not my scene, I'm afraid, old chap.

Ah – you were green, Charlie. Had to explain to you how everything worked, even business.

Charles: The key in the insurance racket, Hennessy taught me, was networking. And rugby afforded more entrées to well-heeled young professionals than, well, I don't know what. Especially if you were a Wanderer. See, because we were tenants in Lansdowne Road, we had access to the best seats in the house for the big internationals – the famous promenade, quote-unquote, at the front of the Lower West Stand. People would have offered their kidneys to get their hands on those tickets.

Hennessy: That, he learned fast. He meets, say, an architect. Knows the guy needs insurance. He's got three or four partners need it too. Wants the company's business. Charlie takes him out to lunch. No pressure. Take your time. Not the kind of decision you rush into. Hey, by the way, what you doing Saturday?

Believe me – everything we know that's worth knowing, we learned from the Prods.

Charles: Their faces when they discovered where they were sitting. Ringside! Within touching distance of Slats and all these chaps. Blew their bloody socks off. Johnny Moroney, for heaven's sake!

Oh, the deal was as good as done – you knew it.

Then back to the Wanderers Pavilion for a hot one – keep out the cold.

'Do you know the Kavanagh brothers? No? Let me introduce you . . .'

'Oh, watch out – here comes Kevin Flynn! Kevin, I want you to meet a friend of mine ...'

Hennessy taught me all this.

Hennessy: Seventy per cent of his business, he did between January and March. Maybe another twenty in the autumn.

Charles: This, I discovered, is what made the world go round.

Years later, when certain so-called tribunals were inquiring as to the origins of my supposed wealth, they didn't want to know about 1968, beating Australia 16-3, or the following year, France put to the proverbial sword, 17-9, first victory over *les bleus* for eleven years. Or 1973 – England told to stay away, under pain of death. But they turned up anyway – IRA be damned – and they got a bloody well standing ovation from us that lasted, what, five minutes?

When I said all this, I was accused of obstructing the work of the tribunal – threatened with contempt.

Hennessy: He dressed like shit, too. Put that in the book.

Charles: I did, I did, I did. Until Hennessy here took me to his tailor – old Abe Taubman, rest his soul, there on Dawson Street. One in every colour – navy, black, grey. Oh and one pinstripe. And then, the *pièce de la résistance*, my first Cole Haan overcoat. Camel-coloured. Which was to become my signature, of course.

Never seen at Lansdowne Road without it.

Of course, Hennessy did more for me than just that. It was he who convinced me to make the leap. Get my own premises. I'd been working out of my father's house, you see. The sixteenth of July, nineteen hundred and seventy-one – that was the day. Took a little office in Fitzwilliam Square, three doors down from where Hennessy here had his. Five flights up and no bloody lift. But that was the start of it all – the empire, for want of a better word.

On the way home, I stopped into a little DIY shop – not sure it's still there – over the bridge there on Baggot Street. Had a second key cut. You know, I think it was the proudest moment of my life when I handed it to my father.

Charles excuses himself, rather unnecessarily given the company, to go to the bathroom.

'His father never used it,' Hennessy says, perfectly deadpan. 'No interest in seeing the place. Matter of fact, he says to Charlie, sitting in an office, shuffling paper – that's women's work.'

I ask him about Fionnuala. It's devious of me, I know, to wait until Charles is out of earshot, but I admit their relationship has me transfixed and I need another perspective on it. What was it that drew them to one another? And what strange traction kept them together for all those years? And draws them to each other still?

Hennessy considers how best to begin. He begins at the beginning.

Hennessy: Maeve's sister – this Joyce I was telling you about – she'd just given up nursing, see, trained as a masseuse. Physiotorturist, I used to call her. Well, like I told you, she was really sweet on Charlie. Really sweet. Year or two older as well. I used to say to him, Charlie, this girl'll teach you things. Saying this to him for years. One day he says, why not? Can never hurt to meet new people.

I tell him, hey, this ain't the kind of girl you need to go talking to. She's a sure thing, know what I'm saying?

Like I said, he was still green. He was maybe twenty-seven this time, but he still didn't know what it was all about.

So I tell him, look, I'll set up a game of mixed doubles. Charlie and me, we were members of Riverview. But Maeve and her sister were in Sandycove. They were Dun Laoghaire girls, see.

Ah – one of the biggest regrets of my life, bringing Charlie out there that day. Why couldn't it have rained? Why couldn't I have got a flat tyre *that* day, instead of the following week, when I was taking this little Mata Hari – devilling with one of my Law Library friends – to this discreet little hotel I knew in Galway, fill her in on the laws of physics?

But no, I take him to Sandycove . . .

Charles arrives back, lurching slightly. He's drunk, too.

Charles: Oh, he's telling you how Fionnuala and I met! Yes, I remember it like it was yesterday.

Well, I'd had a long-standing problem with the rotator cuff muscles in my right shoulder – same injury Ross had later on, interestingly. An old rugby injury, never properly corrected itself. First two sets, everything's fine. This Joyce was nothing spectacular, but a good, solid baseline player. I could play with her. Hennessy and Maeve took the first set, then we took the second, saving two match-points along the way to set up an intriguing finale. I was serving in the third when I felt a tear. Oh, it was pure and utter agony. Joyce even heard it – and she was standing, what, five or six yards away?

Luckily, she's one of these physiotherapists – like he said, Hennessy had mentioned her many times in dispatches – and she goes to work on it straight away. I'm standing on the court like this and Joyce is, as they say, working her magic, rubbing it and so forth, when all of a sudden, across the way – also locked into a tight, three-set match, as it happens, with her friend Angela – is one of the most beautiful women I'd ever laid eyes on.

Hennessy: Hey, you don't have to say that.

Charles: Oh, if you could have seen Fionnuala in her day. To me, she was like a young Geneviève Bujold. These huge, dark eyes. Black, black hair. Oh, she was beautiful. 'Who is that?' I must have asked everyone within earshot.

Hennessy didn't know, but, as it happens, Maeve did.

Fionnuala O'Carroll, it turns out.

And as well as being terribly attractive, she was also, by some considerable distance, the best ladies player that Sandycove had at that point.

Hennessy: Mad Fionnuala, as everyone knew her.

Charles: She was *different*, I'll grant you that.

Hennessy: Mad as a fucking rocking horse. She'd just come back from France.

Charles: Oh, yes, you'll have to ask her about her Paris life. That's where she headed after she broke up with old Conor Hession.

Hennessy: I don't know how long she was there but – ah – she talked in this stupid broken English. Inspector focking Clouseau.

Charles: Of course, Charlie here is immediately smitten. *Had* to speak to her. Now, remember, I hadn't much confidence when it came to that kind of thing. I'd known a few girls, but Helen was really the only – inverted commas – girlfriend I'd ever had and that was some considerable years previously.

Hennessy: Ah, he was gone. You could see it in his eyes. He was stupid for her. But I got a sixth sense for trouble. Prison does that to you, see. So I says to Joyce, do something, will you?
      She says to me, what? What can I do?
      I says to her, *you're* the physiotherapist – follow him into the men's room, pull his wire. You know, same thing you do for me.

Charles: Steady on, old chap.

Hennessy: Maeve says, don't speak to my sister like that.
      Ah, look, even if she'd done it, I'm not sure it would've even helped.

Charles: I waited for her to come off the court. Nothing rehearsed. No idea what I was going to say. In the end, I just plumped for the first thing that came into my head, which was that I thought she attacked the net like no ladies player I'd seen before. Or since, I *could* add.
      'Sank you ferry much,' she says, just the way *I* said it there, the faintest hint of a French accent.

'Hello there,' I said, 'do I detect a slight twang of something?'

Turns out she'd lived, well, a lot of her adult life in France, which, of course, made her even more exotic in my eyes.

Hennessy: Maeve hears her in the ladies' locker-room. Comes in and she says to this friend of hers, he has his own brokerage.

Charles: Let's just say, a coffee was had that day. And, oh, we talked ourselves hoarse, I can tell you. All sorts. Art. Music. The pros and cons *vis-à-vis* Ireland's entry into the Common Market. And her Paris life, which sounded, I can tell you, impossibly glamorous to a boring old fart like me – what, selling insurance?

Oh, she was part of the scene over there. I mean, your chap, Dalí, wanted to paint her. *Paint* her, thank you very much.

And what she didn't know about food. *Coq au* this, *Cassoulet* that. She had totally immersed herself in French culture.

And all these famous names. They all went to the same parties, you see. I remember saying to her one time, 'Are you saying you're *friends* with Zizi Jeanmaire?' You're too young to remember Zizi Jeanmaire. Carmen. Married to Roland Petit. Oh, they were huge at that time.

I remember she laughed and she said, 'Charles, I can understand how that might be an amazing thing to someone like you. But to me that's just normal.'

She was the first to call me Charles. Never Charlie.

Ten minutes in, I thought, uh-oh, you're out of your depth here, old boy.

Well, it was obvious. Her last chap, in France, was a bloody war hero, albeit a much older man. Yes, he was decorated – wounded as well, I think she said – in Algeria. How was I going to compete with that?

But I asked her if she'd extend me the honour of allowing me to take her out to dinner. More in hope than expectation. If, as I suspected, she said no, then I'd still have shared an hour – not to mention two coffees – with one of the most beautiful women I'd ever seen.

But she said yes!

I took her to the Shelbourne Hotel of all places, which was where we later had our wedding reception. Oh, she was no stranger to it. Turns out her father had been taking her there since she was a little girl. Sunday dinner and so forth. *I'd* been going there for a year or two myself, so the staff knew me reasonably well – banter about rugby and so forth.

Anyway, had the most wonderful meal and we're having a coffee afterwards when Tony, one of the waiters, whom I knew well, came over.

His face suddenly takes on a grave aspect.

Charles: Said, 'Charlie, there's a phone call for you.'

Well, it turned out to be Mr Lebzelter, the lovely Jewish man who lived next door to us. 'Your father's had a heart attack,' he says.

I asked if he was okay and . . . Silence on the end of the line. Then, 'Charlie, I'm so sorry. He's dead.'

Seems the old boy keeled over while mowing the lawn. The old ticker. Mr Lebzelter heard the little motor going. We had a petrol mower, one of the first, certainly in the Blackrock slash Booterstown area. Everyone else was using the old reel ones. Oh, they used to come from miles around – kids mostly – to sit on the wall and watch *Dad* – quote-unquote – tackle that lawn with the Victa.

Anyway, old Mr Lebzelter would listen out. I think he used to time him, see how long it would take. Forty minutes, forty-five. He was retired, don't forget – probably nothing else to do.

But this day, twenty minutes and then the motor suddenly cuts out. I expect he thought, hello, he must be clearing some obstruction or other from the blades, wet grass and so forth. But then when it didn't come back on again, he decided to investigate.

Went upstairs, looked out the bedroom window and saw the old boy lying there.

Hennessy: Dead.

Charles: Well, for as long as I live, I'll be grateful to Fionnuala for being there for me that night. Our first date – can you imagine! She came with me to the hospital. St Michael's in Dun Laoghaire, for whatever reason. He was laid out on the bed, on top of the sheets, still in his gardening clothes.

But Fionnuala was wonderful.

Hennessy: I can't listen to this shit.

Charles: Steady on, Hennessy. Lot of drink and so forth.

Hennessy: Her first thought was the house. Ah – she knew Charlie was an only child. Lot of folding stuff coming his way. Should have seen her at the funeral. Black coat, black gloves . . . black veil! Like Jackie fucking Kennedy. She only knew Charlie a week. And Charlie and his father weren't even close.

Charles: Well, we didn't see eye-to-eye on very much, the old boy and I. But I'd like to think I made him proud in his final years, especially the way I grew the brokerage.

Hennessy: Black handkerchief. Dabbing her eyes. Front row with the family. Ah – it was some performance. Worthy of an Oscar.

Funeral's in Deansgrange. Afterwards, we go to Gleason's or whatever it was called then. Might have *been* Gleason's. And she's fussing over him. Brandy's bad for your heart, she's saying to him, have a whiskey instead. I mean, she's there as Charlie's *girlfriend* – this after one date!

I says to Maeve, I'm telling you, it's the house.

Charles: Well, you've always had your view and I respect that. And, okay, there was no happy-ever-after for Fionnuala and I. But I shudder to think how I'd have coped through that whole period without her.

Hennessy: Ah – you'd have coped fine. *Her* big success was convincing you that you needed her. You were vulnerable. There for the taking.

Charles: Well, we started to, em, *date* is the expression they're all using these days. Quote-unquote. And, yes, I'm not too proud to admit it, *I* did most of the chasing. I was dogged in my pursuit of this . . . *stunning* young lady.

Hennessy: See, Charlie's raw. Guy's looking for love from somewhere. And here *she* was, rationing it out, controlling the measures, so as to always keep him hungry. So this one time, say, she gets this photo of Charlie and his old man at Leopardstown. Where she got it from, I don't know because I never saw one of them together, not as adults. So she gets it put in this fancy frame and she gives it to him. You know, nice. Nice thing to do. A week later, it could have been, they're out to dinner and she tells him – what's this phrase she used? – there's aspects to his personality that she doesn't like. *Aspects* to his personality. This is Charlie she's talking about. Stupid, lovable bastard. Up to that time, never met anyone with a bad word to say about him. And she says this to him, what, two weeks after his father died?

Charles: In fairness to Fionnuala, I wasn't terribly cultured. Knew literally nothing about art. Nothing about wine. Fionnuala will tell you, I didn't know how to hold a knife and fork!

Hennessy: He rings me one night in tears, tells me all this. Aspects of his personality. Two weeks in.

I says, Charlie, do yourself a favour – get out. A broad would want to have two goddamn vaginas for *me* to take shit like that.

Now, though, Charlie thinks there's something up with his personality. And that's what it's all about – if she can get the guy questioning himself, then he's weak and she can control him.

Charles: I think the point Fionnuala was trying to make – and I know you were never terribly fond of her, Hennessy – was that she was used to, you know, very charming men. Urbane, sophisticated, that type of thing.

Hennessy: She says shit to him like, you know, I really love men who are like this, I really love men who are like that.

I says, what are you, Mr fucking Potato Head?

Charles: Well, we all change, we all adapt, *within* relationships.

But whatever the rights and wrongs of it, I was spending every spare hour I had with this wonderful woman.

And there was dancing, I can tell you that. This was still the early seventies — seventy-three, seventy-four — before that awful bloody disco music came in. You could still hold a girl in your arms.

There was Donie Nugent and his band. Anyone who was around Wanderers at that time will tell you about Donie and his band. Chap on clarinet, chap on sax, chap on double bass and then the man himself on piano. You see, every other band was still doing Elvis. Donie was doing The Duke. 'Take The A Train'. Chopin in A minor and whatever you're having yourself.

And Fionnuala — oh, could she move. She was a classical dancer, you see. Flamenco and all sorts.

Hennessy: Next thing I know, he's gone. I mean, he's fallen off the face of the Earth. I don't see him. Weeks go by. Doesn't call. You know, he's not even playing rugby any more.

Charles: It's true. If anything, it was tennis, tennis, tennis.

Hennessy: But one day — don't know how I did it — I get him on the phone and I get him to come out, play a round. Elm Park.

He played like shit, by the way — head gone. After seven holes, we go back to the bar. Says he doesn't want a brandy. I say, what? Says, think I'll have a Scotch, old boy. Bad for the heart and he pulls this face — remember my old man is what he's saying.

A brandy never hurt no one. *Her* again.

So I ignore him, get him a brandy. A double. Put it down in front
of him. Say, there you go, Charlie. Looks at me and says, would you
mind not calling me Charlie, old boy?

I say, it's your fucking name, isn't it? He says, yes, but Fionnuala
doesn't like it.

Charles: She didn't. That's where Charles started, you see.

I don't think it would be overstating it to say that over the next
couple of years Fionnuala really helped to straighten me out. Especially
my backhand. I had a tendency to consider the shot completed once
contact had been made with the ball, instead of swinging through it.

Hennessy: Not good with dates, but it must have been the following year – think it was the summer of seventy-five – he comes to
me and he asks me can I get him tickets for Wimbledon. I says, yeah.
Could get my hands on all sorts of shit – still can.

Charles: Hennessy very kindly acquired Wimbledon tickets for us,
through his – quote-unquote – *channels*. The two finals days, if you
don't mind. Well, if you could have seen Fionnuala's face. She was
terribly impressed by the whole business.

Centre court, if it should please m'lud!

Hennessy: I think, why's he going to all this trouble? I mean, it
wasn't Charlie. He was a take-me-as-you-find-me kind of a guy.
And he's going to all these lengths . . .

Charles: A client of mine – a bloody good anaesthetist if you're ever
looking for one – he recommended the Cumberland Hotel, Marble
Arch.

Hennessy: Then I think, he's not going to do something stupid, is he?

Charles: So we sit down at the tennis – strawberries and so forth
– and we watch Arthur Ashe famously beat Jimmy Connors. First
black chap, *etcetera, etcetera*.

Fionnuala's loving this, of course.

Although she was *all* for Connors. She loved the, em, bad boys – is this what they're called? Năstase was another.

Then the following day, Billie Jean King beat Evonne Goolagong, the little Aboriginal, in straight sets. Only dropped one game. *One*, can you imagine?

I remember Fionnuala turning to me and saying, 'You'd almost feel sorry for the little coloured, wouldn't you?'

Oh, the most wonderful weekend. Two people very much in love.

Hennessy: He is – he's *going* to do something stupid.

Charles: The best laid plans of mice and men and so forth. The fates seemed to be conspiring against me. The Cumberland was all the things it was said to be – oh, very respectable establishment.

It did, for some reason, though, attract a lot of these hooker types. Prostitutes, not to put too fine a point on it. They tended to hang around the reception area.

Anyway – night of the ladies' final – we were going out to dinner to a wonderful restaurant, again recommended by my anaesthetist chap, when I realized that I'd left my wallet in the room. Won't be a minute, says I. Took the stairs, two at a time.

Of course, you can guess what happened. Fionnuala was looking absolutely wonderful – fashions of the day and so forth. The concierge came along and asked her to go and ply her business elsewhere.

Oh, you can imagine Fionnuala's response: 'How *dare* you!'

It was like he'd never seen a short-cut fur coat before.

Oh, she was furious. Wanted to check out and return home immediately. Three gin and tonics later, I managed to calm her down, which was good news for everyone, because we had reservations for the Hungarian Csárda on Dean Street, Soho.

One of the best restaurants in London. Very elitist. Very expensive. Impossible to get a table, naturally.

Roger Moore was there. Do you remember *The Saint*? *And* Joan Collins, who actually leaned across and admired Fionnuala's coat.

And recommended the Mecsek Highwayman's Dumpling Soup. Turned out to be everything she said it was.

All of the food, in fact, was extraordinary. And what's more, I had the chaps with the violins come to our table to serenade Fionnuala. And it was at that moment that I got down on one knee . . .

Hennessy: What an idiot.

Charles: And posited the idea of perhaps getting married.

First phone call, after Fionnuala phoned her father obviously, Angela and one or two friends, was to a certain Mr Hennessy Coghlan-O'Hara, BCL, Dip. Emp., PhD in Public Liability Law.

Hennessy: He rings me from a payphone in the restaurant. I'm in the bar in the Berkeley. Knows where to get me because it's Sunday night, see. Says, tonight, old scout, I asked Fionnuala for her hand in marriage. And she said yes! That's what he kept saying! She's only gone and bloody well said yes!

I mean, what else was she going to say? I'm holding out for Warren Beatty?

Charles: Hennessy's sat at the bar in the Berkeley – picture this – working on his book. *Personal Injuries and You.* See, this was a whole new area in Ireland – Hennessy was one of the pioneers. You really don't get enough credit for it, old boy. That book – would you believe that's how he wrote the entire thing, sat at the bar in the Berkeley. The entire thing – longhand, using that trademark eighteen carat, rhodium-coated Caran d'Ache fountain pen of his. On hotel notepaper, if you don't mind. Then he used to hand the pages to his secretary to type up, didn't you?

So anyway, here's his famous sidekick, jousting colleague and whatever else I was to him, phoning him up, disturbing all this work, to tell him he's getting hitched. Have you ever heard the like of it?

Hennessy: I told him he was making a terrible mistake.

Charles: That was about the measure of the banter all right.

Hennessy: Hey, you knew I was serious.

Charles: Then I cleared my throat, deep breath, and said I would consider it a signal honour if he would agree to serve as my best man.

Hennessy: I was his best man all right. You want to know the best day's work I ever did for him? Okay, his old man's house gets sold. Charlie doesn't want to live there.

Charles: Well, I felt I needed a break from the past.

Hennessy: Like I told you, his old man was an asshole. Anyway, he moves out and he rents.

Charles: Ah, yes. Croswaithe Park in Dun Laoghaire.

Hennessy: Real cosy. Two rooms. Bed. Cooker. Fridge. It's temporary.
So the money from the house sale comes through the weekend he asks me to get him the tickets for Wimbledon. Maybe it's fifty grand, some shit like that. So I got this in my head − he's gonna do something stupid here.
Because his head's up his ass.

Charles: You gave me some sound business advice is what you did.

Hennessy: I say to him, Charlie, you got to do something with this money. So he mentions some shit about a pad on Marlborough Road in Glenageary − a big pad. See, she's already in his ear.

Charles: In all fairness to you, you predicted that commercial property was going to go through the roof in value.

Hennessy: You want a house, I says, get a mortgage, like I got a mortgage. You want to make a success of that business of yours, you got to get your own premises. Renting's dead money.

Charles: Happened just as he said. I said, 'Okay, old chap, I'll leave it in your capables.'

Hennessy: See, I already know there's a building for sale on the other side of Fitzwilliam Square, the South. Five-storey Georgian – a hundred grand. We could buy it between us – go fifty-fifty. Perfect for him because he's already having to take on more staff. And me, well, I knew a good business opportunity when I saw one. Fully renovated. I get it for cheaper, maybe ninety. What – thirty years later? – it sells for twelve million.

Of course, the Revenue took that.

Charles: I think anyone who was fortunate enough to be there will remember our wedding as a smashing day. Really super. Third of August, nineteen hundred and seventy-six. Got married in the University Church on Stephen's Green, which would have had huge social cachet at the time.

As for Fionnuala, what can I say? Oh, she looked stunning. Wore a dress that was very similar to the one that Princess Anne wore when she married Mark Phillips – embroidered Tudor-style, with a high collar and medieval sleeves.

Father gave her away. Whispers to me at the altar, 'You make sure and look after my little princess.'

I ask why he and Fionnuala decided to take one another's names.

Charles: Well, there was little or no debate about it. Never any question of Fionnuala giving up *her* name. What, Fionnuala Kelly? You couldn't picture her as a Fionnuala Kelly, could

Fionnuala O'Carroll with Conor Hession, her first love, Enniskerry, 1968. 'It was like she was playing out a part in some nineteenth-century romance ovel,' Conor said. 'I remember one night she handed me a book of poems and got me to read to her.'

Charlie Kelly and Helen Joseph at a dance in Blackrock Tennis Club, 1966. 'When he was on the dance floor, he was a danger to other people,' Helen remembered. 'I'm sure people were maimed by him.'

Fionnuala standing outside the Élysée Palace, Paris, 1971. 'I had the most wonderful time,' she recalled. 'I'm sure you can imagine. Very cultured, very *avant-garde*, very non-conformist . . . Sexually – *very* liberating.'

Charles and Fionnuala on their wedding day, Newman University Church, St Stephen's Green, Dublin, 1976. 'Any time anyone admired the dress,' Audrey Mannion, one of her bridesmaids, recalled, 'she mentioned this Princess Anne thing – it's supposed to have been modelled on the one *she* wore – but then she kept saying, "Yes, *she* married a commoner too, didn't she?"'

A much less svelte Fionnuala with four-month-old Ross outside the O'Carroll-Kellys' former home, Glenageary Wood, 1980. 'This wasn't the Glenageary *I* knew,' Fionnuala said. 'The people, they breathed through their mouths. They paid for their TV licences with stamps … I made a quiet promise to myself – Fionnuala, this is as low as you're ever going to let yourself sink.'

Ross, with his *viola da braccio*, on his first day in Montessori School, 1985. 'I admit it,' says Fionnuala. 'I was looking forward to it being just Alexis, my darling Pomeranian, and I at home.'

The famous *Irish Times* cartoon re-creating the moment when Conalswood, the brainchild of Charles O'Carroll-Kelly and Hennessy Coghlan-O'Hara, was conceived, 1985. 'Robert Emmet, how are you?' said Charles, recalling Hennessy's 'famous' speech. '"Ireland won't always be like this," says our friend there. "A backward, potato-eating island on the edge of nowhere…"' Oh, he knew what buttons to press.'

Father Denis Fehily with Fionn de Barra, Ross O'Carroll-Kelly,
Christian Forde, JP Conroy and Oisinn Wallace, the nucleus of what
would become the Castlerock Dream Team, 1994. 'These boys were
Denis's project,' said English teacher Eoghan Clark. 'I mean, Mary
Shelley couldn't have written it.'

Sorcha Lalor and Ross on the night of the Mount Anville debs,
1997. 'If Sorcha mentions the hickeys I had on my neck that night,
it was from paintballing,' Ross said. 'And I focking mean that.'

Ross's infamous 'gesture' to the St Mary's crowd after scoring the winning try in the quarter-final of the Leinster Schools Senior Cup, 1998. 'Of course, then it was open season on me,' he recalled.

The O'Carroll-Kelly extended family portrait. *Clockwise from top left:* Fionnuala, Charles, Erika, Ronan, Ross, Honor and Sorcha. The photographer has revealed that it was the worst assignment he'd ever undertaken in a career that bore witness to the conflicts in Northern Ireland, Bosnia and the Hostel Wars in South Africa.

you? So the compromise was that we would amalgamate the two.

Then the famous honeymoon, which is still talked about. Had to be France, of course – scene of, I think, possibly the happiest times in Fionnuala's life.

I remember saying, I hope we don't run into that bloody racing driver – French chap who'd been pretty keen on her when she lived in Paris. Seems he'd been writing to her recently, promising all sorts in return for her hand. 'If we run into him,' I said, 'God help me, I'll punch him on the bloody nose.'

We toured the Champagne region. Stayed in the most fabulous hotel in Reims. Five stars all the way. Saw all the sights – Palace Royale, Forum Square, Saint Rémi Basilica. Tastings in only the very select Champagne Houses. Had a fabulous time.

Hennessy: Till Charlie drops his bombshell.

She's in his ear about this house she's seen. Might have been on Adelaide Road, somewhere like that. Again, lot of poppy. She wanted to give up the teaching . . .

Charles: No, she wanted to go part time. She loved that school, you see. She was teaching Home Economics in the Loreto Convent there in Dalkey.

But, yes, I did tell her that we might have to scale back our ambitions somewhat.

Hennessy: Then he tells her about the money.

Charles: It was just a tiff, old boy. Fionnuala wanted to know, naturally, how we were going to afford a house.

I said, 'We'll get one of these mortgages, like other folk.'

Oh, she burst into tears. I tried to reassure her. I said, 'Everyone has a mortgage these days, Darling.'

Hennessy: So she packs her bags. Says she's going home.

Charles: Well, I'd have put a different spin on that. There was only, what, two, three days left anyway. Oh, we'd had our fill of *brut* this and *cuvée* that and something else the other. We were excited about getting back and looking for somewhere to live.

Hennessy: All that night she's trying to get me on the phone. I'm in Buck Whaleys. Come home, it's maybe five in the morning. Maeve says Fionnuala rang, seven, eight times. I says, Charlie okay? Says, I think so. Then she says, she was furious – kept saying she wasn't going to be some PAYE monkey for the rest of her life. I says, hey, the broad's a nut. She says, poor Charlie. I says, poor Charlie is right.

Interview Tapes 16 and 17
Wednesday 1 October 2008
Fionnuala O'Carroll-Kelly

With a long, blood-red talon she indicates the grandfather clock at the foot of the stairs. 'A genuine Morbier longcase,' she says with the recitative manner of a museum guide, then conducts me into a large drawing room that conjures up images of world leaders in greatcoats smoking cigars and discussing peace.

'There are three of what *you* would probably call *living* areas. But this, the main one . . . I remember, when I was designing it, thinking, "Fionnuala, it *has* to be mid-Georgian."'

'As you can see, it's got eight tapestry panels, each depicting scenes from famous hunts in the eighteenth century, *in* the classic style, of course. A fabulous Neo-Palladian chimneypiece. Beautifully coffered ceiling, with a stunning ornamental dado rail, featuring designs inspired by those in the dining room in the Provost's House in Trinity College. Carpet, Baroque-style, reflecting the design of the ceiling – again, *my* idea. And the furniture, all classical – antique day-beds, that type of thing . . .'

But my attention has snagged on the longcase in the hall. The House That Fionnuala Built – was it a home for her family or an approximation of the life she expected to have with Conor Hession?

She asks me if I like *maiale con timo e risotto*. I tell her I expect so and she leads me down another long hallway to a shrilly lit kitchen. I sit on a high stool at an island of glass and chrome and warm maple, while she measures various ingredients into pots.

I try to make small talk. I mention the Government bailing out the banking system. 'Four hundred billion,' I say. 'That's nearly ten times the national debt. It's mind-boggling, isn't it?' and she says, 'Hmmm,' and smiles inwardly, as if I were a shopkeeper commenting on the softness of the day.

Are the O'Carroll-Kellys so wonderfully wealthy, I wonder, or are they simply in denial?

'Oh, I *must* show you the larder,' she says. 'A larder! I can only imagine how that must sound! Very Jane Austen. Very Maria Edgeworth. *Both* wonderful writers, you could put in – big inspirations to me.'

I tell her the house is quite stunning and she agrees. 'Oh, I knew *exactly* what I wanted. I had all these drawings, all these plans, that I'd made over the years. Even when I was in France . . .'

'*Tell* me about France,' I say. I'm genuinely interested.

Fionnuala: Well, when I split from Conor, I thought, 'Okay, Fionnuala, now it's time to be selfish, to look after number one.' Which is why, after I finished my H. Dip., I decided to go to Paris for what turned out to be three years.

Had the most wonderful time, I'm sure you can imagine. Very cultured, very *avant-garde*, very non-conformist – that was the scene. Lot of galleries, lot of parties . . . Lot of affairs. Short, passionate. One with Michel Lamerre, a surrealist painter – very, very close to Salvador Dalí. Sexually – *very* liberating.

Oh, I really was an innocent abroad until I met Michel. He showed me how to position my legs in certain ways to heighten my orgasms, sustain them for longer . . .

He loved to paint me, too. Naked, of course. In fact, more often than not, he'd finish a portrait of me, then five seconds later we were making, oh, torrid love to one another on the floor of his studio, both of us covered in paint, our faces flushed.

Sancerre *et l'amour*.

This Jane Birkin/Serge Gainsbourg tableau is, I suspect, Fionnuala O'Carroll-Kelly's greatest ever work of fiction. Yet it's difficult to feel anything other than sympathy for her. After the humiliation of her broken engagement, she had few friends to fall back on. She went to Paris, why? To hide? Regroup?

Parts of the picture are beginning to resolve themselves now. She came home, single and in her late twenties. It's easy to imagine her, looking into the future and catching sight of herself as an elderly schoolmarm, teaching convent girls how to boil the perfect egg, then going home every evening to a lonely house.

She met Charlie Kelly. *He* found her physically attractive and she found him not too repulsive. And he was easy-going enough to ignore her casual selfishness and clear lunacy.

And *she* presumed – wrongly as it happens – that he had money.

While she stirs the pot, I ask her about the early years of their marriage. She answers as if I've asked her about their first house.

Fionnuala: Well, it was still under construction when we went to view it. The whole *estate* was.

Can you believe that word – estate?

We each had to put on one of these *hard hats* to look around. I remember turning to Charles and saying, 'Are there going to be *people* living in all these other houses?'

'Of course,' he said.

I said, '*All* of them?'

I could *not* believe it.

The day we moved in was the closest I've ever come to just total and utter despair. This wasn't the Glenageary *I* knew – the people, they breathed through their mouths. They paid for their TV licences with stamps. Awful, awful stuff.

What stopped me commiting suicide – I would have to say, looking back – was my belief in myself. I made a quiet promise to myself – Fionnuala, this is as low as you're ever going to let yourself sink.

'What about the arrival of Ross?' I ask. 'That must have given you an enormous boost.'

Fionnuala: Well, yes, of course. For a time. But then he started in the Montessori and it was then, of course, that I started becoming more and more well known for being active in the whole charity area.

I mentioned Rwanda to you before, but I suppose the one I would have been most associated with in those days would have been Chernobyl. Well, who *wouldn't* have been moved by the images we saw on our screens that day?

That was the first of my famous cake sales. I remember baking myself *beyond* the point of exhaustion. I baked angel cakes, I baked clafouti, I baked chocolate pea puddings. I must have made a hundred pots of my famous rhubarb and ginger jam, which Charles and Ross will tell you has to be tasted to be believed.

Big piece about the event in the *Times*. Everyone who matters takes the *Times*.

I don't know what we raised to help those poor unfortunates, but it was in the realm of hundreds.

Of course, the way it is with charity, you know, you're constantly asking yourself, is the money getting through? Is it making a difference to people's lives *on* the ground?

I think I had also reached a point in my life where I was becoming more concerned with matters, shall we say, closer to home. I mean, who was I to try to help these desperate, desperate people when I myself was living in the most appalling conditions?

So I made a decision – that other stuff, leave it to Adi.

I mention that I drove through Glenageary Wood this morning and found it nothing at all like she describes. It's a quiet, largely unremarkable, middle-class housing estate. She stops stirring, pins me with a look, then continues as if I'd never spoken.

Fionnuala: I mean, the terrible things we were bearing witness to, the grinding poverty, day in, day out, it would just crush your soul.

I had to tell the neighbours to stop talking to Ross over the *back fence*. I just didn't want him ending up with one of these Dublin accents you hear.

The last straw for me, I'll never forget this, was one morning, I got up, as usual, for work. It was just over a week before Christmas. I drew the living-room curtains and there, in the middle of the road, is this – oh, I can barely bring myself to say it – *motor coach* outside.

A bus, yes. Just parked there, without a by-your-leave.

The driver, he's sitting there, not a care in the world. I said, 'If you don't move this *thing* immediately, I shall phone the Gardaí.'

Then I notice that all the *wans* from the estate are sitting in it. I had to ask. I said, 'Where are you all going?'

Someone – I don't know *who* it was – shouted, 'Newry.'

I said, 'Newry? In Northern Ireland? Why on earth would *anyone* want to go to Northern Ireland? There's a bloody war on.'

'Cheap beer,' comes the answer from the back of the bus. Then, of course – big cheer.

Eight o'clock in the morning and they're already drinking cans of *lagger* – even the *women*.

'Cheap beer?' I said. 'I expect there's cheap biscuits in the Lebanon but you wouldn't go *there*, would you?'

But they probably would have.

Awful, awful people. Might as well have been living among the beasts of the field. So when Charles came home from work that evening, I said, 'That's it – we're moving.'

He said, 'Moving? Where?'

Dalkey, Foxrock, Sandymount – I really didn't care.

'We couldn't possibly afford a house like that,' he said. 'Not on what I'm bringing in.'

That's when I told myself, okay, Fionnuala, *you're* going to have to do something here to pull the three of us out of this living hell.

She serves the *maiale con timo e risotto* and it's every bit as good as it sounds.

'So all this,' I say, indicating the house, 'was paid for by flowers?'

She smiles.

Fionnuala: Charles is on the record somewhere as saying that when they sit down to write the definitive account of the Celtic Tiger, there'll be an entire chapter dedicated to Fionnuala O'Carroll-Kelly – *if* there's any justice. And I have to admit, the success of my floristry business is one of the great untold stories of our times.

The way it all came about was that Audrey Mannion, who I was reasonably good friends with – she was a bridesmaid at my wedding, though she's not worth talking to now, you'll get only poison out of her mouth – she knew this lovely old lady, Mrs Goad, or Alma, who had a wonderful little florist shop in Stillorgan called

Buds . . . or something like that. I think she'd been friends with Audrey's mother, going way back.

Alma was a lovely little *thing* – a widow – very, very nice, and at that time she just so happened to be looking for an assistant.

She was well into her eighties, you see, and starting to find the work a bit tough-going. Half-blind as well.

And, of course, neither of her girls had the slightest interest in taking over the place. Eliza married an optometrist and moved to Aberdeen and Harriet was pollen intolerant. I mean, *she* couldn't put her head around the door of the place.

Now, marvellous as she was, Alma didn't know the first thing about running a successful business in the modern age. I mean, the place was going to rack *and* ruin before I walked through that door.

The position was for an assistant manager, which implied a certain level of responsibility. Which suited me. I said the money was fine for the time being, but I made it clear that I wouldn't do menial work. And by menial work I meant *sweeping up* or anything that sounded remotely . . . janitorial.

I told her I didn't consider it a fitting application of my talents and, as it happens, I think she was inclined to agree with me.

I can honestly say, when I went in there, I would not have known the difference – honestly – between a polyanthus and a wild primrose. But what I *did* have – what I've *always* had – is a good artistic sense. So it wasn't any kind of surprise to discover that I had a real flair for flowers. If you were to ask me what my strong points were, I would say I was imaginative in the arrangements I put together, very innovative – I was the first person in Ireland to put delphiniums together with snowballs and Ecuadorian roses, for example – and I think, very quickly, that became known far and wide.

Alma was – and I don't wish this to speak ill of the dead – a dinosaur. She was still wearing shawls. It was like dealing with Peig Sayers. I mean, Peig Sayers was probably very nice, but try doing business with her.

At the same time, very quickly, I could see how the flower business was going. People were diversifying, there was no question. It wasn't just funeral wreaths any more and a big run on roses on Valentine's Day. Something was happening. Sending flowers was becoming more and more a means of heartfelt expression in people's lives – this is the mantra I started repeating to Alma, day in, day out. But she was too set in her ways. Too old, if the truth be told.

An example. I suggested baby baskets to her. Now bear in mind that no one – and I mean *no one* – in Dublin was doing baby baskets at the time. A lot of women get very sentimental when they have babies. This was perfect. If it's a boy, you put carnations, chrysanthemums, even some some irises, into a darling little wicker basket, with a balloon attached saying, 'It's a boy!' and maybe even a little bear.

If it's a girl, some gerberas, some alstroemerias obviously, some lilies – all soft colours – again in a darling little basket, tied with a bow.

I might as well have been talking to the wall.

Another simple idea. Gourmet fruit baskets. Fresh fruit – lychees, kumquats, dewberries, Surinam cherries – arranged in a super little wicker tray, with some bright, pretty flowers – I *adore* asters – some chocolate and some assorted herbal teas and infusions.

Again, I could have been talking Hungarian to her.

Eventually, after months and months of this, I asked to see the books, out of concern more than anything, because I had my suspicions about how badly things were going. I mean, on the surface it looked like a thriving business, but underneath I suspected all was not well – it couldn't be, with all the things I was seeing.

I showed the books to my father. I mean, he was in the bank. He knew numbers. He had a look and uncovered – let's just say – all manner of sins. The shop was haemorrhaging money. And it was little wonder, the way it was run.

She takes away my empty plate. I watch her rinse it under the tap, then place it in the dishwasher and I wonder could this woman really have conned a frail old pensioner out of her business. The answer, I've already decided, is yes.

'So why did you and Audrey fall out?' I ask.

Fionnuala: Oh, she accused me of *stealing* from Alma one day –
just like that. I remember, I was adding eucalyptus stems to some
bouquet-length cream, pink and peach roses, and I said, 'Audrey, get
out of the shop now or, God help me, I'll murder you with this faux
lead crystal amphora.'

Oh, I'd have done it.

I was the one trying to keep the show on the road. I was the one
putting in six- and seven-hour days, trying to stop the business literally haemorrhaging money.

And all my ideas, which I was prepared to let Alma have, for the
pittance that she was paying me, *all* because I wanted this shop to
work . . .

Stillorgan needed it – I truly felt that.

But I was the only reason that Alma still had her neck *above* water.
Let us not forget that when the bills started to stack up, I was the one
who went to see my father and arranged a personal loan for her of
twenty thousand pounds. And when she defaulted on that loan, I was
the one who went back in to my father and pleaded her case.

Anyway, between the jigs and the reels, it was decided that the
best way forward was for me to buy the business, lock, stock, fix-
tures and fittings.

Oh, she got a good price for it, especially for a woman of her age,
and with *her* knees. Well, what I mean is, she wasn't going to be
travelling on any expensive holidays, was she? And of course, she
got to keep her house – or at least stay in it until she died.

The name of the shop, Ross told me, was changed overnight to *Tulips To
Say I Love You*.

Fionnuala: And then, well, we all know what a success I made of
the business. Turned it around in a very short space of time. Not a
crime. And what I could say – but I won't – is that its success was
built on the ideas that Alma had spent the previous two years pooh-
poohing. It wasn't rocket science. There *was* money in this country
in the 1980s, just as there is now. You just have to find out what
people want and give it to them at the right price.

Gourmet baskets. Seasonal wreaths – not just for funerals but for happy occasions, too. Fabulous silk arrangements. Standing sprays for churches. These were all *my* ideas. Twenty years ago, most people in this country hadn't heard of alstroemerias, if you can believe that. I would still claim I was single-handedly responsible for their renaissance.

Inside twelve months, not only was the shop in Stillorgan showing a healthy profit, but I'd opened two more. Then another in the year after that. And a fleet of eight vans. I'd see them on the road – *Tulips To Say I Love You* blazed across the side, then underneath, Stillorgan, Foxrock, Sandycove, Donnybrook – and it made me feel so proud.

I thought, 'Fionnuala, you deserve this.'

I thank her for lunch.

'You're one of only two people who's *ever* seen me make my risotto,' she says, as she air-kisses me, 'and you're sworn to secrecy.'

When I make for the back door instead of the front, she asks me where I'm going. 'To see Ross,' I tell her. 'And Ronan, I think.'

She looks through the kitchen window, askance. 'Are they down there?' she says.

'I presume so – Ross's car is in the driveway.'

'Very unusual,' she says, 'for him not to stick his head around the door and say hi. I wonder if they are hungry. Perhaps I'll do them some of my crockpot Cajun-style buffalo wings.'

Interview Tape 18
Wednesday 1 October 2008
Ross and Ronan O'Carroll-Kelly

A bomb shelter. Given the way the country's going, they could soon be selling spaces in here.

Ross and Ronan are playing pool, moving, between shots, in a jerky, freeze-frame manner to the heavy pulse beat of Busta Rhymes. 'I was leaving the house when I saw your car,' I say. Ross shushes me because Ronan is in the middle of explaining the American subprime mortgage crisis to him. That's worth repeating. Ronan (11) is explaining the American subprime mortgage crisis to Ross (28).

Ronan: An awful lot of people who bought houses in America over the last few years are what they call subprime borrowers. In other words, people who got money from lenders that didn't have the same strict loan criteria as the established banks and building societies . . .

Erika was right. He's almost unrecognizable from the little boy I last saw. He's grown in height, to just shy of Ross's shoulder. Puberty has shorn the soft edges from his features and his voice has dropped an octave. I should also say, since it's the most eye-smarting thing about him, that he's wearing glasses and a bow tie. There's an array of different-coloured pens lined up in the pocket of his white, short-sleeved shirt and his hair has been brushed upwards in the manner of a cartoon 'mad professor'.

Ronan: So a couple of years ago, when house prices started to fall, mortgage delinquencies went through the roof and securities backed with subprime mortgages, which were held mostly by financial firms, lost their value. This resulted in the collapse of Government-sponsored

Enterprises, most notably Fannie Mae and Freddie Mac, and a large decline in the capital of all the major US banks. This, in turn, resulted in credit being tightened all over the world.

Ross is grinning at me idiotically and pointing at Ronan like he's a dog who speaks Esperanto.

Ronan pots the second-last striped ball off two cushions.

Ronan: It caused panic in financial markets and convinced investors to take their money out of risky mortgage bonds and shaky equities and put it into commodities. The declared bankruptcy of Lehman Brothers helped trigger the biggest drop the Dow, the Nasdaq and S&P500 had seen since the terrible events of 9/11. The House of Representative's rejection of the US Government's $700 billion bailout for Wall Street resulted in a further catastrophe for stocks.

He fluffs a long-shot. There's an ugly clack of balls and the black drops into the middle pocket.

'I didn't catch a focking word of that,' Ross says to no one in particular. 'I'm just glad this whole thing's not going to affect me.'

Without taking his eyes off his father, Ronan retrieves the black from the pocket, then rolls it back into play.

There's something about this child genius story I find unconvincing. His account of the world financial crisis sounds like something that's been learned by rote, with no real understanding or appreciation.

'So, Ronan,' I say, 'you're *off* school at the moment.'

'Yeah,' he says, potting the final stripe with a flourish. 'We're after being looking for nearly a year – aren't we, Rosser? – for one that caters for kids with my abilities . . .'

Then he starts re-spotting the balls again.

'But sure, you already know pretty much everything,' Ross tells him. 'And even the things you don't know, the internet's there for that – that'd be my attitude.'

Then he turns back to me. 'The old dear,' he says, applying chalk to his cue in slow, circular movements, 'did she cook for you?'

'Er, yeah,' I say. '*Maiale con timo e risotto*. I think she's doing you guys buffalo wings.'

He shakes his head. 'I focking love her wings. She's an unbelievable cook, isn't she? The ugly smelt.'

'Why do you always do that?' I ask.

'Do what, Dude?'

'Well, it's the only time you ever say anything nice about your mother, when you're talking about food. It's always, "She's unbelievable, the things she can do with a Le Creuset and a sprig of tarragon," and then it's like you suddenly remember yourself and you feel the need to say, "the stupid whelk" or "the ugly sprat".'

'So?'

'Well, I just think it's interesting that the only kind thoughts you seem to have about your mother involve the giving of . . . sustenance.'

I suppose what I'm really asking him is whether he was denied the breast as a baby.

I think he recognizes where the conversation is taking us because he jabs an angry finger at me. 'Have *you* spoken to Audrey yet?'

'I've left messages,' I tell him, which is true. 'I'm not sure she wants to talk.'

'What about those two reporters?'

'Yeah, I'm meeting them tomorrow.'

'Well, that's something,' he says. 'Don't be wasting any more time talking to her, though.'

'Well, I think her life history is very relevant to yours,' I tell him. 'Anyway, this might interest you – tonight, Loreto Foxrock are having their ten-year reunion in the Champagne Bar in Ron Blacks.'

He shrugs. 'What's that got to do with the price of kohlrabi?'

I watch Ronan flex his hands and lower himself to break. There's a loud crack and the balls scatter in every direction. One or two find their way into pockets with the help of his hand.

'I just thought, you know, there'd be a few girls there who might remember you.'

A smile somersaults across Ross's face. 'Yes!' he shouts. 'At last! See, this is the kind of shit the public *wants* to know about me.'

Interview Tapes 19 and 20
Wednesday 1 October 2008
Notes from the Loreto College Foxrock
Class of 1998 Reunion

Naoisa Scully: Oh my God, I was, like, *so* mad about him for half of fifth year and then a little bit of sixth year as well? I ended up actually *being* with him after the Mass of Remembrance one year and then, like, a week later he totally blanked me in Annabel's. I was like, 'Oh my God, oh my God, oh my God . . .' Ended up making a total fool of myself, though I'm pretty sure my drink was spiked. Emma Maher, Nadine O'Loughlin, Susan Cooney – they were all, like, dragging me away, going, 'He's not worth it, Naoisa – he's *so* actually not?' and I was like – oh my God, *so* embarrassing – I was like, 'Ross, I love you,' and you know what he was like? He was like, 'Yeah? I love me too.'

Holly McFarlane: Have you ever heard of the Battle of Beaufort? Oh! My God! There used to be this, like, hockey tournament between all the Loretos – we're talking Foxrock, Dalkey, Beaufort, the Green, even Bray. Ross was kissing, like, a girl from our school – Samantha Ryan – one from Dalkey and one from, like, Beaufort, as in Olwyn Blackmore, who actually went on to play for Ireland. So he turned up on the actual day and everyone was like, 'Oh my God, who's he actually here *with*?' So there's all this, like, tension? The next thing, this girl from, like, Dalkey trips Samantha and – oh my God – all hell breaks loose. There was a, practically, riot. Players, supporters, everything – fighting. There was, like, broken hockey sticks everywhere. Jenny Dale – this, like, girl I know? – she had, like, a huge lump of actual hair torn out. She ended up having to wear, like, a bandana in school for the next two months. Even though bandanas *were* actually in.

Chloe Allen: I was with him, like, a few times. There was one night – it was at, like, a house party – and I caught him checking his watch while he was actually kissing me. His friends were all behind me and he was telling them with his eyes, you know, basically, let's hit the road. I was like, 'Oh my God, what a wanker!' *I* finished it with *him*, though, which a lot of girls *can't* actually say? And I'm with an amazing guy now who owns, like, three of those new apartments opposite Dundrum Town Centre and he treats me, oh my God, *so* well. So any regrets? I *don't* think so?

Amber O'Riordan: He was a total and utter, oh my God, wanker. At the same time he was seeing me, he was also seeing Jenny McSweeney, as in one of my best friends? There was one night he rang me from town – the little-boy-drunk act – and he was like, 'Any chance of a lift?' I was like, 'Oh my God, if you *think* I'm getting out of bed to pick you up from God knows where . . .' and he was like, 'Hey, it's cool – I'll ring Jenny,' and I was like, There's no way that bitch is getting her claws into him! So I drove in, picked him up, in my mum's actual car. So the next thing, we're on the Stillorgan dual carriageway and he's like, 'I think I'm going to spew,' and I was like, 'Wait, I'm going to pull over,' and he was like, 'It's cool, I'll do it out the window. Like, the G-Force will take it *away* from the car?' Like, he'd know *anything* about physics! Couldn't stop him. There ended up being puke *all* down the side of the car. And I don't know what he was drinking, but it stripped off the paint. My mum had to get it, like, resprayed.

Beibhinn Flood: I actually met him when our schools did, like, a joint CAO talk? I'm sorry, I get quite . . . emotional. Even now. But we ended up being, like, boyfriend-girlfriend for . . . three or four weeks, even though I found out afterwards he was stringing a few of us along, including (incoherent) . . . This one night? Our two schools had a charity event for, like, homelessness or one of those, and *he* persuaded me to put myself up for the auction – as in, A Date With Beibhinn Flood? He swore to me that he'd, like, top any bid that was made . . . Oh my God, I can't believe I'm actually crying over him still . . . They opened the bidding at, like, twenty pounds and *he* just sat on his hands. I mean, what a focking (incoherent) . . . Of course, he *thought* it was focking hilarious, him and his friends. I ended up having to go on a date with this, like, total weirdo – who didn't *even* play rugby? I'm sorry, you're going to have to stop the tape.

Melanie Mackey: If you see him, tell him that Melanie Mackey said he's a wanker . . . But also . . . But also tell him that I'm, like, *so* over him, because I don't want him thinking I'm not? Which is probably what he *does* think? It's, like – whatever . . . Jessica, do you have my bag? Oh, Amy has it . . . Ross is, like, oh my God, *such* a loser. (shouts into tape recorder) Loser! Focking loser!

Andrea Ruane: It's, like, I *think* I'm over him? But then someone says his name and . . . (interview ends).

Interview Tapes 21 and 22
Friday 3 October 2008
Liam Toft and Brian Hoban

Liam Toft spent six years in Africa as an *Irish Times* correspondent. He once said that the time he spent writing about the planning process in Dublin was the perfect apprenticeship for covering the corrupt regimes of Mugabe, Mobutu and Abacha. 'I said that at a Transparency International conference,' he says, 'and people thought I was being facetious.'

He has a great hacking laugh that's ill at odds with his sad, doughy face.

We're sitting in a quiet corner of O'Neill's on Suffolk Street with Brian Hoban, the *Sunday Independent* journalist who has broken most of the major stories concerning corruption in Irish public life over the past ten years.

'Wait till you see what'll come out now,' he says, putting a pint down in front of me. 'There's a lot of people who've been doing a lot of, let's just say, questionable things . . .'

I notice his nails are bitten blood-raw.

'The kind of stuff we've been writing about,' Liam says, 'if we're honest, you know, very few people cared. Brian, you'd be the same – most of the time you feel like a voice in the wilderness. I think there was a tribunal fatigue that set in in this country and that was understandable. People had money. Nobody cares who else is getting rich when they're getting rich themselves. But now there's *no* money and people are mad as hell. And now they're going to start asking questions themselves – you watch.'

'So,' says Brian, 'how does any of this fit into a book about – what's his name?'

I laugh silently, imagining his response to being called that. 'It's Ross,' I tell him, 'and, well, the way I see it is, the O'Carroll-Kellys were a family who defined themselves purely in terms of wealth and status. I'm interested in hearing the lengths to which they were prepared to go to achieve that wealth and status. *And* the effect that had on their son. Because when I read about Charles's past and I think about Ross's, it's the same themes recurring — that sense of almost blood-borne entitlement, the abuse of power, the effect of wealth without responsibility . . .'

Liam: Okay, I'm telling you this just by way of overview. What's become apparent, listening to the evidence put before the various tribunals over the years, is that Ireland essentially had two separate economies. There was the one in which ordinary workers operated . . .

Brian: Fools like us.

Liam: Exactly . . . worked hard and had their taxes — often accounting for more than half of what they earned — deducted from their pay packets. Then there was the other economy, the one in which the new elite operated — men like Charles O'Carroll-Kelly and Hennessy Coghlan-O'Hara — salting away their wealth in illegal offshore schemes, protected by crooked solicitors and accountants, subverting the real economy, starving public services, such as hospitals, of billions and billions of pounds.

If you go back to the late 1950s, when Charles would have been — I *think* — a teenager, if you got on a train at Heuston Station, travelling west, it was only a few miles before you saw the city disappear. You know, it was fields and hedgerows and boreens. Well, in the 1960s that all changed, mainly due to industrial expansion. But the population was growing and moving out of the city into new housing estates built on what was formerly agricultural land.

Brian: In the seventies and eighties, there was a scramble for land on the outskirts of Dublin. If you think of it as a modern-day gold rush, the western part of the county, by the mid-eighties, was the Klondike. And Merrigan's Farm, the seventeen hundred acres that Charles and his solicitor bought, was Bonanza Creek.

Liam: I didn't look at any figures – I meant to – but they bought it for, what, two point three million, was it?

Brian: It was two point six. Poor Matt Merrigan – he was sat on all this land and he could do nothing with it. Tried to get it rezoned a few times. See, what he didn't have was Hennessy's contacts.

'Rezoned, as what?'

Liam: Well, under the 1963 Planning Act, every piece of land in the county was given a designation – residential, agricultural, industrial, commercial, *etcetera*, *etcetera*. These designations were made by council officials, to ensure a balanced development of the county.

Brian: To make sure houses weren't built without amenities, that people weren't living on top of factories, that housing estates had proper services, like road access and sewage facilities.

Liam: The simple procedure of designating a piece of land for residential rather than, say, agricultural use could increase its value, oh, logarithmically. And by way of a mechanism called a Material Contravention of the County Development Plan, a majority of county councillors were given the power to overrule decisions taken by qualified planners.

In other words, a simple majority of elected councillors, usually with no knowledge of planning matters, could redesignate land or grant planning permission for developments against better advice, sending the value of that land soaring.

Brian: So you can see the potential for abuse. Back then, the dogs in the street knew that the votes of certain councillors were up for sale. And just to give you an idea of the kind of money we're talking about here – they bought that land for two point six million. Charles and Hennessy made, by my estimate, about forty-eight million from it.

'Forty-eight *million?*'

Brian: And this was in the *eighties*, remember.

Liam: Almost all of which went offshore as well. A lot of it's still out there somewhere.

The suburb that eventually sprang from the mud of Merrigan's Farm was Conalswood. Today, the name remains a synonym for bad planning, not just in Ireland but far and wide. Town-planning students from a university in Oslo recently visited it, Brian says, to see how planning *shouldn't* be done.

Brian: When you look at it, it has all the hallmarks of a development that was built on the back of corruption.

Liam: Oh, the classic ugly mish-mash you end up with when you pay bribes to subvert the process that's supposed to ensure proper, considered planning.

Brian: Then again, if your criterion is profit per acreage, then you *could* say that Conalswood is a masterpiece.
  I mean, they went to the best. I don't want to speak ill of the dead, but it's an indicator of the kind of thing Pat Moone was capable of had he not chosen – and I say this with tongue firmly in cheek – a life of evil.

'Who's Pat Moone?' I ask. I get the impression I should know.

Liam: Pat Moone was the architect they used.

Brian: There was no end of problems with Conalswood. Firstly, there was no public transport link. That was the big thing. It wasn't on any bus or rail route. Because it was a development in what was then still a rural area, it took Dublin Bus years to agree to send buses out there.

Secondly, the shopping centre – what's now the Conalswood Mall – was over-ambitious in terms of its scale. There was a recession on then as well, remember. The company they sold it to, once the planning permission had been secured, struggled to find strong anchor tenants and it lay largely empty for years. As did the so-called high-tech business park – another white elephant.

And as for the houses, I've never seen so many people living in that kind of density. Little Kowloon, they used to call it.

Liam: I'm sure they *do* look at it now – the pair of them – and congratulate themselves on their vision. Like they somehow knew that the Celtic Tiger would come about and Conalswood would be swallowed up in the general conurbation. But this wasn't about any vision of theirs. This was about buying land, getting it rezoned corruptly, building cheap, soulless housing estates, then selling it all on for an enormous profit.

It was about greed.

Brian: If you can, get your hands on a copy of the original prospectus, it's well worth seeing. They had pictures of deer, grazing. Not the kind you see in the Phoenix Park either – they were white-tailed fawns, like Bambi.

They had waterfalls, orchards, fountains – and no pictures of the houses themselves, by the way.

Liam: The motion to rezone the land was tabled in, what was it, September of eighty-seven? For six months leading up to that, there would have been quite intensive, let's just call it lobbying, of interested parties – councillors, journalists, one or two groups who were campaigning to save the green belt.

And no expense was spared.

Brian: They were couriering press releases around. One to your office *and* one to your home. And it'd be something, you know, not particularly newsworthy, like, I don't know, an award-winning builder had been lined up to do the first phase of the housing

development – this is before they even had the rezoning permission. There's no *need* to courier something like that. These were the
days of two postal deliveries a day, there were fax machines . . .

But it was that Marshall McLuhan thing – the medium is the
message. And the message – aimed, *I* think, at those who might
have been, say, borderline corruptible – was that we are men with
very deep pockets.

Same thing with the famous helicopter trips. They took a lot of
people up, councillors mostly, to see the land. Whatever it costs to
charter a helicopter for an hour or two – well, you can *see* how
much money was riding on this thing.

Will I tell him about Morris Garton?

Liam: Yeah, but be careful of that story.

Brian: There was a journalist who worked for the *Press* called
Morris Garton. There were one or two environmental groups who
had his ear and, you know, he wrote quite a lot of critical stuff about
the whole plan. So Charles *or* Hennessy – don't know which – rang
him up, all friendly, asked him if he'd be interested in hearing the
other side of the story. Took him up in the helicopter and – well, so
Morris claims – Hennessy opened the door and threatened to push
him out.

Liam: I think you should qualify the story, Brian, by saying that
Morris now runs his own website dedicated to UFO sightings in
Ireland.

Brian: That's true – he *is* a bit strange.

Liam: So you wouldn't know whether to believe him or not.

Going back to the bribes – which Charles admitted paying during the course of his trial, remember – it'd be impossible to link any
of the one point two million or so in payments they made to politicians over the years to any specific decision. But that wasn't how
it worked.

They had a small core of councillors essentially on a retainer. They paid them what they claimed were political donations – the usual guff, money to defray election expenses, entirely legitimate, no favours asked or given – but they paid money into accounts held under false names in Guernsey, Liechtenstein and the British Virgin Islands. Five thousand a month, in one or two cases, every month, over the course of three or four years.

Brian: Then there were others who were bunged occasional amounts, ranging from two to five thousand, with no specific pattern at all. They used Pat Moone as their bagman, delivering plastic shopping bags stuffed with notes to pubs, shopping-centre car parks, petrol-station forecourts . . .

I'll never forget the day of the vote. Like I said, I was only cutting my teeth as a reporter . . .

Liam: Well, it would have been quite typical of those meetings back in the 1980s. The chamber had this tiny little public gallery at the back, which would be full of men in expensively tailored suits. You'd hear them talking among themselves, taking head-counts of who was present and how many votes they were likely to have. And you'd see councillors waving back at them. There was this air of collusion between them, like this was something they were all in together.

Brian: The planners gave *their* verdict. In this case, they felt it wasn't a sustainable development, wasn't consistent with good planning and would be grossly injurious to the environment. Then the council – I should say a majority, not all – voted to completely disregard the advice of the experts and allow it to go ahead.

Then I heard a cork pop. It was all so brazen. Charles O'Carroll-Kelly opened a bottle of Champagne in the public gallery, because I remember the chairman warning him to control himself. Then outside in the lobby, they were hugging councillors, and councillors were hugging them. They really didn't care how it looked.

Then they all went to Conway's and got pissed.

It wasn't until, I think, early nineteen ninety-five that tongues started to really wag about Charles and Hennessy. I think we all poked at the story. It was very difficult to prove anything, though.

Liam: Even the Gardaí couldn't do anything about it. As you said, Brian, the dogs in the street knew that there was corruption in the planning process in Dublin since the seventies. But the resources to deal with complex white-collar crime were, conveniently, non-existent.

You know, there was ample legal apparatus to deal with someone who, say, burgles a house to feed his drug addiction. It was easy to process him, send him off to jail. But when it came to following a complex money trail across three continents, the criminal justice system fell down. Which is why so many tribunals of inquiry had to be set up to establish the truth in these matters.

Brian: We both could have wallpapered our offices with the solicitors' letters we got from Charles and Hennessy over the years. They knew we were asking questions.

But even a phone call to either of them at their offices – their secretaries would say, 'No, he's not available,' and then within the hour, without fail, a courier would arrive with a cease-and-desist letter, threatening all sorts.

'How did Pat Moone die?' I ask.

Liam: Killed himself.

Brian: Shot himself in the head. But I know what you're *really* asking – were there suspicious circumstances?

Morris Garton will tell you there were. He says he was supposed to sit down with him that weekend. Thought for some reason that Pat was going to blow the whistle.

Hennessy's supposed to have told Morris once in a fit of rage that he knew how to kill someone and make it look like suicide.

But look, Pat was depressed. That was the real truth. Pat was gay.

But he couldn't tell his family. He'd a wife and, I think, two kids. It's tragic, really. He was a pretty heavy drinker.

Liam: Brian, you'll remember this. The plans for what would have been the fifth and final phase of Conalswood were submitted, what, a month after Pat died? It would have been the summer of ninety-five anyway. And it was to *South* Dublin County Council, because by then the local authorities had all been reorganized.

I drove out to Tallaght to look at the plans and met you, didn't I, on the way out? And Brian said, 'You're never going to believe this.'

Brian: Yeah, all the roads were called, you know, Moone Avenue, Moone Villas, Moone Drive.

There was even a Moone Walk.

I mean, like Liam said, Pat was only dead a few weeks. And this was something that was done at the last minute because the original names had just been Tippexed over.

It was a bit crass, I thought.

Liam: You did think, you know, the gall of these people. But they'd no embarrassment.

I mean, Conalswood had been an unmitigated disaster. There must have been a couple of thousand houses already built, but, six years on, still no sign of the shops, the school, the church, the library promised in the plans.

Brian: And no sign of the white-tailed deer.

Liam: No, *they* never arrived. There'd have been nothing for them to eat. There was no grass. I mean, anywhere – just giant mounds of earth. Footpaths hadn't been finished. Playing fields hadn't been sown. Roads hadn't been surfaced. There were other roads that went nowhere – just turned into dirt tracks.

Brian: Then there were the problems with the houses themselves, which the people who bought them were only beginning to discover. They were almost literally thrown up. Badly designed, badly built, badly wired. Some of them, it was later found, had no sewage connections, so the toilets were emptying under the houses.

People were literally living in their own shit.

Then cracks started to appear in the walls. *Big* cracks. So you had field mice getting in and raising families in the wall cavities. Then, even worse, the roofs weren't on flush – you know, there were gaps, whoever they used to build them . . . So some of the houses had bats in their attics. Can you imagine that? Bats! Because it was still the middle of the countryside, remember – trees everywhere.

Some poor guy I interviewed, he opened the attic one day and they flooded out into the house, hundreds of them. He had to repaint the entire place.

Liam: So then they turn up and announce phase five – no shame. This time it was going to be some houses, but mainly apartments, which were the new thing at the time.

The apartments I described as being Ceauşescan in character, which got me another solicitor's letter for the collection. But that's exactly what they looked like in the plans – these grey, monolithic, Soviet-era superstructures.

Brian: I remember sitting in the little public gallery at the back of the chamber, a few feet away from the two boys, thinking, they could struggle to get the votes here. See, the political climate had changed. I think there was a growing sense among councillors in general that they were being watched.

Liam: Charles certainly seemed edgy. And he'd obviously read the things I'd been writing that week about the first two phases because he shouted at me outside in the lobby that I was a disgrace to a wonderful institution, by which he meant the *Irish Times*. And that he'd be ringing Conor Brady and telling him he was considering putting his one pound twenty-five a day – or whatever it was – elsewhere.

Brian: The officials recommended that the rezoning motion be turned down for, oh, loads and loads of reasons. One of which was that the developers were still being pursued to try to get them to complete work on phases one to four.

And then, unbelievably, the council turned it down. I think only three voted in favour. It was like, you know – at last!

Liam: I had the unenviable job of phoning Charles the following day for a quote. But it was like we'd been friends all our lives. 'Hello there, Liam,' he says. 'What can I do for you?'

It was quite disarming.

He was very magnanimous about the whole thing, I thought. And quite open. Said they'd probably sell what remained of the land, which they eventually did, of course.

I asked him what plans he had for the future. He said he still had his business, which was insurance or pensions or something.

And then he talked about his son, presumably this guy you're talking about. The funny thing is, having a son myself, it was the first time I actually thought of Charles O'Carroll-Kelly as a human being, with real feelings. He said, 'Wonderful rugby player, you know. You're going to be hearing a lot about him.'

Interview Tape 23
Monday 6 October 2008
Ross O'Carroll-Kelly

He's staring into the camera, with great, popping, basilisk eyes, neck muscles taut, face a furious shade of red and the middle finger of his right hand raised in grim defiance. This photograph was the talk of the country for a week in the spring of 1998. It made the front page of most of the national newspapers, prompting editorials about the nation's youth being out of control, then, once the heat went out of the story, more considered pieces about whether sport in school fosters unhealthy tribal tendencies among boys.

We're sitting in Starbucks on Dawson Street, looking through a sheaf of old press clippings, but it's to this one we keep returning. He has mixed feelings about the photograph today. He says he kept a copy of it on the wall beside his bed for years. But then his voice drops to a lower register and he admits that when he looks at it now, he doesn't recognize himself.

'What kind of provocation led up to it?' I ask.

Ross: See, none of the papers at the time mentioned that. I'm not, like, defending what I did, but . . . You know, the crowd singing, 'Ross O'Carroll-Kelly is a homosexual!' and all sorts of shit. I mean, my old pair are sitting in the stand, actually *listening* to that?

And it wasn't just the Mary's crowd either. They were from all over – we're talking Clongowes, we're talking Blackrock, we're talking Terenure – they were turning up at matches they'd no *even* interest in seeing, just to give me a basically hard time.

See, I'd been with a lot of people's girlfriends at that stage?

Speaking of which, how did it go? As in, Loreto Foxrock?

'Good,' I say, unable to hold back a smile. 'They certainly remember you.'

Ross: Go on then, what were they saying?'

'Look, a mix of stuff really.'

Ross: 'It's all focking true, by the way. I mean, I *was* an actual bastard to women. Still am, I like to think.

By the way, you know Muckross are having *their* reunion tomorrow night? It's in the Clarendon. Be a lot of birds there with stories about my shenanigans. And I'm pretty sure Loreto on the Green are having one soon – I can find out when.

You know what, I'm starting to feel actually better about this book?

I tell him I'm glad. 'But can we go back to the photograph?' I say. 'What was it about that day?'

Ross: Well, there's not a lot else to say. I had a mare, I'd be the first to admit. Missed a lot of kicks. I mean, the crowd were, like, booing and whistling from the second I put the ball down. A true rugby fan would never do that, of course.

Mary's were something like, I don't know, six points up, five minutes to go, looking for any kind of score to kill us off. Next thing, Christian – it's a pity he's not here, he'd have some stories for you about my focking carry-on over the years – he threw himself in front of this, like, drop-goal attempt. Ball spills right at my feet. The Rossmeister here scoops it up, runs practically the whole length of the field, puts it under the posts, then kicks the points.

Then . . .

He stares at the photograph, then makes a farting sound with his mouth.

Ross: Yeah, it was like, 'We're the ones in the semi-final of the Leinster Schools Senior Cup – swivel on that!'

But it's, like, no one would have mentioned it if it hadn't been for that photographer who just so happened to be standing between me and the crowd.

Of course, then it was open season on me.

I've been cross-checking some dates, I tell him. The match against St Mary's came just a week after the death of his grandfather. I ask him if it might have contributed in some way. Because when I look at the photograph, I don't see the rage that everyone else seems to have seen. I see anguish.

Ross: Nah, the thing is, I wouldn't have been, like, *that* close to him?

But what we were talking about before – okay, yeah, that happened. I *was* nice to the old dear around that time. See, he would have died the morning after we beat Skerries in, like, the previous round? I got up, feeling pretty shabby it has to be said, and the old dear was bawling her eyes out in her room. Told me what happened. So I gave her, like, a hug – as you do.

He's nowhere to be seen, of course. Actually, do you want to know where he was? He was in the study, on the phone to the *Times*, giving out yards because they said I scored thirty-six points instead of thirty-eight.

Eventually, he comes upstairs. Big stupid head on him. Goes, 'I know how you feel, Darling – the so-called paper of record, docking the boy a conversion on his famous day.'

'So it'd be wrong to say that you were grieving for your grandfather?'

Ross: Yeah, no, I wasn't.

But then *her* – see, this'd be typical of her now – the day *of* the actual funeral, that actual afternoon, she gets a call from one of her mates on the council to say they're not going ahead with the halting site on Westminster Road – the one she's been campaigning against? And she's, like, all delighted. She's, like, *gloating*, if that's an actual word? I'm like, 'You've just buried your old man!'

'So you went into that match, what, angry because you'd felt sorry for your mother, then saw how hard-hearted she really was?'

He laughs.

Ross: Do you know what your problem is, Dude? You think I'm a lot, I don't know, deeper than I actually am? Have you ever thought there might be a hell of a lot less to me than you think?

'Never.'

Ross: I'm being actually serious.

I laugh then and tell him he's probably right. 'I think I'm still trying to get a handle on why you hate them so much.'

I can't imagine what it was like for him, still just a teenager, finding himself in the eye of a media squall. I heard somewhere that Alan Sutton decided to drop him for the semi-final against Terenure College, but was overruled by Father Fehily on the morning of the game.

I ask him is it true.

Ross: Yeah, that's basically what happened.

I mean, Sooty's told me the story himself. He was awake all night, he said. Decided, maybe six or seven in the morning, to drop me. He's supposed to have had breakfast the morning of the game in Café Java in Blackrock. Sat in the window and picked the team, moving Christian to outhalf – because he was our back-up kicker – and playing Ollie Merriman at outside-centre.

Fehily's supposed to have gone ballistic.

A diary entry that morning reads: 'No more than a hundred empty heads will ever make one wise man, will an heroic decision arise from a hundred cowards.'

'Were you nervous?' I ask.

Ross: I was always nervous. Nerves are an actual good thing. It's like that line I always text Rog on the morning of a big game – eat nerves, shit results.

He loves that.

But yeah, they had to move the match to Donnybrook because of the demand for tickets. After all the, I suppose, publicity, everyone suddenly wanted to see me play. People love a bad boy. You'll have heard that from the Foxrock girls the other night.

The crowd were, like, baying for me. And Fehily said to me, this could go one of two ways. Either you're going to disappear out there or you're going to have the game of your life.

And of course, you know what way it went.

Castlerock, reduced to fourteen men, earned their place in the final thanks to a late try by Ross.

Ross: I never gave Fionn the credit he deserved for that try. Don't put this in the book, but it was *his* tackle. I always say *I* booted it downfield, but I didn't. It was actually Fionn. Pretty similar to the Mary's match – this was, like, five metres from our line. Must have travelled fifty or sixty metres downfield. I focking pegged it. Made it to the ball first, two or three Gick players right behind me, but there was, like, no way they were going to catch me. Put the ball down under the posts – or as good as.

And then . . .

He shuffles through my clippings and pulls out another famous photograph, which he places on top of the pile. After touching the ball down he ran to the Anglesea Road end, where the visiting fans were sitting, and pulled up his jersey. Underneath – I'm looking at the photograph now, of his pouting face – he was wearing an impossibly tight pink T-shirt bearing the line, 'Please don't hate me just because I'm beautiful.'

Everyone, apparently, saw the funny side of it.

Ross: I actually robbed that T-shirt from a bird I was with a couple of nights before. Holy Child Killiney – fock, if *they* ever had a reunion, you'd get some material. Anyway, I was with her – as in *with* with – saw the T-shirt in her room and thought, 'This'll be pretty funny.'

I think that was the real start of it. Rossmania, if you want to call it that. Actually, *do* call it that. You could see everyone – even the Terenure fans – shaking their heads, going, 'You've got to say, there's something about this guy.'

I think I have enough for one day. When I stand up, Ross reminds me about the Muckross reunion tomorrow.

'*If* I'm back,' I tell him. 'I'm going on a bit of a road trip in the morning.'

'A road trip? Hey, can I come along? I'm doing fock-all.'

'I don't know if you'd want to. It's with your old man . . .'

'Oh.'

'. . . and Helen. They picked up some really foul-smelling cheese somewhere and they've found some dealer in Tipperary who's going to take it off their hands. Your dad invited me along for the drive.'

'He obviously wants something.'

'What? What do you think he wants?'

'I'm sure you'll find out tomorrow, Dude.'

Then he says something so unexpected, so out of character, that for a moment I think I misheard him.

'He's not actually that bad, you know.'

'Who?'

'The old man. I mean, I give him dog's abuse, which – don't get me wrong – he deserves. But he can be actually all right, when he's not trying to do the big pals act. Look, I wasn't going to mention this, but you probably should put it in . . .'

I know, word for word, the story he's about to tell. It's usually a special reserve for nights when he's drunk.

Ross: I was watching the *Late Late* this one time, with the old pair – two focking dopes. Next thing there's a kid on and he's got, like, cancer or one of those. Needs to go to the States, some hospital there, only one in the world that can treat him. They need to raise, I don't know, fifty Ks, something like that. The old man gets up, goes into his study, blahdy blahdy blah . . .

Couple of days later, I'm rooting through his desk, looking for focking money to steal if I'm being honest, and I find his cheque-book. Had a look at the stubs and he'd written a cheque to this kid's family — we're talking the full amount.

I mean, you've *got* to put that in, I suppose. Don't see how you can avoid it. Don't put *me* down as saying it, though . . .

I walk up Dawson Street, with my head down and my shoulders hunched against the wind. I've heard that story many times before, but never in the sober light of a Monday afternoon. Why did he choose to tell it then? And there, leaning awkwardly against a display of Tazo tea infusions? It stays on the periphery of my mind for weeks, vague but troubling, like a shadow on an X-ray.

The problem is, I don't believe it.

Interview Tapes 24, 25 and 26
Tuesday 7 October 2008
Charles O'Carroll-Kelly, Hennessy
Coghlan-O'Hara and Helen Joseph

The trouble with Irish people, Charles says, is that when it comes to choosing a meat to accompany cheese, they're so terribly conservative. 'Why is it always *prosciutto*?' he wants to know. 'What about *sorpressata, jamón serrano* or some good old-fashioned German *Speck*?'

'Charlie,' Helen says, wearily. 'Eyes on the road,' and he gives her a big, leathery smile by way of apology.

It seems ridiculous to be discussing *charcuterie* this morning. The Government has brought forward the Budget to today. Everyone looks set to suffer. I can't help but wonder will any of us even remember *prosciutto* this time next year? Will it be consigned to some fond but distant past, like liniment and lyle stockings?

Hennessy is snoring heavily on the back seat beside me, sleeping off the after-effects of the latest in a long procession of retirement parties. It's not clear yet why he's come along.

It's a miserable morning, the rain falling in great gouts. I watch the chequerboard countryside pass as Charles and Helen fill in the blanks in their story.

Helen met Tim through friends. He was an expat, too, from Bandon, County Cork. Chicago was an exciting place to be in the late sixties. It felt like a turning-point for mankind. Tim went into securitization and capital markets. He earned a fortune. Helen wanted a family; Tim didn't. They married in August of seventy-three, thinking this essential difference would somehow resolve itself. Helen was lonely. They moved to Vancouver. The rows and the additional timezones made the home-sickness worse. In the summer of seventy-nine she returned to Dublin to visit her parents. While home, she phoned Tim to say she wasn't

going back. They agreed to separate. One morning, just before Christmas, she bumped into Charles coming out of Switzers. She knew,
through her sister, Francesca, that he was married. He told her he had
a child on the way. They had a brief affair, during which Helen became
pregnant.

'I wasn't altogether proud of myself,' Charles says. 'Marital infidelity
and so forth.'

Helen: I think we both understood – I certainly did – that what
happened between us was – and this is going to sound awful –
for old time's sake. He was a married man with a baby on the
way. You didn't do that kind of thing.

Hennessy is suddenly awake and jackknifed forward in his seat.

Hennessy: Best thing you could have done, Charlie – I told you at
the time, didn't I? – was pack Fionnuala off to the farm, then pick
up where you two left off.

Helen: Hennessy!

Hennessy: Would have been two problems solved in one fell
swoop. Because at that point – I know, Charlie, you never wanted
to hear it – but Fionnuala was deranged. I could have collected a
hundred witness statements, especially from the neighbours, to say
this woman was certifiably off her nut.

Charles: This is not for the book, obviously.

Hennessy: I tells him, let's park friendship for the moment. As
your solicitor of record, I am legally obliged to point out – Helen,
block your ears for a moment – that Helen is a far more attractive
broad.

It was a wonderful opportunity – cheap, too – for you to get rid
once and for all. Clear the decks.

Charles: It was out of the question, Hennessy. She was my wife.

Besides, I wouldn't know how to go about *getting* someone committed.

Hennessy: Ah – we both knew doctors who'd have signed the forms. We played rugby, didn't we? Too loyal, that was you. Too stupid. So it proved in the long run.

So Charles confessed his adultery, but stayed with Fionnuala. Tim wanted Helen back, baby or not. So she went back to Canada. On 20 September 1980, in St George's Hospital, Vancouver Island, she gave birth to a girl, whom she named Erika Bridget. Bridget had been Charles's mother's name.

Every year, on her birthday, Helen sent Charles a photograph of his daughter. Other than that, there was no contact. Erika was raised thinking Tim was her father. Helen and Tim's marriage limped on: In 1984 they moved back to Dublin and bought a house on Waterloo Road. Three years later they agreed to give it up as a bad job. Tim went back to Canada. Helen stayed home.

'And, what, twenty years later,' I say, 'here you are?'

'That's it,' Charles says, smiling at her, 'together, *very* much in love and – dare I say it – getting ready to take the battle to Sheridans. Who, incidentally, are going to go stark raving mad when they find out we're going to be doing the *Tomme Vaudoise*.'

'Is it really, I don't know, prudent,' I hear myself ask, 'to be setting up something as specialist as a cheesemongers, *in* the current economic climate?'

Using my fingers, I rhyme off the parrot phrases of the day. 'The credit crunch, the recession, the banking crisis . . .'

'Let's not talk about a crisis,' Charles says. 'Let's talk about a *challenge*. You think chaps like us – me and Hennessy back there – are going to roll up in a ball and what-not? What, entrepreneurs? Oh, not on your life. And the world can sleep easily in its beds tonight, let me tell you, because there are more out there like us . . .'

'Are you going to talk to this little shit-kicker or am I?' Hennessy says. He's referring to me. I suspect the reason he's in the car is about to become apparent. The reason I'm in the car, too. Charles clears his throat in preparation to speak.

Hennessy: Little birdie tells us that certain parties have been flapping their mouths off . . .

Charles: Flapping their mouths off? Steady on, old chap. No, no, no, it's just we hear you've been meeting up with our friends. Woodward and Bernstein, as we've been known to call them.

I look at Hennessy, then at Charles, then back at Hennessy. 'Are you having me followed?' I ask.

Charles: Followed? Of course not. No, you were seen, that's all. No secrets in this town.

'Obviously not,' I say. 'But anyway, I met two journalists – so what?'

Charles: Well, I think *our* concern – and I'm taking the unilateral liberty of speaking on your behalf here, Hennessy – is that the facts are presented in a fair, balanced *and* objective manner.

'Okay,' I say, rather peevishly, 'present away.'

Charles: Well, the facts – as it happens – are known. The media had a bloody free-for-all at the time of the trial. What was absent from the coverage, however, was a little context.
   I don't know how well you remember Ireland before the – inverted commas – boom, but I can tell you, it was a bloody wretched place.

Hennessy: We were the Albania of western Europe.

Charles: The banks opened at ten, closed at three and somewhere in between took a bloody hour for lunch. If you wanted a phone connected, you waited for six months. It's a wonder any business got done.

Hennessy: It got dark at midday.

Charles: It did, literally, get dark at midday.

I have all these people coming up to me – still – and they say, 'Never mind your Feargal Quinns – *you're* the one who should be in the Senate. *And* that wife of yours – ex now, obviously – *she* should be on the board of a dozen semi-states.'

And I say, well, thank you very much, old scout, but don't hold your breath. Don't expect any of our so-called politicians to heed your call. Because that would mean acknowledging that this economic miracle everyone was talking about until very recently was no miracle at all.

It happened because of people like Hennessy and I, entrepreneurs who were prepared to stay in this country when tens of thousands of others were emigrating – no offence, Helen – to stoke the dying embers of what could loosely be called an economy.

Hennessy: You name me a country – a worthwhile country, mind, not some tuppence-ha'penny tinpot in the sun – that wasn't built on corruption.

Charles: I'd put that word in inverted commas, Hennessy. I'd make that distinction.

Hennessy: The States, Germany, France, Japan, Italy, Britain – you think in *their* first hundred years of nationhood they didn't use grease to make sure the wheels of progress ran smooth?

Charles: Did they go rounding up *their* founding fathers and putting them in front of these star chambers we call tribunals?

No.

No, sir.

They said, thank you very much for doing the state some bloody service.

Sorry, Helen – getting all worked up.

Helen: It's okay, Charles.

Hennessy: That time, ah, you'd a fucking mania in this country for fields. Protecting them, like they was a dying species.

Wasn't a country in the world more hostile to the idea of development than this place. You tried to build a factory, a supermarket, a DIY store – nothing but objections, dragging it on so long that in the end you said, 'Ah, stick it in your fucking hat.'

Quarter of the workforce unemployed, fifty thousand emigrating every year and we're trying to protect – what's this they called it? – the green belt.

Jesus, the country was *covered* in fields. What the fuck did fields ever bring us, except bad potatoes and worse ballads?

I repeat what I can remember of Liam Toft's line, about the County Development Plan being there to ensure a balanced development of Dublin.

Charles: It was drawn up by glorified landscape gardeners . . .

Hennessy: Grey men with set squares. And their pretty maps. Agriculture here. Heavy industry there. Houses in the middle. Ah – all very nice, I'm sure. But let me tell you something. It has nothing to do with nothing.

Charles: What Hennessy means is, they weren't planning for Ireland's *economic* future.

Hennessy: If they had their way, we'd be living on fucking dandelions today.

Charles: Ireland's biggest problem, you see, was underdevelopment. Young people needed jobs. They needed homes.

Enter the man of vision in the back there.

Still remember the day like it was yesterday. It was the same day Ireland drew fifteen-each with France in Dublin, thus being denied the famous Grand Slam, which means it was 1985.

Eight o'clock in the morning, Hennessy arrives at the door – still in Glenageary at the time – says he has something to show me. So there we are in Hennessy's sedan, which I was telling you about, pointed west, with me feeling like some modern-day Magellan, half expecting to drop off the side of the Earth at any moment.

We pull up. Middle of nowhere. I mean, it's barren. I doubt it appeared on any map. Hennessy turns to me – do you remember this, old chap? – and he says, 'I'm sorry about this, but I'm going to have to kill you.'

Hennessy: Ah, you little pissbag. Should have seen your face. 'But, but, but – we've got tickets for the match! It's the Grand Slam! Doyler and so forth!'

I says, you know too much, kid. You're going to take a little dirt nap. There's a shovel in the trunk – I want you to make your own bed.

Charles: Hennessy's idea of a joke, of course. Oh, we laughed and laughed, eventually.

Then Hennessy says, 'Come on – something I want to show you.'

Got out of the car. Legs still a bit shaky, if the truth be told.

Still wasn't sure if . . . Well, I was still in shock, I expect. And Hennessy has that way of walking – always *looks* like he's carrying a gun, even when he's not.

So, like I said, we're out in the wilds. Bally Go Bloody Nowhere. We walk up this little hill affair. Hennessy turns to me and he says, 'Charlie, what do you see?'

What was I *going* to say? 'Not much, old boy. Lot of cows and not a lot else.'

'Funny,' he says, 'because *I* see the future.'

Hennessy: The Temptation in the Wilderness – that's what the papers later called it.

That cartoon in the paper, I got it framed.

Charles: His famous speech. Robert Emmet, how are you?

'Ireland won't always be like this,' says our friend there. 'A backward, potato-eating island on the edge of nowhere . . .'

Oh, he knew what he was saying. What buttons to press. We're in the EEC now, he says. It can't stay like this forever. Can't!

And I'll never forget, he said to me, 'See that Bobby Fischer?'

And here's me finally getting a word in edgeways. I said, 'Only Bobby Fischer I know, old scout, is the chap who plays the chess.'

'That's the one,' he says. 'You want to know what makes him the greatest chess player who ever lived?'

Hennessy: I says, when I look at a chessboard, I see black and white squares – forty-eight, sixty-four, whatever there is. But black and white squares. That's all. Nothing else. But when Bobby Fischer looks at a chessboard, he don't *see* squares – he sees moves, strategies, opportunities. That's what makes him great.

Charles: He said, 'Ninety-nine point nine per cent of people, you bring them out here and what they see is fields. You want to know what *I* see? I see concrete. I see see steel and glass. Over there, an industrial park. High-tech, because – mark my words, Charlie – computers are the way this world's going. Offices – there, there and there. That field behind it? Retail. A shopping mall, big as the ones they got in the States. And over there, apartments, block after block.'

I said, 'Apartments? In Ireland?'

'That's how people will live,' he says. 'Giant fucking ant farms. And there, where I'm pointing, that's where the motorway will run.'

I said, 'A *motorway*? You hand me that hip-flask this instant – you've had enough. Honestly, it's still four hours till kick-off.'

'A motorway,' he repeated, just like that. 'And you'll have to pay a toll to use it. And people will sit for an hour or more, snarled up in traffic, to get from the industrial park over there to the apartments over there. But they'll be happy. Because they'll be sat in big fucking German cars and they'll be *living*, Charlie – *really* living.'

I mean, what he said that day, it was Churchillian.

Hennessy: Yeah, I point my finger and I say, you see that little farmhouse over there? Okay, follow my finger. You see that mass of buildings there – the piggery? Okay, keep following my finger. See the end of that road over there? To where we're standing. How'd you like to own it? I mean, own it *all*.

Charles: I said, 'Own it? Must be half a bloody county there. Wait a minute, what county are we even in, old boy?'
    'Dublin,' he said.
    Couldn't believe it, of course.
    Two point six million of your old pounds.
    Hennessy said, get a mixture of zonings – commercial, industrial, residential – and it'd be worth, well, a lot more than that. He must have seen the shock on my face because I'll never forget what he said. 'Chess ain't my game, Charlie. *This* is my game.'
    Cut me in for half, didn't you, old boy.
    We sat down with Pat Moone, Lord rest his soul, with his famous bow ties . . .

At the mention of Pat Moone, I can feel Hennessy staring hard at me. Or maybe I'm imagining it.

Charles: Architect friend of Hennessy's – played second row for Terenure, or maybe Mary's, at one point – and we drew up a plan for the land.
    Well, essentially we were building a new town, which was terribly exciting . . .
    Just like Hennessy said – houses, factories, offices, a shopping centre.
    The rest is history.
    Go back to your newspaper pals and tell them to take a look at Conalswood today. One of *the* most prestigious addresses west of the R112.
    The houses – held their value, even during the current ups and downs.

The shopping centre, thriving – they're all in there, all the big names.

The business park, ditto . . .

I have no idea whether Hennessy is capable of killing a man, but I admit I feel safer for having Charles and Helen in the car. I'm sure I come across as far less nervous than I am when I say, 'You make it sound like it was all about, I don't know, philanthropy. The judge at the trial said it was naked greed.'

Hennessy gives me a cold, hard stare.

Hennessy: Let me tell you something about greed. Greed is the only reason any of us is still here. You buy something for five, you sell it to someone stupid enough to pay six – only thing that keeps the world turning. Greed gave us the Celtic Tiger. Greed got us into the mess we're in today. And greed, my friend, is what'll get us out of it.

Interview Tapes 27 and 28
Tuesday 7 October 2008
Notes from Muckross College
Class of 1998 School Reunion

My phone rings at five o'clock in the morning. It's Ross. 'Dude,' he says, 'do *not* hang up. Unless you *want* me at your front door singing "Ireland's Call".'

My mind manages to process this, despite the early hour, and I decide to hear him out. 'What are you doing up already?' I ask.

He says, 'Your question should actually be, why aren't you in bed yet? And all I'll tell you is this – it's a story that's not fit for any book.' Then he adds cryptically, 'Take my advice – *never* get involved with a bird whose old man calls her Princess. Rossism number one hundred and thirty-two. Write it down . . .'

'I will. Where are you, by the way?'

'A place called Leixlip.'

'Leixlip?'

'Mad, isn't it? I don't even know where it is.'

'I'm pretty sure it's in Kildare.'

'Kildare! Can you believe that? I'm beginning to think this story would work better as a movie . . .'

I laugh. I can't help myself.

'Dude, I'm serious. Here I am, walking the streets of some strange focking town. Commando, I might add, because I had to leave in a hurry. Can't get a Jo. Two hours to kill before the next bus back to civilization . . .'

'Aha! I was going to ask to what did I owe the pleasure. You're looking for a lift.'

'A lift?' he says, appalled. 'I wouldn't take a lift in that bucket of rust.'

'You're bored then.'

'Yeah, I am a bit. But it *would* make a good film, wouldn't it? And I'm telling you now, Dude, you're writing it . . .'

'Thanks.'

'Who would they get to play me? Maybe Matt Damon – *if* he bulked up . . .'

'Ross,' I tell him, 'I really do need to sleep.'

'Okay,' he says, 'but just before you go, did you make it back for the Muckross reunion?'

'Yeah.'

'Uh-oh – this'll be good. Did you get a lot of shit on me?'

'I got a few stories. They haven't exactly started a fan club in your honour.'

This seems to please him.

'Go on then,' he says, 'give me a little taster.'

I switch on the lamp, resigned now to being awake. I wait for my eyes to adjust to the light, then take my notebook off the locker and flick back through the pages.

'Okay,' I tell him, 'I'm going to just give you the sober ones . . .'

'What do you mean, the sober ones?'

'Well, you broke a lot of hearts, Ross. Four Cosmopolitans in, things started to get a bit emotional. Any I spoke to after eleven o'clock, I didn't even bother transcribing.'

'A lot of tears, I'd say.'

'It was like watching *The X Factor*.'

'Give me the not-so-damaged ones then.'

'Okay,' I say, 'Nadine McCaul . . .'

'Nadine McCaul! There's a blast from the past.'

'*Ross O'Carroll-Kelly is an arsehole and put that in. I went out with him for, like, three or four months – it would have been when I was in, like, sixth year? Then, oh my God – this one night? – he ended up being with Anna Dunford in, like, Annabel's. He was, like, seen? But of course, he couldn't admit it . . .*'

'I know where this is going.'

'*He tried to tell me he'd an identical twin . . .*'

'Oh my God – Ralph!'

'*A twin brother he'd never mentioned to me before . . .*'

'Yeah, I got away with murder because of Ralph.'

'*And I actually believed him. Oh my God, I'm, like, so embarrassed about it now. But all of his friends, like, backed him up? They were all there, "Yeah, yeah, they're twins," even though nobody I knew had ever seen them together. But any time I'd turn around to him and go, "Ross, were you with Jenna Carroll at Sadbh Mulvey's eighteenth last weekend?" or "Ross, did you collect Alannah Kelligan from hockey practice on Thursday night?", it'd always be, "No, no – it was Ralph."*'

He laughs hysterically.

'Classic,' he says, when he retrieves his breath. 'You have *got* to put that in.'

'Zala Desaleux.'

'Oh, yeah, *her* old pair were French. What's her story?'

'*I was with him, like, once or twice. There was this one night, I invited him over to watch, like, a DVD? Mum and Dad were at something in the National Concert Hall. Anyway – whatever – somehow he managed to lose his mobile phone. Looked everywhere for it and I was like, "Oh my God, my parents are going to be home any second now." So then I was like, "Oh my God, I am so dumb – why don't I just ring it from my phone," which is what I did. Turned out it had actually fallen down the side of one of the, like, sofa cushions? So I pull it out and it's still ringing, but I'm just, like, staring at his caller ID. He had me in his phone as Emergency Score.*'

'Brilliant,' he says, almost convulsing now. '*I* couldn't have told that better. Put in, though, that she was actually with me – as in *with* with? – loads of times even after that.'

'Ella Brady . . .'

'Oh my God – now this is vintage Ross O'Carroll-Kelly. Go on . . .'

'*I invited him to the Muckross debs . . .*'

'*Pre*-debs.'

'My mistake. *I invited him to the Muckross pre-debs. But then, like, two or three nights before it was on, I ended up getting back with my ex, as in Stephen Spacey – he was, like, captain of CBS Monkstown that year?*'

'She blew me off for someone from CBS Monkstown!'

'*I explained it to him over the phone and he seemed, like, cool with it? Then he rang me later and he was like, "Can I just call over?" and I was like, "Ross, there's no point, I've already, like, made my decision?" and he was like, "No, I just want to return a few things," because he had my scarf and one of my CDs – it was actually the Lighthouse Family? So he calls around and he's got this kid with him . . .*'

'Yeah, that was Oisinn's little brother . . .'

'Ross said he was giving him chemistry grinds. I mean, the idea of Ross giving anyone grinds . . .'

'Harsh, but continue.'

'This kid kept, like, coughing — it sounds really bad — but all over me. I was like, "Ross, is he okay? He sounds really sick." Anyway, Ross was all, "No hard feelings — as it happens I want to keep my options open on the whole bird front." So anyway, the coughing continues, always in my direction and I was like, "Oh my God, would he not put, like, his hand over his mouth?" Woke up the next morning with, like, gastroenteritis? And yes, I ended up missing the pre-debs.'

I have to ask. 'You, what, presumably *paid* a child to infect a girl with gastroenteritis?'

'Dude,' he says, 'you have no idea how much we hated CBS Monkstown.'

'Lucy Skirrow . . .'

'Weird,' he says, 'I don't remember a Lucy Skirrow.'

'I actually met him at a cousin of mine's going-away-on-a-J1 party? He seemed, I don't know, really nice. He asked me did I want to take it into the bedroom, private party and whatever. I was like, "Cool." And, like, nothing happened? As in, he was a total gentleman? I mean, I was actually puking my guts up in the en suite. But he was lying flat on the bed and what he kept doing was banging the headboard off the wall, obviously to let his friends think that he was, you know, getting it. The next thing, I hear this — oh my God — crash, as in really loud. My cousin had, like, a fish tank on a shelf above the bed and Ross managed to, like, bring it down on top of himself. He was, like, covered in water, glass everywhere, and there were, like, fish jumping all over the bed. He ran out of the house screaming.'

'Don't even *think* about putting that story in,' he says, then hangs up.

Interview Tapes 29 and 30/A
Wednesday 15 October 2008
Audrey Mannion, Delma Dean
and Angela Hutton

Avoca Handweavers this morning is a henhouse of clucking women, fes-tooned with bright scarves and smelling of jasmine and sandalwood. I edge my way through the confusion of tables to where they're sitting and introduce myself. Audrey Mannion is pretty, if slightly porcine, with big red lips, russet cheeks and sixties-style horn-rims, while Angela Hutton is small and heavily made-up with a slightly querulous face. Delma Dean – or Dee Dee, as she's known to her friends – is a striking, statuesque blonde with angled features and hair cut in a man's crew style that, at a quick glance, gives her the look of Sharon Stone.

Fionnuala despises Audrey and Audrey feels much the same way about Fionnuala. Yet they've both remained friends with Angela and Delma, dividing up their weekday mornings in the manner of a custody agreement. Fionnuala gets them on Tuesdays and Thursdays, in the Gables in Foxrock or the café in the National Gallery. Audrey has them on Wednesdays and Fridays, either in Bianconi's in Ballsbridge or here, in Kilmacanogue.

For twenty years the arrangement has worked well for everyone, though Audrey's antipathy is never far from her lips.

Audrey: *I* was one of her bridesmaids, if you can believe that now.

Angela: Yes, the three of us.

Audrey: But *me* – I always found that very odd. I didn't know her terribly well. Angela, you were at school with her. You were too, weren't you, Dee Dee?

Delma: No, I boarded in Rathnew. But I knew her through tennis.

Audrey: Well, you knew her a long time. Which *I* didn't. I mean, I only met her after she came back from France. With that ridiculous accent. And those ridiculous stories. Angela and Dee Dee introduced me to her in Sandycove one day. I remember thinking . . . Well, I won't tell you *what* I thought. The point is, I didn't know her that long *or* that well when she asked me to be her bridesmaid. I said to Bart, my husband, 'Does she not have any friends, this girl?'

We arrived at the reception and, well, there was your answer.

Angela: Audrey, that's unfair.

Audrey: Oh, is it?

'The reception was, where – the Shelbourne?'

Audrey: Yes, and there must have been three hundred people there. It was the biggest wedding I ever saw. And Charles and Fionnuala knew hardly anyone there.

Angela: Well, we were there. And all of Charles's rugby friends . . .

Audrey: It was mostly Fionnuala's father's friends.

Angela: Well, he paid for the wedding . . .

Audrey: His friends and clients, all in their fifties, sixties, which was ancient to us.

The other thing that stands out in my memory was that anytime anyone admired the dress, she mentioned this Princess Anne thing – it's supposed to have been modelled on the one *she* wore – but then she kept saying, 'Yes, *she* married a commoner, too, didn't she?'

Angela: I never heard that.

Audrey: This was right in front of Charles. She didn't care that he heard.

Delma: She might have been drunk, Audrey.

Audrey: Well, remembering it now, I think, you know, the woman was teaching Home Economics to teenage girls in a convent school – who the hell did she think she was?

Angela: Like I said, I'd be very surprised if she said that. Very surprised, Audrey. But I think, looking back, they would *both* admit now that their marriage was a mistake.

'Do you think she married Charles on the rebound from Conor?' I ask.

Angela: Not exactly the rebound. Quite a few years *had* passed.
  I have to admit, even as her oldest friend, I would have seen very little of Fionnuala during our final year of school and then college as well. I think, socially, we were just moving in different circles.
  I met Eduard, my husband, who was very involved in student politics. He was a Marxist then; he ended up in hedge funds, which we always laugh about. But the crowd Fionnuala was knocking around with – they wouldn't have been *his* cup of tea at all. They would have been hanging around the New Am Coffee House – that would have been the centre of their world.
  It's hard to believe it now, but it was the first place in Ireland where you could get what they used to call a frothy coffee. It used to attract all sorts. A lot of boys from Gonzaga, but also a lot of music and art students – these were the type of friends Fionnuala had. All very bohemian.
  In school, there would have been a lot of jealousy of her, of course, because it got around that she and Conor were going out to restaurants. I mean, no one went to restaurants in those days, only

the super-rich. She was only seventeen. It just seemed like such an impossibly grown-up thing to be doing.

Delma: Jammet's – wasn't that the one? On the corner of Nassau Street and Grafton Street?

Angela: Yes, Conor's family had an account there. Fionnuala would come into school and say, you know, Monsieur Jammet does the most wonderful *poulet basquaise* I've ever tasted. Apparently, even French people who ate there couldn't believe that a restaurant in Ireland could serve French food like that.

Audrey is listening to this exchange with a look of scorn.
'The years Fionnuala spent in Paris,' I say, leading, 'they sound very, I suppose, glamorous . . .'

Audrey: Oh, *please!* That was all in her head. None of it happened. The first time I ever met her, she told me she was in love with a bullfighter called Jorge Montenero. Oh, she had it all worked out. He was in Paris recuperating after being gored by a bull. But *she* ended the affair when he told her he wanted to go back to Madrid to fight the same bull again.

Another day, she told me she'd been in love with a Russian dissident writer called something Baltacha who liked to tie her up and slap her face while they had sex . . .

And I see you looking at me, Angela, but this has nothing to *do* with Alma and the shop.

I asked her once did she have any photographs from her time in Paris. All she ever showed me was one of her in this tiny Sonia Rykiel sweater – which were the height of fashion in those days – standing in front of the Élysée Palace, sucking her cheekbones in, a faraway look in her eyes.

I kept asking could I see more. I wouldn't let it go, which was a bit mean, I know, but I was like a dog with a bone.

All these stories of glamorous lovers. I mean, you'd *have* photographs, wouldn't you?

Delma: Not necessarily. They were very carefree years for her.

Angela: Exactly.

Audrey: Oh, come on. Bart has this friend. Worked for years in the Irish Embassy in Paris. Well, long story short, about two years ago we had dinner with him and his wife, Treasa, who, it turns out, *knew* Fionnuala in Paris. *She* had a whole other story, which was just as I suspected.

Angela: You see, this is why we agreed to *never* talk about Fionnuala . . .

Delma: Well, what did this woman say?

Audrey: What do you think? There *was* no bullfighter. No artist. No stormy affair with a married Government minister, which was another story she used to tell. Two nights a week she taught English to second-level students in a language school. The rest of the time she worked as a kitchen hand in a restaurant in the Gare du Nord . . .

Angela: *I'd* know that if that were true.

Audrey: Angela, it gives me goosebumps to even think about it, but Fionnuala spent, what, three years of her life, *in* Paris, working as a pot walloper. Miserable, according to Treasa. And she invented this parallel life for herself, in the hope, presumably, that this boyfriend of hers, Conor whatever he was called, would hear about it and . . . do what exactly?

Delma seems suddenly convinced by Audrey's account.

Delma: I mean, *I* worried about her – because of some of the things I would have seen. I mean, I myself personally.

Angela, she told Oprah she was engaged to a soldier who fought in Algeria. He was tortured by the ALN to the point where he lost the use of his left arm *and* his sense of smell.

She never mentioned that before.

Audrey: Ever.

Angela: Well, she mentioned it to me. Several times.

Delma: I mean, I'd *always* defend her myself. I'm just saying, there were times when, you know, I would have worried that she was going the same way her own mother went . . .

Angela: It's not hereditary, Dee Dee.

Delma: Well, I don't know if it is or not. All I'm saying is that *at* that time, her behaviour *was* what you would call, you know, odd.

Conor broke her heart, remember. We've all had our hearts broken. But I always felt sad for her, that she didn't have a mother to confide in.

You know, there was a definite sadness in Fionnuala when she came back from France. A loneliness. You know, the same one you see in her now sometimes . . .

'They were married a good few years before Ross came along,' I say. 'Presumably they were delighted.'

Angela: Well, obviously . . .

Audrey: Not as far as I could see. I thought she regarded Ross as some awful growth she was waiting to have removed . . .

Angela: Audrey!

Audrey: It's true. She never wanted children. All the talk was of, you know, all the things she was going to do when this *thing* was out of her.

Top of the list was obviously getting out of Sallynoggin . . .

Angela: It was Glenageary, Audrey, and well you know it.

Audrey: And throwing herself into charity work . . .

Angela: For which she never sought recognition, I might add . . .

Audrey: She wanted a Women of Europe Laureate Award . . .

Angela: The number of times she asked for her name to be kept out of the papers . . .

Audrey: It killed her that Adi had one. Oh, you couldn't mention Adi in her company.

Delma: She was always very kind, Audrey. You can't deny that.

Audrey: Oh, she was *full* of kindness for people, wasn't she? Oh, yes. As long as they lived in Africa. As long as the council wasn't trying to settle them in a halting site around the corner from her brand new house in Foxrock . . .

I'm talking about Bridie Codd.

Angela: You were as against that idea as anyone.

Audrey: But you know the reason Fionnuala was against it? Because one of the neighbours gave Bridie a bag of clothes – just being charitable. And in that bag of clothes was a Gerry Weber jacket – black, grosgrain – identical to one that Fionnuala had. She ran into her one day outside Thomas's – both of them wearing exactly the same thing.

That's why *she* was against the halting site.

Delma: None of us were *against* the halting site. It was just generally felt that something like that wasn't appropriate for somewhere like Foxrock.

I mean, she herself wouldn't have been happy living among people like us.

They continue pecking at one another in this manner for a few more minutes. I'm anxious to hear Audrey's memories of how her relationship with Fionnuala became fractured.

Audrey: Well, one of the first things she did when she went to work for Alma – it might even have *been* the first thing – was to have a bell fitted to the door of the shop. That was to warn her that a customer – a member of the public – was on the premises. She hated dealing with people. She left that to Alma. She'd immediately slip into the little office at the back of the shop and wait there until she heard the customer go out the door.

Delma: Dealing with customers wasn't her forte, Audrey. Her real strength – I think *you'd* agree, Angela – was doing the arrangements. Then the business side of things as well . . .

Audrey: And we all know what happened there. Look, it wasn't a particularly sophisticated fraud. It was just theft. Once or twice, I sneaked a look at the books and Fionnuala, as far I could see, was simply skimming money off the top of the daily take . . .

Angela: Now that is libellous.

Audrey: In time she forgot her aversion to customers, you see, and now *insisted* on serving them. And by sheer coincidence, of course, that was when Alma's financial troubles began . . .

Angela: You can't keep saying these things, Audrey . . .

Audrey: In the two years that Fionnuala worked for her, the shop lost money hand over fist. I remember saying to Alma – I mean, she'd have been my mother's best friend – I said, 'Alma, does that not seem suspicious to you?'

Fionnuala was somehow operating two tills. Or at least there were two sets of till receipts – the real ones and the ones she declared to Alma.

Angela: Not true.

Audrey: I thought it was very suspicious, for instance, that credit card sales were still going up, year on year. See, that side of things, it was more difficult to steal, because there was an electronic trail. But the *cash* take was down something like sixty per cent over twelve months.

Delma: But that would have been the case with most retail businesses, Alma. I had the cake shop in Sandycove at the time – everyone was switching to plastic. Especially a florist's. It was suddenly all phone orders. Fionnuala told me that herself.

Audrey: She was keeping a book, this little ledger – all her ideas for when she took over the business. Posy baskets, orchids, Surinam cherries. Pages and pages and pages of ideas. A Balloon and a Boost. That was her Get Well Soon idea. A bunch of flowers and a foil balloon filled with helium. She thought this made her Gina Rinehart, of course – all these drawings and notes.

She was even trying out different names – La Dame De Fleur, Serenity, Chelsea Garden, Tulips To Say I Love You . . .

Angela: I'm sorry, Audrey, but you've got a very selective memory. That shop was in trouble before Fionnuala ever went to work for her.

Audrey: It was not.

Angela: Audrey, you told me yourself – you met Alma in Bewley's in Stillorgan one day. She said to you, 'What am I going to do, Audrey?'

Do you remember that?

Audrey: That was *after* Fionnuala started stealing from her.

Angela: No, it wasn't. Because you were pregnant with Sophie at the time and I remember Fionnuala was pregnant with Ross. Which was, what, five or six years before she ever went to work for Alma?

Audrey's eyebrows are suddenly knitted in thought.

Angela: And you asked Eduard if he'd look at the books. Give Alma some advice. Do you remember that?

There follows a silence worthy of Pinter.

Angela: Yes, Audrey. She was in trouble even then. That's why her daughters – what were they called? – that's why they didn't want to know. Until Alma died and they realized there was next to nothing in her will. Then you started filling their heads with all this nonsense.

Audrey: I told them to phone the Fraud Squad. And I make no apologies for it to this day. Alma only lasted another year after what happened. Suffered a massive stroke. Lost almost three-quarters of her brain function. Lingered on for months in Harold's Cross . . .

Delma: But Audrey, that has nothing to do with Fionnuala.

Audrey: I blame her for it. And I make no apologies for saying that. Let her sue me if she wants . . .

They agree to drop it with an equanimity that suggests the ground has been covered many times before. Angela asks Delma about her son, Lloyd, a quantity surveyor, who it seems was earning €150,000 a year last year, but now can't even get an interview. 'It's either take an office support job for a third of the salary,' she says, 'or take the family to Dubai.'

Audrey says she read somewhere that Tesco have reported a three hundred per cent increase in sales of home hair-dye kits. They all agree that
this is awful.

I sit through the conversation, but my mind is elsewhere. Of all the
salty stories I've heard about Fionnuala over the years, the swindling of
Alma Goad was the one I was most prepared to believe. Now, I don't
believe it at all. But Audrey said at least one thing that suggested a certain
truth in something I hadn't been prepared to believe.

Interview Tape 30/B
Friday 17 October 2008
Ronan O'Carroll Kelly

Ronan is standing outside Dr Quirky's Good Time Emporium, sucking the last glow of life out of a filter cigarette. I see him before he sees me, which bothers him greatly.

'Losin' me touch,' he says.

'Maybe it's because you're not wearing your glasses,' I say.

He stares hard at me, like we both know he's been caught out. He retrieves them from his inside pocket and puts them on.

I notice, for the first time, that the glass in them is clear.

'Taking a break from the books,' he says, going through the motions anyway.

I nod. 'You're wise,' I tell him. 'Watching the news – feels like the world has slipped on its axis, doesn't it?'

'Er, right enough,' he says, 'yeah.'

'You might as well enjoy yourself.'

He drops his butt on the ground and grinds it under a white Nike Air Max. 'Be long enough looking at the lid,' he says, 'wha'?'

I laugh. 'That's true. By the way, Ross was saying you're still having difficulty finding a school . . .'

'What caters for fellas of my abilities, yeah.'

'Well, I hope you don't mind, but I made some phone calls for you and I found one or two. Did you know that DCU has a course?'

'Does it?'

I pull out a sheet of paper that's been folded in four. 'There's actually a couple of numbers there. I was going to give them to Ross.'

He looks over both shoulders – habit, I suppose. 'I'll, er, give them to him meself, if you like,' he says.

'Are you sure?'

'No problemo,' he says, snatching it from my hand. 'No fooken problemo at all.'

Twenty yards down the road, I turn back to see him pinching the
piece of paper between two fingers while trying to get a flame from his
disposable lighter.

Interview Tapes 31 and 32
Wednesday 22 October 2008
JP Conroy, Oisinn Wallace and Fionn de Barra

'Hook, Lyon and Sinker today became the first major estate agent to go to the wall as a result of the slowdown in the housing market and the uncertainty over the world economy. As he closed the doors for the final time on the business he established more than forty years ago, Barry Conroy said the days when people were prepared to pay seven figures for a ratbox in Ringsend may be over forever.'

I mute George Lee and pick out JP's number on my phone. He sounds surprisingly upbeat. When you've been living so long in a state of stasis, even bad news can be a relief.

I offer my condolences. 'Everything on Earth,' he says, 'has its own time and its own season.'

He asks me how the book is coming along.

'I don't know,' I say. 'I mean, they're all a lot more complicated than I expected. More interesting, I suppose. See, I thought writing a biography was just like adding beads to a string. But it's more like, I don't know, shell games. I _mean, you lift up one and underneath it's never what you expected . . .'

'Oh,' he says, like he only asked out of politeness.

'I've got, I suppose, one or two theories about various things. Are you and the guys around over the next day or two?'

'Well, what are you doing now?' he says. 'We're all meeting in Cullen's. A sort of redundancy party.'

Ballsbridge is unpassable and I quickly discover the reason. Motorists are slowing to a crawl to take in the sight. The Hook, Lyon and Sinker office has been gutted. All of its contents – from the medium-density fibreboard furniture to the giant electronic scoreboard on which JP and Ross kept account of their commissions – have been piled into a skip and set alight. I narrow my eyes and through thick whorls of smoke can make out JP's father's famous pinstripe suit – his Lucky Louis – lying amid the flames like a Guy resigned to its fate.

JP is at the bar, calling a round for Oisinn and Fionn. Oisinn mentions that he hasn't been to bed for thirty-six hours, though he doesn't say why. He looks wretched.

There's a television on with the sound turned down. There were marches today – old-age pensioners and students letting the Government know what they think of the Budget.

'You know what?' Oisinn says with a mordant smile, 'they're the best-dressed student protesters I've ever seen. Shit the bed, have they never seen *Reeling in the Years*? You've got to at least *look* like you're hard-up . . .'

'The Ugg Boot Revolution,' JP says to great roars of laughter. He was always good at coining a phrase. He thought up 'Athlone – Gateway to Dublin' after all.

'I was talking to Charles and Hennessy the other day,' I tell them. 'They seem pretty confident this recession is something we're going to ride out. I mean, a cheesemongers! That's confidence, isn't it?'

They all laugh. I'm the only one not getting the joke.

'Well, it's an obvious front, isn't it,' JP says, 'for something else? Look, those two will have already worked out a way to make millions out of all this . . .'

'And it'll have nothing to do with cheese, of that you can be sure,' says Fionn.

Of course. How could I have forgotten the money they squirrelled away in Andorra? Twenty euro for a block of *Caprino Noccetto*? Twenty-five for the Lincolnshire Poacher? It's their way of laundering the millions they managed to hide from the Revenue and the Criminal Assets Bureau.

'Is Ross coming in?' I ask.

'He won't come to Cullen's,' JP says. 'He's burnt a fair few birds from the bank centre over the years. Too much hassle.'

I laugh and shake my head indulgently.

'I've been to a couple of ten-year reunions,' I tell them. 'Foxrock. Muck-ross. Ross was pretty insistent I include some of his crimes against women in the book. Jesus, he's been with a lot of girls in his time, hasn't he?'

Oisinn and JP nod their heads.

'A hell of a lot,' I repeat. I think about the size-ten footprints on the inside of the GTI window. 'It's almost as if he's, I don't know, compensating . . .'

I let it hang there, but no one takes the bait.

'But the thing I can't get a handle on,' I say, 'is the whole thing with his parents. He *says* he hates them, but they say they have, I don't know, a normal, happy relationship. I mean, what's the story with that?'

'You've met them,' Oisinn says. 'They're all right, his old pair.'

I make a noise that doesn't commit me either way.

'His old dear's pretty hot,' he says. 'Mad as fuck, but you'd have to say big-time MILF material. And Charles is pretty cool . . .'

'They're always at matches together, him and his old man,' JP says. 'I mean, he talks like he hates them – and I've heard him say, like, the *odd* thing to them? – but I think he exaggerates.'

'What about you, Fionn?' I ask. 'He *seems* to also hate you at times. You've obviously read some of the things he's written about you over the years. Always seems out to humiliate you . . .'

'Ross and me,' he says, pushing his glasses up on his nose, 'that's, er, complicated . . .'

I admit it. I steal a look at his feet.

Lack of sleep has accelerated the affect of the alcohol on Oisinn. 'Go on, Fionn,' he urges, 'it's part of the story.'

Fionn: Well, you know you were asking about Ross being bullied. Well, I suppose dominance hierarchies are a major part of . . .

Oisinn: Ross got the shit kicked out of him. Guy called Gary Gest, who *I* know from the yacht club. Him, Seth Dwyer, Joel Chambers. There was a few of them.

Fionn: It started – the bullying – when we were in the junior school.

Oisinn: Yeah, like I told you, Ross was a weedy little thing. I saw them make him drink water from a puddle once. He was down on his hands and knees, lapping at it, like a dog.

JP: Yeah, I was there. Gestie had his foot on the back of Ross's neck. There was a crowd around him, laughing.

I notice JP's father on the far side of the bar, inviting us to raise our glasses in a toast. He's tottering drunk. 'I'm not going out all bitterness and recrimination,' he shouts, a man with no control over his volume. 'Make hay while the sun shines, they say. And we *made* hay. Oh, that's as sure as I'm going to be in Legs of Lower Leeson Street tonight – where women with a past meet men with no future ...'
    JP smiles, vaguely embarrassed.

Oisinn: Like, mostly it was just harmless shit. The whole Sallynoggin thing – batter burger and chips, all that – or *even* the odd thump. It was mostly only bullying. You took it, then when you got older, you dished it out yourself. That was the way it was.

Fionn: It was when we joined the senior school that it started to go way beyond that. It crossed a line.

JP: I don't know how the cops were never called.

Fionn: Ross has this story in one of his books – I've heard him tell the story himself – about how he and Christian stood up to them one day and how they suddenly respected him and left him alone. Well, that never happened.

'So *what* happened?' I ask.

Oisinn: See, the whole school knew about the special treatment we were getting – the steaks and everything – because we were supposed to be, like, the stars of the future. Gestie and Joel would have been on the S that year. I mean, they were shit, but I suppose their noses would have been out of joint.
    So this lunchtime, Ross is having a hit-and-miss and Gestie comes up behind, punches him in the back of the head and Ross's head went – bang! – off the wall. He still has a scar from that. They

gave him, whatever, a kicking, then they grabbed the toilet brush – you know those focking brushes, covered in shit and piss and God knows what else – and they scrubbed his face with it.

My stomach lurches.

'He could have got, I don't know, hepatitis,' I say, like that's the worst thing I can imagine.

Fionn: I was the one who found him. I was the one who brought him down to Fehily's office . . .

'So he gives you a hard time, why? Because it's the only way of dealing with the humiliation of you seeing him like that?'

Fionn just shrugs.

His feet, for what it's worth, could well be size ten. But of course that doesn't mean anything.

Interview Tapes 33 and 34
Monday 27 October 2008
Charles and Ronan O'Carroll-Kelly

He unfurls it with a magician's flourish – even saying, 'Ta-da!' – but it takes a few seconds for all the lines to resolve themselves into something. 'Oh,' I say, 'these are the plans for the hotel.'

'Yes, they are!' Charles says. 'Yes, sir! Oh, yes!'

'The Mountjoy,' Ronan says, projecting the words into the air, 'where it's a pleasure to *do* time.'

We're sitting in the lounge of the Shelbourne Hotel, waiting for Hennessy to arrive for their three o'clock meeting at the Office of Public Works.

Whatever else you may say about Charles O'Carroll-Kelly, you have to admire the man's energy. 'So, when did you do all this?' I ask.

Charles: When I was *in* there, of course, languishing away in Joshua Jebb's folly. That's what you do when you're cooped up, you see. You escape. Not literally – although Hennessy did have one or two ideas in that regard, which we ruled out for reasons of safety. No, no, in your mind, you rise above the sheer awfulness of your circumstances. You try to envisage a better place.

That's where it came from, you see – the idea.

I'd be in my cell at night and I'd say to poor Lex, 'Fancy tottering down to the lobby bar for a late one, old scout?' and he'd say, 'Why not? I'll just get my smoking jacket.'

The lobby bar! The idea of it! Oh, that was about the colour of it, you see – the banter.

Then one night it hits me. St Paul on the road to what-have-you. They're building a new prison, aren't they? Another couple of years they're going to be moving the chaps out. The Government are going to be looking for someone to take this place off their hands.

I said, 'Lex, I've just gone and had one of my world-famous ideas. Give me up that roll of toilet paper, will you? And my good Mont Blanc.'

Ronan says, 'I think it's a great idea, Grandda,' and Charles reaches across, musses his backcombed hair and says, 'Thanks, little chap.'

Watching the easy camaraderie between them, I can't help but think about the letter that Charles sent to Ronan's mother while she was still carrying him, warning her to stay away from the O'Carroll-Kelly family. Situations often have a way of righting themselves.

'Give him the pitch,' Ronan says, taking his glasses off for dramatic effect.

Charles looks at me. 'Wouldn't mind running through it one more time,' he says. 'Make sure it's right in my head.'

'Fire away,' I tell him.

Charles: Welcome, friends – old *and* new – to the Mountjoy, Ireland's newest and most luxurious maximum-security, six-star hotel. Situated in one of the city's most venerable quarters, the Mountjoy captures the magical character of – inverted commas – real Dublin. Its unique architectural design, revelling in its former life as a prison, evokes an atmosphere of Victorian ease and relaxed grandeur, with windows opening to reveal streetscapes of charming red-brick terraces.

The North Circular Road has been described as Dublin's very own Notting Hill. While retaining its traditional character, it is also the hub of Ireland's terribly exciting multicultural revolution.

Step through our famous revolving doors and discover the most spacious and luxurious accommodations in Dublin, to say nothing of our comprehensive and advanced conferencing and banqueting facilities.

The rooms, all stunningly appointed, are situated in four wings, which have been retained from the original prison structure. A-Wing contains the Presidential, Premium and Executive Suites, B-Wing features our excellent Deluxe Rooms and C-Wing our high-quality Superior Rooms.

D-Wing offers – quote-unquote – thrill-seekers the opportunity to experience Mountjoy as its previous denizens experienced it. Our two hundred euro-a-night Quality Cells sleep up to five people in a space no bigger than the average family bathroom. The absence of in-cell sanitation means guests can experience, inverted commas, slopping-out – doing their business in a pot or milk carton, then disposing of it when the door is opened the following morning.

Excelling in quality service and the art of hospitality will be the cornerstone of our success. Guests will enjoy fine dining in any of our bars or restaurants, including the Rasherhouse breakfast lounge – built on the site of the former women's prison – and our lobby café, A Hungry Feeling.

The Works, our modern, contemporary restaurant, will offer the finest in cooking and also a number of traditional prison staples, which will be given the gourmet treatment – venison sausages with beans and chips, as well as a special dessert of porridge, with demerara taking the place of broken glass.

Ronan: Ah, nice touch, Grandda.

Charles: Bit of levity often helps.

The Mountjoy is more than just a hotel. It is also Ireland's premier Conference and Leisure destination, offering superb facilities, including the 5,000-capacity Kevin Barry Conference Centre, not to mention the Brendan Behan Luxury Spa.

And if you're in Ireland to golf, the Mountjoy offers a comprehensive helicopter service. Our chopper – the *Seamus Twomey* – will have you on any golf course in the Dublin area within fifteen minutes.

So retreat from the outside world to a place that combines the luxury of contemporary comfort with the old-style warmth of Dublin hospitality.

The Mountjoy . . .

Off you go, Ronan.

Ronan: Come in and visit – our door is always revolving!

'What's that?' I ask. There's a room to the west of the reception area that's the size of two football pitches, but it doesn't have a use ascribed to it.

'That's the casino,' Ronan says. '*Like A Bad Penny.*'

'The casino?' I say. 'We don't have casinos of that size in Ireland, do we?'

Charles shifts uncomfortably in his seat. 'Obviously,' he says, 'it would require a change in the existing legislation. It's just, em, tentative at the moment. Wouldn't really want it publicized. Oh, you'll get the exclusive when it happens – you mark my words.'

'A shut mouth . . .' Ronan translates, his bow tie alleviating the edge of menace that his voice usually carries.

So this is it, Charles and Hennessy's grand plan for the future of the Irish economy. Preying on the gullible and the desperate with the vulgar promise of money for nothing. I suppose it's not unlike the property market in which they made their first fortune.

'We'll, em, tell them it's a ballroom for now,' Charles says. 'No point in upsetting too many applecarts.'

'Some ballroom,' I say. 'Two hundred and twenty metres by one hundred and forty metres. What's that in square metres, Ronan, off the top of your head?'

The question catches him off kilter. 'Er . . .'

'Look at his little brain working there,' Charles says excitedly. 'Oh, he's his father's son all right.'

'Must be, what, twenty thousand, six hundred and fifty-seven?' I suggest. 'Sorry, fifty-eight.'

'Bang on,' Ronan says. 'That's exactly what *I* was going to say, if you'd given me a chance.'

Hennessy arrives and signals to Charles without coming over. 'Must be double-parked,' Charles says. 'Wish us luck,' which we do, then he leaves Ronan and me sitting alone.

'Better be off meself,' he says, my stare clearly discomfiting him. 'Meeting Bla from school . . .'

'That still going strong, is it?'

'Er, yeah,' he says, standing up. 'Two year now.'

'I mean, she hasn't been, you know, frightened off by the vast intellec-
tual chasm between you?'

He sits down again, a degree of resignation about him.

'So how did you fake the IQ test?'

'Ways and means,' he says.

'All that stuff about the subprime mortgage crisis . . .'

'Wikipedia,' we both say at the same time.

'So what *have* you got – like, a photographic memory?' He nods. 'So
you can memorize huge amounts of information, then regurgitate it
without any appreciation or understanding?'

'Exactly.'

'You'll probably get maximum points in your Leaving Cert. so,' I tell
him. He laughs. 'But, what, you hate school?'

'I don't fit in,' he says, 'all them fooken rich kids. They already know
what they want to be, most of them.'

'I'm sure Ross'll love you no matter what you are,' I tell him. 'Even if
it's just, I don't know, a *criminal* genius.'

He nods like he understands. Then he points at me, then at his mouth
and says, 'Keep *that* fooken *dúnta.*'

Interview Tape 35
Friday 31 October 2008
Gary Gest

'Name?'

I tell her my name.

'From?'

My least favourite question in the world. I hesitate.

'What company?' she says like a woman fast running out of patience.

'No company,' I tell her. 'I'm just . . . *me*.'

For a moment, I think she's going to ask me to leave. Then she remembers. 'You're the one who's been ringing,' she says. 'I'm sorry, he's been literally tied up all day . . .'

She asks me to sit. The soft leather of the sofa yields under my weight. My eyes follow the pictures wainscoting the benign cream walls – images of whales and elephants and cheetahs with captions underneath about grace and beauty and other such folderol.

Literally tied up. I somehow doubt it.

Gary Gest is not at all what I expected. He had become some terrible monster in my imagination. But in reality he's short and thickset with an open face and thinning sandy hair. 'I can't give you long,' he says.

'Busy?' I ask

'Opposite,' he says. 'I'm being let go.'

I respond, I think, in a neutral way.

'Ah, it was coming. Conveyancing, you know . . .'

'Nothing left *to* conveyance?' I say.

'Twelve of us in the department, all called in last week, told there's only three jobs after Christmas. We had to re-interview for them . . . and apparently I *don't* have the X Factor.'

'What are you going to do?'

'*Retrain*,' he says, his heart clearly not in the answer. 'I mean, that was the mantra, wasn't it, back in the bad old days?'

We go through the polite expedients of what passes for conversation these days, making full use of all the clichés.

'Yeah, but it was never middle-class professionals hearing it, was it? It was people with trades. People with *jobs* . . .'

'And there's no America to run to now. No England . . .'

'So,' he says eventually, 'what's this about?'

What *is* it about? I don't know why I'm here. I don't have any questions to ask him and I don't expect he has anything to say that's insightful, or even useful.

In my mind I try to formulate something clever-sounding.

We all bear the weals of adolescence on our backs. I'm trying to find out the extent to which your treatment of Ross shaped his personality . . .

But that would be a lie. I'm just here to see the monster.

'Well, like I said to you on the phone, I'm writing this sort of biography about Ross O'Carroll-Kelly and, well, apparently you bullied him. Pretty badly.'

He nods thoughtfully.

Gary: One of the things you have to do when you accept the Lord into your life is to take responsibility for all the hurt and pain you've caused by not following His way. I hurt him – no question. Him and lots of others . . .

'There was a story of an incident in a toilet . . .'

Gary: Yeah, that happened. Probably a lot worse as well. We were out of control. *I* was out of control.

'From the description I heard, there seemed to be, I don't know, almost a pornographic dimension to the violence.'

Gary: Look, I'm not trying to, you know, hang the blame on anyone else here, but what did the school expect? Fehily created us. Alpha males going out to battle, beta males and females on the sidelines urging us on.

We were kids. They were the adults – Fehily and Sooty and the rest of them. They're drilling it into you that you're the greatest thing that ever walked the Earth, you start to believe it. So you beat up one or two first years and nothing happens. I mean, teachers literally stood and watched.

And if you can, I'd like you to mention Tom McGahy, because he was the only one with the decency and the integrity to stand up and say that what's happening here is wrong.

'Whatever about beating up one or two first years,' I say, 'what happened in the toilet that day – the way it was described to me . . . I mean, *you* studied law – that's aggravated assault.'

Gary: *And* I was eighteen. Old enough to be charged. If I didn't play rugby, they'd have called the police. But will I give you a laugh? That wasn't even the reason I was kicked out of the school.

'It wasn't?'

Gary: The real reason I was kicked out was because my name appeared in the sailing column in the *Irish Independent*, two days before we were supposed to play St Michael's in the S. You know Fehily had this thing about *other* sports?

'He didn't approve.'

Gary: Well, at the time, I was pretty serious about my sailing. So anyway, I got this mention. Said I was one for the future, tipped to make the Olympics one day in Laser class. I mean, Fehily was just looking for an excuse.

'You certainly gave him one,' I say, 'what you did.'

Gary: Like I said, I deserved it. And more. My parents came up to the school, offered Fehily a blank cheque to take me back, but he wouldn't budge.

And this is kind of funny, I can laugh at it now, but when we

were leaving the office, he started singing, 'Row, row, row your
boat'.

In German.

I ask him about the fable of Ross and Christian standing toe-to-toe with
him and his friends and earning their respect. He shakes his head ...

Gary: I read that in one of his books and I thought ... You know,
I even *said* it to him. 'Where did you get that from?'

'You *said* it to him?'

He immediately gauges the depth of my surprise.

Gary: He didn't tell you about this? I presumed you knew the
story. Well, I went to see him a couple of years ago. The church I'm
involved with now, they do this thing like ... you know the ninth
step from AA? Make direct amends.

Well, that took up the guts of a year, I can tell you.

No, I met Ross for a coffee. I apologized to him. And he apologized to me, even though I told him there was no real need.

'Ross apologized to *you*? Sorry, I'm clearly missing part of the story here.'

Gary: Clearly. Ross never told you what he did to me?

'To be honest, we didn't talk about you at all.'

Gary: Okay. It would have been February or March 1998 – actu-
ally it *was* March because it was a couple of days before the Senior
Cup final – I was in Dun Laoghaire. It was a Saturday. Just at the
East Pier there, getting ready to go out.

I had this dinghy, brand new, which I'd had shipped all the way from
Australia. Top of the range. Cost a fortune. But the Irish Sports Coun-
cil was starting to come on stream and I got money from them. Then
I would have had two or three sponsors as well who supported me.

I would have been, I suppose, an outside bet for Sydney.

I'm about ten feet from the pier and I'm untying the ropes and doing whatever little bits I had to do. The next thing, I look up and I see these three guys. The one I recognized immediately was Oisinn Wallace, who I knew to see, mostly through his old man, who was in the George as well. Oisinn used to collect him, have the odd drink in the bar.

I didn't recognize Ross at first – I mean, he'd bulked up, seriously bulked up, since I'd seen him last. I don't know what he was bench-pressing, but it must have been . . .

The other guy was . . .

'Christian?' I ask.

Gary: Christian Forde – that was it.

I didn't see where Ross pulled the bottle from, but I presume it came from inside his jacket. It's, like, a vinegar bottle, the ones you get in the chipper. Without a word of warning – without a word of anything – he sends this jet of whatever's in the bottle ten feet into the air and onto the dinghy.

It's petrol. I immediately know it's petrol.

He emptied the bottle. Poured the last of it onto the ground next to his feet. Didn't take his eyes off me once. His eyes, let me tell you, were crazy.

I'm standing in the boat, remember. I said, 'What the fock are you doing?'

Actually, I didn't say anything. Didn't get the chance.

He whips out a Zippo, flicks the little wheel, then just drops it on the ground. The fire went like that – *fffttt* – straight across the water and to the boat.

I don't even remember thinking about it – I just jumped head-first, overboard.

I thought it was instinct. Now I realize it was Him.

The boat went up like you wouldn't believe.

I'm in the water, thrashing it to a foam, trying to get away from the flames. Reached some rocks, turned around and . . . you know, just watched her burn.

Ross was laughing like a maniac. The other two, I don't think they could believe he did it.

End of the Olympics for me.

'You said his eyes were . . .'

Gary: Crazy.

'Did you get the impression that he might have been *on* something?'

Gary: You mean drugs? I would say definitely.

I thank him for his time, but especially his candour. He tells me to give Ross his best if I see him.

I think about Gary Gest for the rest of the evening, finally feeling like a current is taking me towards the story's end.

Interview Tape 36
Monday 3 November 2008
Ross O'Carroll-Kelly

There are a lot of people in trouble. Circling the drain. Those circles ever tightening. Last night, the drain claimed someone we all knew, someone Ross dearly loved.

The credit crunch, the property slump, the world financial crisis. Oisinn was beset from all sides by the perfect storm of disasters. Everyone has a snapping point.

At half-seven last night, he drove his silver Mercedes C Class into the short-term car park in Dublin Airport. He left the keys to both the car and his Shrewsbury Road home, as well as his mobile phone, credit cards and various loan agreements, on the front passenger seat. Then he boarded a plane. To where, the Gardaí haven't said, but I expect somewhere he won't be found. Somewhere he can blend into the beige of everyday life and not be reminded of his failure. I can't help but think about Fionnuala in Paris.

We're sitting in the Merrion Inn, Ross nearly on the point of tears. 'He took his Senior Cup medal with him,' he says, looking for some measure of comfort. 'I suppose that's something.'

It seems I don't know the half of it. 'What I don't get is, you know, Oisinn's a big name in the world of international fragrances. Wouldn't a new perfume have, like, turned his fortunes around?'

Ross: *Eau d'Affluence* was, like, five years ago. The holy water was, what, three? What's he done since? He hasn't worked. His head's gone. The thing with Oisinn is, it's not *just* the whole current economic tiger thing. He's got, like, addictions . . .

'Addictions?'

Ross: Mostly gambling. Not actual *bookies* gambling? We're talking poker. We're talking internet poker.

He's been at it for, like, a couple of years? But it's like he said himself, no one ever has a gambling problem when they're good at it. I mean, he *was* good at it. He was even talking at one stage of going professional.

When we were all in Vegas for Christian's casino opening, he stung some dude from – I don't know – China or one of them, for, like, two hundred Ks. This was on the actual tables.

Comes home. Thinks he's . . . I don't know *who* he thought he was.

The thing about doing that shit online is, you never know who's at the table with you. Could be a couple of dudes in some internet café in whatever country, double-teaming you. It could be, like, four o'clock in the afternoon for them and four o'clock in the morning for you.

I think four o'clock in the morning is when we're all at our stupidest.

And you do stupid things anyway when you're, you know . . .

He stops and looks at me like I should know. But I don't. 'When you're what?'

He makes a loud snorting noise.

'*That?*' I say, though I shouldn't be surprised. In the world of high fashion, it's as common as coleslaw.

Ross: See, the thing about that shit is, they say it makes you feel, I don't know, invincible. And that's a bad feeling to have when you've got two pairs and the other dude has a royal flush and your credit card limit is – whatever Oisinn's *was*.

'How much does he reckon he's lost?'

Ross: In two years, three big ones – as in mills.

'Jesus!'

Ross: But, like, it's not just what he lost online? Like I said, the dude hasn't done any actual work. He became pretty much, I don't know if it's a word, but nocturnal?

He just let everything slide. Then the whole property thing and the shares . . .

It's weird, I honestly didn't think this whole economic thing was going to affect *me*.

It's not yet November, but there's a Christmas ad on the television. 'A nightingale sang in Berkeley Square,' he says, shaking his head. 'The focking nerve of these people.'

I tell him there's something serious I need to ask him and he arranges his face into a look of concern. 'Look,' I say, 'I know you probably want to forget about the book for one day, but, you know, we were talking about drugs there and I wanted to ask you about them.'

He plays dumb. 'Drugs?' he says.

I ask if I can read him another extract from Father Fehily's journal.

'It is *mein* intention, I wish to state now, for all of humanity and for all the ages, to create a new breed of fighter – a supersoldier, who will push back the bounds of what we understand to be man's capacity to endure.

'These soldiers will be strong, virile, alert. They will not know the meaning of surrender and they shall fight as if death and glory are the only possibilities.

'The materials to create this army of supermen are simple. I shall give them chemicals . . . and Wagner.'

'Okay, forget the Wagner,' I say, 'bad and all as it probably was for you – what are these chemicals he's talking about?'

He sticks out his bottom lip and shakes his head slowly from side to side. 'The only thing I can think of,' he says, 'is, like, creatine.'

'It *wasn't* creatine,' I snap. '*Everyone* was on creatine at the time. You told me yourself, you were on it from, what, the start of second year? This is, like, sixth year . . .'

'Yeah,' he says, 'weird, isn't it?'

His hand goes to his chest. He fidgets with his medal.

'Ross,' I tell him, 'I *will* find out.'

'Okay,' he finally blurts out. 'Focking Columbo. Just don't make it sound bad, all right?'

Ross: Okay, we *were* actually taking creatine – two spoonfuls in your tea, five times a day, or whatever it was. I don't know how that shit works . . .

Whatever. I mean, we *all* bulked up. Especially me. I was, like, huge. Leaving Cert. year . . .

'We're talking about the first time you sat the Leaving?'

Ross: Yeah – don't focking rub it in. Start of that year, Fehily calls me into his study one day. I mean, yeah, he's got the classical music on and whatever.

At the time, you've got to remember, everybody was looking for an edge. It was all, did you hear that Blackrock are running half-marathons in training? Did you hear Terenure are running up the Sugar Loaf with breeze blocks tied to their waists?

That kind of shit.

Bear in mind, I'd have done anything for Fehily. Loyalty, blah, blah, blah. I mean, he's the guy who taught me how to read. Kept teachers off my case. He was more like a father to me than my actual father, who, as you know, is a dickhead. Plus, he made me feel like I was this basically amazing rugby player.

So anyway, he produces this little bottle. And, well, I'd have to say a syringe . . .

'A syringe?'

Ross: Yeah, he was all, 'We must be stronger than our enemies. We must enjoy the edge – physically, psychologically, chemically . . .'

I was like, 'What *is* this shit?'

He was like, 'It's insulin.'

I was like, 'Yeah – cool.'

See, I didn't *give* a shit? I wanted to win – end of.

I read an article recently about insulin use among professional cyclists. It said it force-feeds glucose into the muscles and, when used in conjunction with creatine, approximates the effects of anabolic agents like testosterone and growth hormone.

Ross: I mean, it was, like, insulin – it wasn't banned or anything, was it?

'Not if you can find a doctor who's prepared to say you're a diabetic.'

Ross: The old man knows plenty of doctors.

'I doubt it matters now anyway. What about the others – did they take it?'

Ross: No, Oisinn would have been pretty much where he wanted to be in terms of size. Christian was scared of needles. Fionn was too much of a wuss. I think JP would have had one or two concerns about, like, safety and shit? He asked Fehily was it safe and Fehily was like, 'Perfectly so, my child.' Then he asked us to sign a waiver, so JP was like, 'Er, maybe not then.'

'The drugs, how did it make you feel?'

Ross: Honestly? Like an actual animal.

I ask if he wants another pint. Unusually, he doesn't. He pulls on his sailing jacket and says, 'I need to start looking for Oisinn.'

He could be anywhere in the world by now. But that doesn't faze him. Erika was right. Hearts don't come much bigger than Ross's. And rugby, for all that Tom McGahy might say about it, has formed bonds between him and his friends that are stronger than tempered steel.

'I just wanted to let you know,' I say, 'I'm going to need to talk to Tina.'

I don't know why I feel the need to tell him. He looks suddenly worried. 'Tina? Er, *why?*'

'Because she's, like, Ronan's mother? *And* she was the first girl you ever . . .'

'She was far from the first, let me tell you that.'

'Really?'

'*Far* from the first . . . No, she wouldn't have much good to say about me – definitely skip that one. But hey, did you find out when the Loreto on the Green reunion's on?'

'I don't need to go to any more reunions.'

'I wouldn't be sure about that. I did a serious amount of damage in that place. In other words, emotional.'

'I think I've enough of those stories.'

'Oh, *do* you? That happens to be one of the schools that got an actual High Court injunction to stop me going to their debs. It's, like, respect to the Rossmeister.'

I tell him I'll consider including the story and we high-five our good-byes. I'm close now, I sense, two or maybe three conversations away from some real answers.

Interview Tapes 37 and 38
Tuesday 4 November 2008
Anthony and Tina Masters

Antonio's, on Lower Ormond Quay, is an identikit Italian restaurant – all wooden floors, red-and-white cheesecloth and wildly gesticulating waiting staff, high on espresso. Today's specials are *calamari con mandorla e menta, linguine di cozze e vongole* and *vitello con fagioli*, but I tell the *maître d'* that I'm here to see the owner, Antonio himself.

Or Anto as he's known to his friends.

He's nothing like the caricature Northsider that Ross has drawn for me. He's not angry and threatening. He doesn't even have the pronounced Dublin accent that Ross slips into whenever he's mocking him.

He seems a happy soul, if charged with nervous energy, with a voice that's impossibly husky for one so young and the faintest smile permanently on his lips, like he finds everything in the world just a little bit ridiculous.

He indicates a table by the window and tells me he'll be with me in a minute.

In the ambiguous world of O'Carroll-Kelly family relationships, Anto is Ross's brother-in-law of sorts. More certainly, he's a brother of Tina, uncle of Ronan and once, a long, long time ago, the sixteen-year-old who swapped homes with Ross for two weeks as part of a cultural exchange programme.

It's no secret that he's been to prison, serving eighteen months of a three-year sentence for ram-raiding a Finglas off-licence, an event that always seemed to be more of a juvenile prank than a serious crime warranting jail time.

Happily, it didn't determine the course of his life. His restaurant is one of the most talked-about in the city. The *Dubliner* praised its 'modest excellence' and Paolo Tullio described it as 'a hidden treasure'.

There's even talk of a Michelin star.

I'm here, not for the food, but to hear about the two weeks that Anto spent in Foxrock in the spring of 1996. And, once Tina arrives, the story of how Charles and Fionnuala threatened her, then eventually bribed her, to keep Ronan a secret from Ross.

Today is going to be a day of surprises. The first is lunch. Anto returns from the kitchen with a dish he describes as pork slices, marinated in thyme and caper paste, with red wine, shallot and mustard risotto. The smell fills my nostrils. A memory hits me, like sunlight flashing off glass.

'I've *had* this,' I tell him. 'Is this . . . *maiale con timo e risotto?*'

'Yeah,' he says, pulling up a chair opposite me.

'One of Fionnuala's recipes?'

'Yeah, she's an investor,' he says, like I should have known. 'She owns half, I own half . . .'

All Ross ever told me about the so-called Urban Plunge is that Anto went through Foxrock like a crimewave and that meanwhile, on the other side of the city, he exacted some measure of revenge by bedding his sister, Tina.

Anto and Fionnuala in partnership offends that particular narrative.

'We were going to do it years ago,' he says. 'But then, I had me troubles, which you've probably heard about . . .'

'But you and Fionnuala,' I say, still trying to get a handle on the story. 'How does that work? Or even just, you and Fionnuala – *how?*'

He laughs. 'Ah, Fionnuala's great,' he says. 'We'd never a bother. She used to write to me when I was inside. Be recipes mostly . . .'

'So, what, you bonded over food? You know what, I'm going to switch this tape recorder on. Tell me the story – day you arrived in Foxrock . . .'

Anto: Well, I don't think either of them knew what to make of me – Fionnuala *or* Charles.

Got off the bus at the church. Had to walk up to the gaff from the dualler – no buses. Found the gaff – massive gaff. Ring the bell – bing, bong! – even the bell was posh.

So *she* comes to the door. Fionnuala. Bit up herself, *I* thought.

Very funny. I always say this to her and she laughs. First thing she says to me: 'We have everything, thank you. Don't call again.'

Thought I was going door-to-door, selling shit. I says, 'It's me, Anthony. From the school.'

Me ma said to use Anthony – fit in better.

She's looking at me and I can see she's not one bit impressed. Because she's, like, a lady, isn't she?

I says, 'Are you not gonna ask me in?'

Sort of shamed her into it, like. 'Wait in the vestibule,' she says. 'I'll have to phone the school.'

She thought it was a mistake. So I give her the paperwork. 'It's all there,' I says. 'That's your address, isn't it?'

Anyway, cut a long story short, in I go. I'm standing in the kitchen – kitchen's bigger than our entire gaff – and she's looking out the window, at the shed. I swear to God, she was thinking about putting me in there.

In *he* comes then – Charles. Ah, a nice oul character. I looked after him in prison – he'll tell you that.

He shouts at me, like you would to a foreigner. 'How . . . are . . . you . . . settling . . . in?' Spelling out every word.

Then – mad shit – Fionnuala says, 'Do you want to go and freshen up before supper?'

Freshen up before supper? This is another world. But I'm thinking, all right, might as well play along here. I go up to me room, splash a bit of water on me face, then back downstairs. 'Oh,' she says, 'you're not going to *dress*?'

They had different clothes for sitting eating in.

So she's there, tossing this salad and I says to her, 'Ah, walnut and Rocquefort – I love that.'

Next thing, she stops what she's doing. She says, 'How on Earth do *you* know about Rocquefort?'

See, I was mad into cooking, even then. All I ever wanted to be was a chef.

So I starts giving her tips. 'Try it with sesame oil rather than the olive. Brings out the flavour of everything.'

'A pinch of cayenne pepper in the chowder – not telling you a word of a lie, Fionnuala.'

And that was it – we just hit it off.

She says, '*What* did you say your name was again?'

So the Jack B. Yeats original sketch – *Two Hares*. The Boehm porcelain swans that Fionnuala got as a gift for her work on behalf of the Move Funderland to the Northside pressure group. The trophy that Charles won with Des Smith and Ronan Collins in a charity pro-am in Portmarnock. All the things that Ross claimed were stolen from the house – I'm wondering now, did he simply make it up?

Anto: Charlie'd try and talk to me about the rugby, which I knew feck-all about. 'Well, young Anto – do you *still* think Murray Kidd's the man to lead us to rugby's, inverted commas, Promised Land?'

She used to bring me out, show me off to her friends. We were forever in that place she likes . . .

'The Gables?'

Anto: That's it. What were her friends called? Angela and Delma – that was it. They used to get the Eggs Benedict in there and Fionnuala reckoned it was the best Eggs Benedict anywhere in town. And it *was*, it was unbelievable. So, this is a test for me – she says to me one morning, asks me what I'd do to improve it. I says, 'You couldn't improve on that, Fionnuala – except maybe thrun a few chives into the sauce, chopped.'

You'd want to see her face. Bursting with pride. Only way to describe it is, it was like I was her son.

That's exactly what I was thinking.

'The idea,' I say, 'of the restaurant, it came from . . .'

Anto: Well, what happened was, one day she took me to Donnybrook – there was a Sancerre she liked, you could only get it in Terroirs – and she spots this, you know, vacant unit, one or two doors down from where Donnybrook Fair is now. What she wanted to do was open a little café and get me to help her run it.

I was sixteen and I'd a pain in me hole with school.

The kind of café it was, as she says herself, it wasn't *copying* Avoca Handweavers – although she always said she *was* a huge admirer of what they were trying to do – but improving it.

Sweet *and* savoury roulades, for instance. Her *pescado frio con guacamole*, which I loved. And couscous. One thing she used to always say to me: 'There's no shame in couscous.'

Tina arrives just as I finish eating. She, too, bears no resemblance to Ross's colourful description. No ski pants. No perm. No machine-gun laugh.

She's attractive rather than pretty in the conventional sense – short and busty and bristling with personality. The mystery as to where Ronan got his brains and sense of humour is cleared up immediately.

I ask her if she remembers her first impression of Ross.

Tina: Well, I was away on holidays when he arrived, so he'd already been in the house about a week. But they had him terrified, they did. Me da had this greyhound, y'see . . .

Anto: Ah, Roy.

Tina: We all remember Roy. Never stopped barking, morning, noon and night. Da told Ross he had him trained to hate South-siders and the reason he was barking was he wanted to get in the house to savage him.

Ross says, 'Is he, like, tied up and shit?' and of course they all thought this was the funniest thing in the world. They were all copying him then. 'Is he, loik, toyed up and shit?'

Anto: Me da and me ma used to take it in turns to get him to say things: 'Say, park the car,' and he'd say, 'Pork the cor.'

Tina: Very, very funny.

'Ross said you were on holidays in, where, Santa Ponsa?'

Tina: That's what he said. He's always made me sound like a knacker in them books.

'You weren't in Santa Ponsa?'

Tina: I've never been to Santa Ponsa in me life. I was in Santorini.

Anyway, I came home, walked in and here's this fella – never saw him before – with his feet up on the kitchen table, watching the little portable.

I'd no change left for the taxi – all I had was a twenty – so I asked me ma and she'd nothing. So I asked my dad and he'd nothing. So this fella – Ross – I ask *him*. He gives me a tenner and says, 'Get me a receipt – I'll claim it back from the school.'

I says to me ma, 'Where did we get him?'

Me ma says, it's one of these exchange programmes, *like* the Spanish students, except in Ireland. Our kids go over to the Southside and their kids comes over here.

'Did you fancy him?' I ask. She smiles.

Tina: Ah, yeah. I mean, he was lovely lookin'. Even *with* the nose. He was a couple of years younger than me, but ... yeah, I did fancy him.

'Ah, come here,' Anto says, standing up from the table. 'I can't listen to this. Tina, do you want something to eat?'

'No, just a coffee,' she says.

He points at me. I tell him I'll have a coffee, too. He takes away my plate.

'I've been re-reading *his* account of the, er, famous night,' I tell her.

Tina: Which was a pack of lies.

'A pack of lies?'

Tina: A *pack* of lies.

'He said *you* came on to *him*. You went into his room when he was in bed and started showing him your tan lines . . .'

Tina: That was all rubbish. I said it to him: 'Ross, that's all made up.'

He came to *my* room. Said he was sorry if his eyes were out on stalks when I walked in. He says, 'I've never been more attracted to a woman in my actual life.'

Ah, he was full of it. It was funny, though.

So we started kissing – he *was* a good kisser – and he's giving me all his lines. He really fancied himself.

The thing is, he'd never done it before.

He was only sixteen. There was no reason why he should have, but I still laugh.

Tina: Still a virgin – but full of talk, you know. 'I'm going to do this to you. I'm going to do that to you.' But when it came down to it, I had to talk him through it.

'So fast-forward then – what, you missed your next period and then . . .'

Tina: I missed my next period. Rang his house the minute I knew. I did two tests, then went to the doctor and he said, yeah, I was four months gone.

Ross's account, I tell her, is that Fionnuala said, 'Why would a girl of your type be phoning our son?' and when Tina told her the news, she slammed the phone down on her.

Tina: No.

'No?'

Tina: They were honestly fine with it, his ma *and* da. A bit shocked, yeah, but there was none of that. I mean, I read what Ross wrote – what Charles is supposed to have said . . .

I read it out for her. 'We know what you're like – you and your ilk. No education, no prospects – that's why your lot are *having* these babies. So you'll get all sorts. House. Whatever social welfare payments are going. I'm sure you already know your entitlements – know them *verbatim*.'

Tina: That never happened. Matter of fact, I'll tell you what Fionnuala said to me. She said it was typical of the Kellys – can't keep their bloody seed to themselves.

I guess it would require sanctimony on an enormous scale for Charles to pontificate to anyone about babies born out of wedlock.

Anto arrives back with two coffees.

'So what about *this*?' I say, searching through my folder, looking for my photocopy of the letter that Hennessy sent to Tina. I read it out.

Dear Ms Masters,
Re: Paternity of your unborn child

I act on behalf of Mr Charles O'Carroll-Kelly in the above matter. I respond to your correspondence with my client and your unsubstantiated claim that his son, Mr Ross O'Carroll-Kelly, is the father of your unborn child.

I enclose a cheque in the amount of £50,000 (fifty thousand pounds). This once-off payment is made purely in recognition of your difficult circumstances and does not represent an admission of liability on the part of my client's son.

It is made subject to the following conditions:

• No consent is given to register Mr Ross O'Carroll-Kelly as the father of the child;

• Neither you nor any member of your family will attempt to contact Mr Ross O'Carroll-Kelly now or at any time in the future;

- Mr Ross O'Carroll-Kelly will remain without knowledge of this settlement;
- No proceedings seeking a Declartion of Parenthood will be taken at any time.

This is in full and final settlement of all discussions to date. We do not expect to receive any correspondence from you in the future.

Yours sincerely,

Hennessy Coghlan-O'Hara

'Is this letter not genuine, then?' I ask.

Tina: It is genuine. Like, I *got* it. But it was his solicitor who wrote it. Charles didn't know anything about it.

Anto: Charles actually rang you, didn't he, Tee?

Tina: He did. Before it even arrived. He said there was a letter in the post and to ignore it. He hadn't approved it.

'Are you saying the whole thing was handled amicably?'

Tina: Yeah, Charles and Fionnuala couldn't have been better. They agreed to pay a certain amount every month – I won't tell you how much it was, but it was a lot more than I would have ever asked for. They said they'd pay for Ronan's education, wherever we wanted to send him.

'But they didn't want Ross to know . . .'

Tina: Not until he was older, no. Which I thought was a bit unfair. But he *was* only sixteen. I think they thought he might go off the rails.

Anto: But Charles and Fionnuala couldn't have done enough for her. Birthdays, Christmases, holidays – money always arrived, didn't it, Tee?

Tina: Always.

Interview Tape 39
Wednesday 5 November 2008
Sorcha O'Carroll-Kelly

Barack Obama is the new American president-elect. Sorcha looks tired – she was up until after four watching the results come in. I wouldn't have called so early had I known, but she says it's fine. 'I just can't believe we did it,' she says. 'I'm actually thinking about sitting down and watching the entire *West Wing* again, from, like, episode one.'

She asks me if I want coffee and I tell her no – I just have one quick question and I'm sorry it's so personal. She sits down, looking faintly worried. 'Okay,' she says, dragging out the word.

'The kick that Ross missed in the 1998 Schools Cup final,' I say. 'I've watched it, like, a hundred times on YouTube. I've read all the comments on it. I've heard Ross's account. And, to be honest, I'm dubious. He *said* his head was – I think he used the word melted – because you told him you thought you were pregnant . . .'

She unconsciously balls her fists.

Sorcha: Can I just say, I've read where he's, like, said that in the past and it's not *actually* true? I mean, do you even want to know the background to this?

'Of course.'

Sorcha: Well, even though we'd actually broken up, we were with each other at the Arts Ball – as in *with* with? Of course, as usual, he does a total Chandler on me afterwards – he's like, 'Commitment? Aggghhh!' – won't return my calls, totally blanks me at the next match. It was like, *Oh!* My God!

So I went to see him, just to, like, finish it once and for all? And he ended up being *such* an arsehole to me that I just went, 'I *hope* I get my next period.'

Which is something all girls say.

'Well, exactly. I mean, Ross must have heard it dozens of times over the years.'

Sorcha: Does that, like, answer your question?

I think it answers quite a number. I tell her I'll see her tomorrow, then I drive the short distance to Donnybrook, where a friend who works in the RTÉ archive has promised to let me look through some old tapes. Twenty hours later, I still haven't found what I'm searching for. But I step out into a rimy November dawn, seeing at last what I think is the full, unexpurgated picture.

Interview Tapes 40, 41 and 42
Saturday 8 November 2008
Ross, Fionnuala and Charles O'Carroll-Kelly

So here we are, back where the journey began, in the lounge of the West-bury Hotel. Fionnuala suggested it and I agreed, partly because of the neat way it rounds off the story, but mostly because I need a drink.

Penguin thought it would be a good idea to commission a family por-trait for the centre pages of this book. The photographer confided in me darkly that it was the worst assignment he'd ever undertaken in a career that bore witness to the conflicts in Northern Ireland and Bosnia and the Hostel Wars in South Africa. A job that should have been finished inside an hour took four times that long, with the subjects, rather than the artist, insisting on reshoot after reshoot. Fionnuala felt the light was doing no justice whatsoever to her blepharoplasty. Charles felt he didn't look states-manlike enough. Ross was sure his pecs were more defined. Sorcha was sure the photographer was actually *trying* to make her look fat? And Ronan, for some reason, kept removing his glasses and his bow tie and had to be persuaded to put them back on.

By the time the fill lights were switched off and the shoot declared over, I even noticed a little tension tugging at Erika's smiling features.

We walked the short distance to the hotel. Grafton Street was deathly quiet for a Saturday in November. Sorcha said it's not that people are scared to spend money, it's that they're scared to be *seen* spending money. Conspicuous consumption is out. Hairshirt asceticism is in.

'Apparently Hermès – the one on Madison Avenue? – they've started offering customers the option of a plain white bag,' she said, 'instead of, like, a monogrammed one? Which is, like, *such* a good idea. Erika, we *so* should do that.'

Erika agreed, then said she was returning to the shop for an hour. Charles said he'd see her later. He and Helen were taking her to Bentleys. Something was clearly on her mind.

The rest of us trooped up the carpeted stairs. There was no shortage of tables, but Fionnuala insisted on telling the waitress that she was a writer and that she was always here. She and Charles agreed to share a bottle of Sancerre, Ross ordered a pint of Heineken. Ronan asked for a sidecar, which his father translated as a Coke, and Sorcha dispatched the waitress to the kitchen to find out how many food miles were in their orange juice.

I suspected quite a few – not known for its citrus fruits is Dublin 2.

'So,' Charles says then, an air of finality in his voice, 'you've seen us now, up close, warts and all. What do you think?'

It's a good question. What *do* I think? My conversations with Ross, his parents and the people who've known them have added colour and shade to the bare lineaments of the account of his life that Ross told me. But maybe I still should talk in terms of what I *think* I know.

So what do I think I know?

It goes like this. Once upon a time, there was a little boy called Charles and a little girl called Fionnuala. When they were still infants, they both lost their mothers – Charles to TB, Fionnuala to some form of mental illness that may or may not have been stamped on her own DNA.

They both grew up slaves, to varying extents, to the overweening ambitions of their fathers. When they were teenagers, they both fell in love. Then in their twenties, they lost it. Cut adrift, Fionnuala went to Paris, experiencing some form of breakdown, and dreamt up a fictional life for herself because she wanted to suffer whatever mental anguishes she suffered quietly and with dignity. Charles, meanwhile, threw himself into business, in an effort to prove himself to his father, which I suspect he's still trying to do, albeit posthumously.

Chance threw the couple together one day in Sandycove Tennis Club. They were both long past the age at which social convention said they should be married. They considered all they had in common and decided it was a sound basis for a life match.

Fionnuala wanted to live in a big house. She took over Alma Goad's ailing business and made a success of it. Charles fell under the spell of a rogue solicitor called Hennessy Coghlan-O'Hara, who used him to front a highly successful get-rich-quick scheme. *And* who may or may not be a murderer – I can't decide.

Charles also fathered a daughter, which hurt Fionnuala's pride, though she understood that her husband would always love Helen Joseph, just as she would always love Conor Hession. So they put a sticking plaster on the wound. They might not love each other, but they liked each other a hell of a lot more than most couples they knew.

In time, Fionnuala settled into the genteel life she imagined having with Conor, a world circumscribed by the common round of South Dublin, middle-class life – long lunches, campaigns for the sake of campaigns and acts of charity born of a mix of kindness and a need to feel satisfied with herself.

And in the middle of all this is Ross, who hates his parents – or at least talks about hating his parents – with a passion that most boys grow out of in their teens. Yet of all the things in life he could have excelled at, he chose rugby, allowing his father to live out his own vicarious fantasies. And of all the pretty girls he used and abused over the years, he married the one who most reminded him of his mother.

I've never heard any of the awful put-downs he claims to use almost as a matter of course to his parents, but there's no doubt he harbours a deep resentment towards them. But why? Because they were too busy to see that he was being bullied? Too involved with their own lives to notice he couldn't read?

A little, perhaps. But I think it's something other than that.

'What do I *think*?' I say. 'I think . . . you're no more complicated than any other family.'

The air is taut with something. From the corner of my eye, I can see Fionnuala staring hard at me. 'You didn't tell me you were going to speak to that woman,' she says evenly.

She means Audrey.

'I spoke to Angela as well,' I say. 'And Delma. For balance, like.'

She'll already know that. She'll have interrogated her friends mercilessly to discover everything that was said. I get it. She's a writer. And writers hate not being in control of a story.

'I told him to,' Ross says, quite unexpectedly. 'I told him she knows you better than anyone.'

Fionnuala doesn't look at him. I suspect she has much to say, and it's like sepsis ready to burst through the surface.

Over the course of the next few minutes, the supporting cast oblig-
ingly falls away. Sorcha heads for Circa to check on Erika, taking Honor
with her. Ronan goes to meet Blathin, but tells Ross there's something he
needs to talk to him about later. He says he'll bell him.

Oblivious to the gathering storm, Charles says, 'I wanted to, em, have a
word with you two alone. *Before* I make the big announcement. Last night,
in a certain restaurant not a million miles from here, I asked Helen how
she'd feel about marrying an old fool like me. And would you believe it, she
said yes.'

'That's wonderful,' Fionnuala says, and then more enthusiastically,
'That's wonderful,' like an engine sputtering to life. She gets out of her
chair and grabs Charles, still seated, in an awkward embrace. 'Charles, I'm
so happy – for both of you,' she says, appearing to mean every word. I
think I notice a tear escape her eye.

Ross doesn't stir. 'Married?' he says. 'What are you, twenty-two?'

Fionnuala shoots him a look.

'And Ross,' Charles says, 'I have a very special request to ask of you.
Helen and I would consider it a signal honour if you would agree to be
my, quote-unquote, best man.'

'You can shove your wedding up your actual hole,' Ross says. 'I won't
even *be* there. You can be guaranteed of that.'

Charles raises a hand. 'Save the banter for the big day,' he says, then
turns to me. 'You can imagine the speech, can't you? That's something
you'll want to record, no doubt.'

'Are you focking deaf? I said I wasn't going to be there. Listen to yourself, will you? You're actually pathetic.'

'Stop it!' Fionnuala suddenly shouts, causing every set of eyes to
rivet in our direction. 'Just . . . *stop* it. Charles, I don't know how you
do it. I don't know how you keep up that jolly front while *he* talks to
you like that. Talks to *us* like that. Well, I can't, Charles. I can't do it any
more . . .'

'*You* have a jolly front?' Ross says, with an ugly edge. 'Never seen any
evidence of it myself.'

She shakes her head. 'The things I could have said,' she says, nodding
once in my direction, 'to *him* – but held back.'

'Go on then,' Ross says. 'Let's hear it. Let's hear the actual truth.'

She sits down again, then looks at me with a disaffiliated smile. 'What did Audrey tell you?' she asks.

I hesitate. 'She said you never wanted kids. That you talked about Ross like he was some, I think she said growth, you were waiting to have removed . . .'

'Nonsense,' Charles shouts. 'We all know what Audrey's problem is – jealousy over Fionnuala's success. Fullpoint, new par.'

Fionnuala asks if the tape recorder is running. I tell her it is. She enjoys a little inward laugh, then says Oprah is going to kill her.

Fionnuala: No . . . I mean Audrey's right, I never wanted children.

Ross: Er, *excuse* me? I can't believe you're actually admitting it.

Charles: Well, let me just say, you fooled me – and millions like me. Because you took to motherhood like the proverbial what-have-you . . .

Fionnuala: Charles, please. This is important . . .

Ross: Go on, this should be good . . .

Fionnuala: Well, I *didn't* want children – I won't lie. I had no idea how to relate to someone as a mother because I had no relationship with my own. I still don't know.

Ross: No arguments there.

Fionnuala: I mean, the whole thing was a bloody inconvenience to me. Remember, I was always very, very ambitious – you just have to look at my charity work over the years to see that. I've raised, literally, thousands.

And I had this list – at least in my mind – of all the things I wanted out of life. And I'm sorry that you have to hear it, Ross, but children didn't figure on that list *at* all.

When I found out I was pregnant, I didn't want to face it.

Angela . . . she didn't tell you anything did she?

I tell her no, though I did suspect she knew a lot.

Fionnuala: Well, it was Angela – oh, my dearest, dearest friend – who persuaded me to confront it, face facts. Over coffee, which we often had, in her place in Ballsbridge. Fabulous mock-Tudor house, on an acre. Immaculately kept grounds. Bought it for next to nothing – one sold just like it two years ago for fifty-eight million.

I'd just been sick again. Umpteenth time. And Angela said, 'Fionnuala, do you think there's any chance you're pregnant?'

I said, 'Of course I'm not pregnant. I'm not *ready* to be pregnant.'

I can see you're shocked by that. But the way I saw it was, you know, some women are born hardwired for motherhood. I wasn't. I just somehow found myself in this situation.

So eventually, I had it confirmed, as one does. And, well, I was quite literally devastated.

Ross: Now do you believe me?

Charles: Fionnuala, stop this now.

Fionnuala: I know it's hard for you to hear, Ross, but I must have cried for an hour in Angela's kitchen. I remember saying to her, 'I'd better go home, phone Charles. Discuss our options.'

'Options?' Angela said. Oh, she was horrified. 'Fionnuala, you're married! You're thirty-four! What do you mean by *options*?'

All that.

I told her out straight. I didn't want children. Never did. They're so . . . *needy*. And so bloody messy. You could never *have* anything nice.

I had friends who had babies and, oh . . . shit and Liga everywhere.

And then my figure!

I remember saying to her that this wasn't what I wanted. And Angela said something along the lines of, 'Well, what *do* you want, Fionnuala?'

I looked around – we were in the kitchen, but really I was referring to the entire house – and I said, 'I want *this*, Angela.'

I nod with what I hope is empathy.

Fionnuala: And *being* pregnant was nothing short of a nightmare.

I remember very early on, waking up one morning, with my face
just covered in this . . . *acne*. Covered. Now, bear in mind, you're
talking to someone who went through her entire teenage years
without a single spot.

I read all the magazines, of course. Found out that, you know,
when you're pregnant, your hormone levels increase and your seba-
ceous glands start to produce more and more oil.

I drank gallon upon gallon of water, moisturized four or five
times a day and waited for my oestrogen levels to increase and the
acne to disappear. But you know, it never did.

In fact, every day there was a new outbreak and it wasn't just on
my face either. It came up everywhere, especially my back. I still
have the scars to this day, which is why I famously never wear
strappy tops and backless dresses.

Charles: That wouldn't be my memory at all. Fionnuala, you were
glowing . . .

Fionnuala: A combination of increased blood pressure, hormonal
sweat and my skin being stretched across a wider area.

Come on, Charles, you know what I went through.

I was sick, I think, every morning of the first *and* second trimester. My gag reflex was so sensitive, literally any kind of smell was
liable to set me off. I'd be in school. I'd have the girls cooking something relatively straightforward, perhaps an asparagus and shiitake
risotto, or a gingered salmon and herb en croute. I only had to smell
food – someone would crack an egg or start frying the Arborio –
and I'd have to run immediately to the ladies' room.

Between that and the blinding headaches I tended to get in the
early afternoon, it got to the point where eventually I could no

longer work. I just physically could not do it. And that was hell for me. Sheer hell. As anyone will tell you.

My breasts would leak – *leak!* – and always at the most embarrassing times.

Ross: Jesus! Basic! Christ!

Fionnuala: And of course people expect you to be happy about it, don't they? They look at you, smiling like idiots, with their heads cocked to one side, and they say, 'Isn't it a wonderful time?'

I remember I said to this particular woman – it was in the middle of Pamela Scott – 'Oh, yes, nine months trying to convince my husband to fuck a frumpy frau – then there's labour to look forward to at the end of it.'

Ross: You're a focking disgrace, you know that?

Fionnuala: And it's ironic, isn't it, Charles, that you ended up a cheesemonger?

Charles: Oh, don't Fionnuala.

Fionnuala: Because I ate nothing *but* in the second trimester . . .

Charles: All of this is *off* the record – I hope I don't need to state that.

Fionnuala: I remember Angela coming to the house one morning, the place in Glenageary, and catching me eating a piece of *Vacherin-Fribourgeois*. She said, 'Fionnuala, what are you doing? You're not supposed to eat unpasteurized cheese.'

I knew all *about* listeria, of course. I was a Home Economics teacher.

Ross: I can't believe you're actually admitting all this.

Fionnuala: So what happened then was, I don't know, Angela might have snatched it out of my hand and put it back into the fridge. She certainly *opened* the fridge because she was suddenly confronted by this, just, sheer wall of soft cheeses. There was Brie. There was Cambozola. There was *Torta del Casar*. Wensleydale Blue. And, well, it was immediately obvious to her that I'd been to Superquinn. No question.

She bagged it all up and put it into the boot of that lovely Nissan Maxima she was driving at the time. Got rid of it.

Ross: Like you were trying to get rid of me?

Fionnuala: I did, towards the end of the second trimester, *endeavour* to think of this thing as something other than a terrible accident that had destroyed my life. I mean, it was an effort, but I did it.

I started going back to the gym, not going at it like a woman possessed, mind, but doing a sensible amount, half-an-hour on the bike and some aerobic exercises.

I started generally looking after myself. Did everything the books said. Took the prenatal vitamins, a hundred grammes of protein a day, two tablespoons of fat. Then the folic acid, which Audrey had told me about.

It said in some magazine or other that the average home is full of tiny molecules of chemicals that come from carpets, from paint, from simple stains, and that house plants are the best way to filter them. So I literally filled the house with plants. Filled it.

So you can't say I didn't *care*.

And – yes, Ross – I was experiencing very, very severe guilt feelings over the way I'd behaved.

But as I developed a sense of this baby – you, Ross – growing inside me, I started to think you were, you know, privy to my thoughts. That my ambivalence and – let's face it – downright hostility towards the idea of motherhood had somehow been communicated to you through the amniotic fluid.

I remember Angela took me out for a drive one day. Something innocuous was said – might have been names or maybe even schools

– and all of a sudden I started sobbing, absolutely uncontrollably.

Angela had to pull in. She'll tell you. On Sorrento Road. 'What's wrong, Sweetie?' she kept saying. 'What's wrong?' and eventually I just blurted it out. 'What if he hates me?'

She said, 'Well, for starters, you don't *know* that it's a he yet?'

'Believe me, it's a boy,' I said. 'And he knows. He knows everything.'

Angela said, 'You're being ridiculous. Your baby is quite unaware of the world outside your womb.'

Of course, in those days we didn't know the things about foetal memory that we know now.

Charles: Well, I'll tell you how *I* feel about all that. It's absolute nonsense – and that's *on* the record.

Fionnuala: The kicking started way, way back, though I didn't tell you, Charles.

Then one night we were at home, watching television, and the wind was suddenly taken out of me. I mean, I couldn't hide it. I went, 'Oooph!' and all of a sudden Charles's little face there was all lit up: 'Was that a kick?'

I wasn't going to deny it. I was doubled over. So then we end up having it – this scene I just dreaded.

Charles: Well, I remember it very differently. I remember him kicking away in there and I remember saying, 'He's going to be a number ten. No question. He's in there practising his technique . . .'

Fionnuala: With every kick, I could almost hear him say: 'I hate you! I hate you! I hate you! I hate you!'

Charles: Of course he wasn't.

Ross: I'd say that's exactly what I was saying.

Fionnuala: Not long after that, driving home from Westwood one morning, I got this sudden taste for avocado. I mean, it was more than a craving. I simply *had* to have one. Felt like a life or death thing.

I stopped off in Foxrock village. Thomas's, naturally. Bought two, sat in the car and – oh – devoured them. *Bit* through the skin to get at the fruit because I had nothing to peel them with. Then I went back in. Six more.

The next morning, I woke up – same thing, although of course I couldn't go back to the same shop. I had to pick a different one. But I ate probably six again that day. Could have eaten more.

This went on for two, three weeks, possibly longer, but by the end of it – you can imagine – I was the size of a bloody house.

Avocados are seventy-five per cent fat.

I put on, I would have to say, a colossal amount of weight in a very short period of time, to the point where Angela almost passed me one day coming out of Monica John. I was literally unrecognizable from the Fionnuala she knew.

Yes, it was avocados. But it was also – if you can believe this – deep-fried food. I'll tell you how bad it got. One day, it's Friday lunchtime, I get in the car and I drive to one of these *chip shops* in – oh, I can hardly *say* the word – Sallynoggin. I mean, the idea of it now. Anything could have happened.

I walked in and I said, 'Three fresh cod and three singles, please.'

I don't know *how* I knew what to ask for – I just did.

The man behind the counter – oh, he was like something from *Strumpet City* – he said, 'What was that you said there, love?'

I said, 'Three fresh cod, three singles. They're not for me. We've got some, em, *workmen* in.'

'No, but what did you say after that?' he said.

'Well, I think I said please.'

He said, 'Yeah, I thought you did,' and then he started laughing. 'Don't get many of your kind around here.'

And everybody in the shop started laughing at me. I just took the bag, threw the money at him and ran out of there.

It was awful, standing there among all these people who'd do bloody murder before they'd do a day's work. But that's how far gone I was. They're the kind of risks I was taking. The kind of risks I was being *forced* to take.

Ross: Yeah, definitely make sure you put in a photograph of her when she was a baluba.

Fionnuala: I put on thirty-four pounds.

Ross: And the rest.

Fionnuala: And I was convinced it was all Ross's doing. Because the cravings would change from time to time, but it was always things that were high in calories. It was profiteroles. Or pizza. Or sour cream by the bloody carton.

I was simply convinced that Ross was controlling it.

I went ten days overdue, convinced – again – that he stayed in there just to spite me. And when he finally made his appearance he *had* to humiliate me.

I was in the National Gallery with Angela. We'd had a coffee. No, I had freshly squeezed orange juice. I'd stopped drinking coffee – that's how much of an effort I was prepared to make. Anyway, we're walking around, looking at the paintings – *as* one does. We were stopped right in front of Gabriel Metsu's *A Woman Reading a Letter* when I suddenly felt this really intense urge to pee.

Or what I *thought* was an urge to pee.

My waters broke, there and then, before the contractions had even started. He literally flooded the floor.

Ross: For fock's sake!

Fionnuala: Oh, it just kept coming – buckets and buckets of it.

Angela said, 'We'd better get you to Holles Street.'

I said, 'No, no – I'm having him in Mount Carmel.'

'Fionnuala,' she said, 'there really isn't time. The traffic – it's half-four. Holles Street is only a couple of hundred yards down the road.'

I remember gripping her hand in the back of the taxi – I might have even sunk my nails in – and I said, 'Angela, in the name of all that is holy, do *not* bring me to that awful place.'

But she did.

It's a mark of how we feel about each other that our friendship managed to survive that.

I don't want to go into the details of the labour. Other than to say I swore that day that I would never do it again and, unlike a lot of mothers, I meant it.

The second I started pushing . . .

I'll say flatulence. I'll say vomiting. I'll say diarrhoea. And we'll leave it at that . . .

Charles: I expect you were emotional, Fionnuala. Don't forget hormones and so forth. I'll take over the story from here. Because Charles here arrives on the scene shortly afterwards – the worse for wear, I think I've gone on the record as saying before – sees the little chap lying there and is immediately besotted. As I have been ever since . . .

Ross: Never thought I'd hear myself say this, but I think I'd like to hear more from *her* . . .

Fionnuala: You were a teenager the day you were born, Ross.

Ross: What does that mean?

Fionnuala: It means you were born old.

Obviously you couldn't verbalize your feelings, but I could tell – you took one look at the world and you hated everyone and everything in it.

Charles: That's terribly harsh, Fionnuala.

Fionnuala: Charles, the things he says to you – just hateful – you let them wash over you. I don't know how you do it. I mean,

I've done it too. But that's because I know it's my fault – the way he is.

I remember saying to you, Charles – it might have been the day I was discharged from hospital, back to that awful house – I said, 'Do you not get a *feeling* when you look at him?' *him* meaning the baby.

And Charles said, 'Oh, yes – he'll play for Ireland one day. *And* work for one of the big firms. Goldman Sachs, I expect.'

I said, 'No, Charles. I mean a *creepy* feeling.'

It's an odd thing to say about a two- or three-day-old baby, but when I looked at Ross there was none of the innocence that I saw in other babies. I struggled to put it into words. I said to Charles, 'When you look at him, don't you get the impression that he *knows* things?'

In the hospital – I almost forgot this bit – when they put him into my arms he went straight for the breast.

Ross: You . . . are a focking disgrace.

Fionnuala: I thought, 'Oh no you don't.'

I had these enormous breasts – bloody udders – and as far as I was concerned, that was all down to him, making me eat all that bloody rubbish.

Of course, he couldn't believe his luck when he first set eyes on them. The face on him. All his Christmases.

Ross: A disgrace.

Fionnuala: Bloody Audrey tried to persuade me. I'm sure she meant well, being a midwife. Even tried to tell me it'd help shed the extra weight I'd put on. The body's supposed to burn five hundred extra calories a day while breastfeeding.

But I'd catch him staring at me, at my breasts, like one of these God-awful famine victims watching the relief truck arrive. Big, expectant eyes. And I'd think, no way – *you're* getting the bottle.

Charles: Well, to put a positive spin on all of this. I always say that one of the reasons that Ross and I bonded – quite apart from, obviously, having rugby in common – was all those middle of the night feeds when he was a baby. Myself and m'lado here would often find ourselves – two, three, four in the morning – in the kitchen, the little chap sucking away contentedly on his bottle and his old dad here regaling him with tales of some of the great games and great players it has been my privilege to see down through the years.

That, as the man says, is how we became such fast friends.

Fionnuala: I can't remember how old Ross was – he might have been six months old – but I was trying to play some game or other with him. It was something like, 'Round and round the garden, like a teddy bear . . .'

I'd seen Charles do it with him and when he tickled him under the chin, Ross would just be beside himself. Squealing with excitement. It goes without saying that when I did it, there was nothing. Again, bored. I must have tried it for, what, ten, fifteen minutes, all to no avail. I was quite upset about it – quite *visibly* upset – and as I turned away, I saw him literally sneer at me.

Now, I know that's difficult for some people to believe of a baby, but it *absolutely* happened. The right side of his lip curled upwards – exactly the same way it does today when he's being unpleasant. I watched it, that little supercilious mouth of his form in front of my very eyes.

At that stage, I was under a huge amount of strain. And that's when that incident happened.

The other baby.

Ross: What other baby?

Charles: Fionnuala, I think if Mr Hennessy Coghlan-O'Hara were here, he would tell you not to say another word – and wise counsel it would be.

Fionnuala: I went for what must have been my six-month check-up. Holles Street – again. I *hated* that it was Holles Street.

Anyway, I'd been behaving rather oddly. Angela, Delma, I think even Audrey, were worried about it. So Angela called around to see me when I got back from the hospital. I remember this like it happened yesterday. We were in the kitchen and I was chopping something – something tells me it was Belgian endives – and she happened to look into the carrycot.

Well, she nearly died.

'Fionnuala,' she said, 'this isn't *your* baby.'

'What?' I said.

She said, 'It's not Ross.'

'Isn't it?' I said – didn't even look up.

She said, 'Fionnuala, this baby's Asian.'

'Oh, well,' I said, just like that. Absently. Like it didn't matter. Like I'd taken someone else's golf umbrella and I was going to make do with the new one because they were as similar as made no difference.

She said, 'You've got to bring it back . . .'

Carried on chopping.

She said, 'Fionnuala, his mother will be going out of her mind.'

Oh, I reared up at her. Slammed the knife down on the counter. She would have been quite scared of me, I think. 'Okay, then,' I quite literally screamed at her. 'Just spare me your bloody moralizing!'

Ross: Now you're finally getting the real story of what they're focking like.

Charles: The prams were almost identical, Ross. An easy mistake to make.

Fionnuala: The parents of this little boy were absolutely furious. And understandably. They were from Iran. Something to do with the embassy, there in Blackrock. *He* in particular wanted to press charges. Oh, he was quoting the Koran at me, there in reception. And calling me all sorts of names.

Then the Gardaí arrived. Well, they were there anyway because this other little baby had been reported stolen. They wanted to take me to Pearse Street. But then there was a lovely Bean Garda called Nessa and she showed really wonderful compassion in dealing with the situation.

He knew what I'd done. Ross, I mean. Oh, I was convinced of it. He knew I'd tried to – let's be honest here – abandon him . . .

And while this was all going on, Charles, I knew that solicitor of yours was trying to persuade you to have me committed.

Charles: It was in case you did any harm to Ross.

Fionnuala: Or divorced you and took half the business.

Charles: Well, that's how the mind of a solicitor works, you see – cold, clinical, dispassionate.

Fionnuala: But you didn't, Charles.

Charles: No.

Fionnuala: You could have and you didn't . . .

I ask Fionnuala about Alexis. Was it daughter-envy that led her to bring a dog into the home?

Fionnuala: It was certainly envy – but nothing to do with Erika. Envy at Charles's relationship with Ross.

It was . . . all boys together. Or that's how it seemed to me. I felt outnumbered in my own home.

Alexis was a doty little thing, a little princess, but it was awful what I did, looking back. I treated her as very much a second baby. And a favourite baby. I mean, I fed her before I fed you, Ross. I'd be preparing a bottle and Alexis would start barking and I'd immediately drop whatever I was doing and start preparing *her* food. Awful, awful, awful.

I ask about the day that Alexis bit Ross.

Fionnuala: Oh, *he* provoked her. He did something. I've no doubt about that . . .

Ross: I never touched your stupid dog – get that into your thick skull.

He shakes his head in mock outrage, then sees me staring at him and remembers that one other person in the room knows the truth of the story.

Fionnuala: It happened just before Ross started Montessori. I admit it, I was looking forward to it being just Alexis and I at home.
    I don't know what he did, but I know he did something. And I resented him for it for a long time afterwards.

Ross: You've some balls talking about, I don't know, resenting or whatever. What kind of mother doesn't notice that her actual son can't read? You were a focking teacher – so-called!

Fionnuala: No, you couldn't read, but you could certainly draw, couldn't you, Ross?

Ross: Er, *meaning*?

Fionnuala: Just after you started in the junior school – you don't remember?

Charles: He was just a boy, Fionnuala. Six years old . . .

Fionnuala: Oh, this is worth hearing. Summer holidays must have been coming up. Teacher asked the class to draw what they were going to do when school was finished. Ross produced this picture of the house – the one in Glenageary – on fire, with Charles and I trapped inside.

Ross: I don't remember that.

Fionnuala: We both had these sad faces – you know, two dots for the eyes, then a little upside-down U for the mouth.

I can still see it.

I used to wear this cerise pashmina and he got the shade absolutely perfect, even though it meant mixing red crayon with something else, maybe purple. And of course, Charles's hat.

And Ross was standing in front of the house with a big smile on his face. Holding a rugby ball with a knife stuck through it.

Charles: We were never certain that it was a *rugby* ball, Fionnuala.

I showed it to Hennessy and he agreed – could just as easily have been a Gaelic football.

Fionnuala: Charles, it was very clear what it all meant.

Charles: Blown out of all proportion, if you ask me. The others were drawing all sorts, too – space creatures and what-not. When I was a boy it was cowboys. *I* thought I was Will Kane, for heaven's sake – put that in, give it some proper perspective.

Yes, I must have drawn dozens of pictures of me shooting old Frank Miller – dastardly Frank.

And Grace Kelly, of course, sobbing her little heart out. 'Sorry, dear, I know you're a Quaker and, *ipso facto*, a pacifist, but a man's got to do what a man's got to do. So *you* can do as you please – get on that midday train, marry Prince Rainier III – but I'm going to put bloody manners on these four *hoodlums*.'

Fionnuala: We were called up to the school, weren't we, Charles?

Charles: Political correctness gone mad . . .

Fionnuala: I said to the teacher, 'You're not telling me anything new here. I *know* he hates us.'

'And that doesn't concern you?' she says.

To be honest, I think she was a bit taken aback by my frankness. See, Charles might have been in denial . . .

Charles: Well, she kept referring to it as a *rugby* ball.

Fionnuala: *I* wasn't in denial. I said, 'Oh, don't worry — I stopped taking it personally a long time ago. He hates *everyone*.'

She gave me the number of a child psychologist. I put it straight in the rubbish.

I wish I'd sent you to her now, Ross.

Ross: You're a focking disgrace. I was getting the shit kicked out of me in school.

Charles: *You* were?

Ross: Yes. Bullied. Every focking day.

Charles: I must say, this is news to us.

Ross: They used to put a collar and lead on me, like I was their focking dog. Used to make me bark. Drink from puddles. All sorts of shit.

Do you remember me asking could I start coming home for lunch?

Fionnuala: No, I don't. I'm not saying it didn't happen, but . . .

Ross: Well, *no* is exactly what you said. Too busy with your mates, feeding your fat faces with cake. Didn't want me getting in the way of your focking social life . . .

You know what? I think you'd have preferred actual Anto as your son.

Charles: Oh, the famous Anto. Antonio, as he's known now.

Fionnuala: Yes, I would have, as it happens. He knew more about cooking than anyone I'd ever met. And lovely manners as well. If it wasn't for the way he dressed, you'd never have known where he grew up. *Please. Thank you.* Words I'd barely heard in my own home before.

Charles: Steady on, Fionnuala.

Fionnuala: We'd sit in the kitchen for hours, poring over my recipe books. Oh, he knew how to improve every single recipe by at least twenty per cent. A pinch of this instead of a splash of that. Fry the meat to seal it before putting it under the grill. Marinate it for an hour less than they say. Who'd have thought of stir-frying cottage cheese?

Ross: You were, like, totally taken in by him. Serves you focking right – he robbed you blind.

Fionnuala: No, he didn't, Ross. *You* stole all of those things.

Ross considers denying it but, after a beat or two, decides it'd be far more fun to tell her the truth.

Ross: So focking what if I did?

Charles: *You* did, Ross? Oh, you could have told me. Hennessy and I spent three days trawling the pawn shops of what *we* would have called Poor Dublin – Meath Street, the Liberties, *etcetera* – trying to get it all back.

Ross: Well, meanwhile, I'm out in Pram Springs, practically dying of malnutrition, listening to Anto's old man banging on about how much he still owes the Credit Union from the Wurdled Cup. And Anto's old dear giving it loads as well. 'He's doin' very well for heself on the utter side – sure thee mightn't *want* you back arawl.'

Fionnuala: Well, I won't deny it, I was dreading you coming home. You and your unpleasantness. I was far from a model mother, but you were no model son. There were times when I was frightened of you – genuinely frightened. You were so angry. So aggressive.

I tell them I might be able to shed some new light on that.

A week or so ago, after my conversation with Gary Gest, I was looking back through Father Fehily's journal, reading and re-reading one line in particular: 'The materials to create this army of supermen are simple. I shall give them chemicals . . . and Wagner.'

The gooseneck lamp threw a circle of light on the blank page opposite, where I could just make out the faint tracery of a word. It had obviously been written on some loose scrap of paper and imprinted itself on the page beneath. By holding it at different angles to the light, I could see that the word was methamphetamine.

A quick internet search filled in the blanks for me. Methamphetamine is a psychostimulant that reduces fatigue and heightens aggression. Chocolates dosed with the drug were dispensed to German military personnel of all ranks and divisions during the Second World War. Pilots called it *Fliegerschokolade*, tank crews *Panzerschokolade*.

Adolf Hitler, Father Fehily's great hero, was administered intravenous injections of the drug by his personal physician as a treatment for depression and fatigue. As an interesting footnote, some historians believe it was methamphetamine that impaired his judgement when he made the fatal decision to tear up the Molotov-Ribbentrop pact and invade the Soviet Union.

I suspect that was why Fehily made Oisinn captain that year – he couldn't predict how the drug would affect Ross's mind.

Ross: So he was giving me drugs. So what?

Charles: We'd probably rather leave that out of the book, if you don't mind. They might come looking for his medals back . . .

I tell him it might help explain his behaviour that year. I tell him I know about Gary Gest's boat.

Charles: Boat? What boat?

Ross: Doesn't matter. Move on.

Fionnuala: There was one day – it was the day of the final that year – I hosted breakfast for the Senior Cup mums. Oh, cooked a whole range of things – my salmon kedgeree, my pancakes jubilee, my devilled kidneys . . .

Ross: Shouldn't have even been you doing it. Oisinn was the captain.

Fionnuala: His mum was having a new kitchen fitted and I was more than happy to do it.

Ross: Oh, yeah, they were *all* there, sitting around, tarted up to the nines. There must have been nothing in Pia Bang that morning except empty focking rails.

And *you* were all, 'Ross, how are you feeling, the day of the big game?' cracking on that we were, like, bosom buddies. 'Will you have a twice-baked individual cheese soufflé before you leave?'

Fionnuala: 'Are you focking deaf?' you said to me.

Ross: Well, that wasn't drugs. I always talked to you like that.

Fionnuala: In front of all my friends. You said, 'I told you, Meno-pause Face, we're having breakfast at the school,' which you hadn't, of course.

Then I asked you for the tickets and you said, 'Are you stupid? They're on the mantelpiece, behind the John Rocha signature votive.'

And when I opened the envelope, it wasn't tickets at all. It was a leaflet for a clinic in Bray that did electrolysis.

Charles: An honest mistake.

Fionnuala: Charles, why do you insist on defending him?

Ross: Guilty conscience, I'd say.

    I hope you're not letting *him* off the hook in this focking book. I had an actual son and he didn't even tell me . . .

'About that,' I say.

    The room seems to tighten. 'I have a friend, works in RTÉ . . .'

Ross: So?

'It's just . . . that story you like to tell, about the kid on the *Late Late Show* who had cancer . . .'

Ross: *What*ever.

'And your dad here wrote a cheque for his treatment . . .'

Charles: What's all this about, Kicker?

'Well, I spent an entire day and night going through old archive tapes . . .'

Ross: And?

'There was no cancer kid. You lied to me, Ross.'

Ross: Horseshit.

'We went through five seasons on fast search. Nothing. Spoke to one or two researchers who worked on the show at that time as well. Ross, there *was* no cancer kid . . . Do you want to know what *I* think happened?'

Ross: Not really. Leinster are playing. I need to start making tracks.

'I think you went into the study, like you said. I think you found your dad's chequebook. But the stubs you looked at, they weren't made out to some kid's parents. Well, not *any* kid's parents. They were made out to Tina Masters . . .'

The colour drains from his face.

'And you knew – you must have known – there could be only one reason why your dad would be sending monthly cheques to Tina Masters.'

Ross: I had a feeling this was going to be a stitch-up, right from the start.

'You *knew*,' I tell him. 'You knew you had a kid, but you pretended not to.'

Charles: Well, he was only a kid himself.

'What was going through your head that day, when you missed that penalty – it had nothing to do with Sorcha maybe or maybe not being pregnant. I mean, she might *well* have said she was, but how many girls have you heard that from over the years? No, it wasn't that you thought you were about to become a father – it was that you already were one . . .'

Ross: Is that what you think?

'That's what I think. That story about you only finding out about Ronan at the wedding reception, it suited you to say that. Because you didn't want to face up to your responsibilities – you didn't understand the concept. Easier to let the school sort your problems out. Or have your dad here write a cheque.'

Ross: So you're an expert on me now, are you?

'And that hatred you *claim* to feel for your mother and father, maybe it *was* your mother's ambivalence, maybe it was that they weren't there for you when you had your problems at school. Maybe it was the drugs. But personally, I think it's self-loathing . . .'

Ross: Oh, do you?

'Self-loathing, turned outwards.'

Charles is staring at me, but his look is unfocused.

Charles: That finger – deep down, I knew it was for us. His mother and I.

Something quite unexpected happens then. Ross starts crying, in the manner of a child, in big, breathless sobs. But that's not what's unexpected. Fionnuala moves over to where he's sitting and stretches a tender arm around him and Ross settles his head in the crook of her shoulder. Fionnuala's eyes are large with compassion, her voice like balm.

Fionnuala: How *could* you have been a father, Ross? You were sixteen. And you didn't have the best role models, did you? The two of us, wrapped up in our own little worlds.

Ross: I took one that day, you know, the day of the match – a twice-baked individual cheese soufflé.

Fionnuala: I know you did. I saw you.

Ross, I was a terrible mother. I was a terrible wife . . .

Ross wipes his face with an open palm.

Ross: You're a terrible writer as well.

Fionnuala's laugh says *touché.*

Fionnuala: You might be right.

You know, Ross, when I see you with Honor and with Ronan, when I see the way you are with your own kids, I think, what kind of miracle is that?

I hope it's not too late to start being a better mother to you now. It's like I said to Oprah – every day is a fresh page in the platen.

Ross nods.

Ross: When are you going back to, like, the States?

Fionnuala: In the morning. But maybe I'll stay another week . . .

Ross: That'd be, I don't know, cool, I suppose.

Fionnuala: We could spend some time together.

Ross: I mean, yeah, do what you want. I don't *give* a fock.

Charles: Well, look at us – happy families again!

Down on the street, there are raised voices. Loud and piercing caterwauls that cause even the pianist to stop playing and tense his face against the frequency. Ross and I lead the rush of curious people to the window and we watch as Sorcha and Erika emerge from the Westbury Mall. Erika is walking with her arms folded in front of her, Sorcha following her like a raptor stalking a kill. She's spitting out words like 'unprofessional' and she's accusing her of walking out 'when you know I have an order of Antik and Taverniti jeans about to arrive'.

When they reach the front of the hotel, Erika turns around to face her. Maybe it's the fearsome expression on her face that causes Sorcha to take a step backwards. A crowd has massed, but it's keeping a nervous distance.

I can't see Erika's face from up here, but I imagine she narrows her eyes when she says, 'I have better things to do with my life than selling smelly second-hand clothes for you.'

'Vintage,' Sorcha answers, with real venom.

'*What*ever,' Erika says. 'I'm not slumming it any more. The place is a focking scabies epidemic waiting to happen!'

Sorcha's mouth becomes a large O. She's still reeling from the blow when Erika applies the *coup de grâce*. 'Do yourself a favour, Girl – just put Vincent de Paul over the door and be done with it!'

Erika's in a taxi and out of sight before Sorcha can formulate any kind of riposte. When she does, it's weak. 'Oh I can't *wait* to see how *you* come through the whole current economic climate thing,' she says to no one at all. A girl from Rococo attempts to put a comforting arm around her. 'Get away from me!' she shouts, shaking herself free. 'Oh, I'd say *you're* loving every minute of this!'

Then she announces that she's left her daughter with – *oh my God!* – a total stranger and stomps back in the direction of the Powerscourt Town-house Centre. The crowd melts away.

Ross is left shaking his head. Charles says he'll have a word with Erika tonight.

I make my excuses and take my final leave of the O'Carroll-Kelly fam-ily. I step out into the jaded light of a November afternoon. On Grafton Street, there are sale signs everywhere and a sense of life retreating to the old mundane rhythms of a time when people had nothing.

I think about Ross and his family and the emotional carnage I've just left behind. I wonder what will become of them all. I think about Fion-nuala bearing her most private scars like that. I think about Charles – his crookedness and happy optimism. I think about Ross's friends and the world they knew slowly dissolving. And I wonder, is this the end? Or is it the green shoots of a new beginning?

Behind me, a voice calls my name. I turn around and I'm surprised to see Ross standing there.

'What about Erika?' he says, smiling.

'I'm not the only one happy to see her back to her old self, then?'

'Are you mad?' he says. 'I just hope somebody filmed it – focking *belongs* on YouTube.'

We both laugh at that.

'Are you okay?' I ask.

He nods.

'Look, I'm sorry – setting up that scene like that. I only did it for dramatic effect and that was, well, no excuse.'

He shakes his head. 'It was shit that had to come out. I presume you're going to put it all in?'

'It's the truth, isn't it?'

'Yeah, no, I'm *saying* put it in . . . Here, don't say I cried, though.'

'You know, I think I will.'

'I *know* you focking will.'

'What happened back there,' I say, 'it's changed everything, hasn't it?'

'I suppose.'

'So . . . what happens now?'

'Kehoe's,' he says.

'What?'

'Kehoe's,' he says again, his arm steering me in the direction of South Anne Street. 'You still haven't heard my Loreto on the Green stories.'

L7932

Acknowledgements

Thanks to my editor, Rachel Pierce, for her tireless work and for those eureka moments that allowed me to see where I was going. To my agent, the extraordinary Faith O'Grady. To Michael McLoughlin, Patricia Deevy and all the fantastic staff of Penguin Ireland. To Vincent Howard and Quicky Fingers for the wonderful www.rossocarrollkelly.ie. To George, John and Ruth for the advice. To Dad, Vin, Rich and Mark. And, especially, to Mary.